HWP
$ 2.00

SALISBURY

Who'll forget Lieutenant Davis+? near the dead line he was shot!
There were many others *murder'd,* comrades cannot be fortgot!
Some were very weak and feeble, but they near the dead line fell!
Then the sentinels get furloughs, while they of their *valor tell!*
Gallant men, by insults goaded, sought release from Salisbury,
Made a charge on guards and dead-line, but a few brave men got free,
And they left the camp for heaven, and their sorrows all have fled
Though our comrades forms my moulder with the cold and silent dead!
Ah how oft when storms did gather, we would think of homes afar,
Homes where there were warmth and shelter, notwithstanding frowns of war,
But we had in frowning Salisbury to brave all the tying storms,
While we wished we had more blankets just to wrap around our forms,
Yonder sky our umbrella, oft the only one we had,
Thank of that and never wonder, that the prisoners heart was sad,
Thank of that and never wonder, that so many had to die,
That so many forms are silent 'neath North Carolina's sky.

"When POW George D. B. DeWolfe of Nashua, N.H. reached Camp Parole, Annapolis, Maryland, on 28 February 1865 he celebrated his liberation from the Salisbury Prison by composing a poem of 12 verses depicting experiences at the prison. This rare document was purchased by Barry Isenhour...."[1]

1. Louis A. Brown, *The Salisbury Prison, A Case Study of Confederate Military Prisons 1861–1865*, 1992.

SALISBURY

Civil War Death Camp in North Carolina

Richard Masterson

Copyright © 2005 by Richard Masterson

ALL RIGHTS RESERVED—No part of this book may be reproduced in any form without permission in writing from the publisher, except by a reviewer who wishes to quote brief passages in connection with a review.

This Burd Street Press publication
was printed by
Beidel Printing House, Inc.
63 West Burd Street
Shippensburg, PA 17257-0708 USA

The acid-free paper used in this book meets the guidelines for permanence and durability of the Committee on Production Guidelines for Book Longevity of the Council on Library Resources.

For a complete list of available publications
please write
Burd Street Press
Division of White Mane Publishing Company, Inc.
P.O. Box 708
Shippensburg, PA 17257-0708 USA

Library of Congress Cataloging-in-Publication Data

Masterson, Richard, 1941-
Salisbury : Civil War death camp in North Carolina / Richard Masterson.
p. cm.
ISBN 1-57249-376-3 (acid-free paper)
1. Read, James E.--Fiction. 2. United States--History--Civil War, 1861-1865--Prisoners and prisons--Fiction. 3. North Carolina--History--Civil War, 1861-1865--Fiction. 4. Salisbury Prison (N.C.)--Fiction. 5. Prisoners of war--Fiction. I. Title.

PS3613.A8199S25 2005
813'.6--dc22

2005051230

PRINTED IN THE UNITED STATES OF AMERICA

Dedicated to Mary, who gave me the story of her great-grandfather, James Reed, encouragement to write, and the empathy to rediscover the heart and strength of a man long forgotten.

Contents

Prologue ix
1 Becoming Soldiers 1
2 Becoming Killers 11
3 Coming Home 31
4 Alien Land 38
5 Strangers Evermore 55
6 At Peace in War 67
7 Enemies Among Us 74
8 Captured 83
9 Libby Prison 91
10 Entering Salisbury 112
11 Pit of Hell 142
12 Rebel Retribution 156
13 Survive Today 166
14 Unbeaten 182
Epilogue 191
Afterword 201
Military History of James E. Reed 203

Prologue

Campground
Outside Buffalo, New York
October 1861

"It matters not a damn," my father had told me. "Killin' of men does no good any time and this foolishness ain't no different!" He hadn't expected a response from me. When he spoke, I listened. "You don't know nothing about why you're joining up, do ya? Is it just to strut about in a uniform? Is it worth hurtin' your mother? I don't give a damn if you volunteer! Your mother's well-being is all I care about. The rest don't matter!"

Sitting here now, listening to this veteran, this survivor, those words my father had spoken came back to me. Did this soldier, who had fought in the first real battle at a place called Bull Run, believe all the death and suffering and sacrifice mattered? Could he quell the doubts that my father had burned in my mind?

> *"This war ain't what ya think,"* the soldier searched for words. *"At Manassas, there was running about and noise and yelling and nobody knowin' what to do. Then the killin' started."*

Not much older than me, smaller in size, he absent-mindedly stabbed his right hand across his chest to touch the empty sleeve dangling at his left side. Having earned the status of wounded hero, he returned home to heal and help train new volunteers to join with the 21st New York that was waiting for us outside of Washington, D.C.

> *"Our regiment pulled back,"* he continued. *"We were to be the rear guard, to protect the retreat."* There was no sound coming from the few of us sitting, listening to this sad man speak. *"There was a lot of bad stuff I seen on the road that night...not just soldiers...."* He paused for a short while before saying, *"It was late and the shootin' had stopped. The road, it was clogged with trains, buggies, columns, and lots of blacks, dozens of 'em, old women and young 'uns mostly, going on some place north. One old woman bent over, alookin' kinda sickly at the edge of the road, not far from me. Her kid, I reckon, 'bout seven or so was to be apullin' at the old woman. Hell! The old one up 'n fell down in the mud. The kid didn't leave hold of her...cryin' 'n pleadin'. 'Get up! Get up!' She was ayellin'.*
>
> *"Nobody did a damn thing but stand there awatchin'...and I'm seein' a cavalry detachment comin' from the north. I had to get to her! Damn! I could barely move! The kid...cryin' and all ascared as hell staring up at me...tears ran down her face...shaking, like to freezin'.*
>
> *"'I'll help—don't be acryin',' I told her. The old woman just lay there. Her eyes were closed. She didn't move any!*
>
> *"God! I thought when I picked her up, she weighed less than my knapsack. My friend named Iglar with me took the girl's hand and came behind me. I told him I was atakin' the old woman to the surgeon's tent.*
>
> *"'We'll come too,' Iglar insisted.*
>
> *"'No!' I yelled to him. 'Take the kid to camp. Git 'er some food.'*

"Iglar saw the woman in my arms was dead. 'Yeah,' he said. 'I'll do that.'

"When I laid the body inside the hospital tent, I looked at the woman's face and saw for the first time a ribbon tied in her hair, thin and blue, tyin' a fist-sized bun at the back of her head...ends dangling in a fashion my mother wore on hot summer days. The dead woman's face was wrinkled; deep-set lines across her forehead, and her sunken cheeks made her look like a skeleton. When I got back to my campsite, the little kid was gone. Iglar's atellin' me she pulled away from him and run toward her people along the road.

"'It was probably best,' I recall Iglar saying. 'It was probably best.'

The veteran looked up from the ground where his eyes had been fixed.

"I want ya to remember that story because it tells ya the kind of monsters you'll be afightin' down there in Virginny; mother-killers and orphan-makers and murderers of men and women like what I seen at Bull Run when they slaughtered defenseless citizens who did nothin' but ride down from the capital carryin' parasols and picnic baskets just to watch the damn goins on.

"I lost my arm that day, but I still got this one!" He jutted his right hand toward the ceiling. *"Only hope the damn war lasts just long enough for me to git my revenge by takin' a few of the arms from them mad dogs."* His tone changed as his voice rose. *"You ain't got to wait none and God has given you the right to wipe out them heathen bastards, to destroy their homes, ravage their land and women and be heroes fer adoin' it!"* He paused to look directly at me. *"But once ya start killin',"* in calm measure

he emphasized each word, *"don't let up and never surrender. If'n they git ya, they'll kill ya slow and you'll be aprayin' fer death to come quick."* His stare burned into my head. *"Don't git captured alive! I pray fer yer soul if ya do."*

1 Becoming Soldiers

Campground
Outside Buffalo, New York
November 1861

The crackling of cornstalk stubble feebly protesting the pressing weight of soldiers' boots quickly faded and was no more. Heard in its place were the sounds of an army on the move. Dust raised by the marching boots floated along the ground beneath the knees of the soldiers, and then began to drift slowly upward until it was above the heads of the men closing the end of the columns. As we passed, it rose, disappearing within the yellow leaves clinging to the top of the white birch trees that bordered the road.

Griffin, our squad leader, was directly in front of me, Jon Pederson to his right and Liam Morgan at my shoulder. Concentrating on Griffin's movements, I fumbled with the Springfield's leather strap to hold the long gun away from my legs as I walked, ignoring Sergeant Hamilton somewhere along the column. An albino, tall and thin, with red eyes shielded within tiny slits that never blinked, a freak of nature, Hamilton had survived the docks of Buffalo. He said little, remaining apart from his men, without a fire through the night, crouched alone beneath a blanket.

"Treat it like a lady," he had told me, holding the musket with mangled hands. "Take it firm and glide the rod in the hole and then thrust it like this!" He jammed the cartridge down the barrel, flashing teeth gritted behind a twisted grin.

As I was one of the volunteers straggling in daily, Hamilton had taken it upon himself to train me separately.

"I can shoot just fine, Sarge!"

"Shooting don't mean facing down a wide-eyed doe out in your pasture, Reed," he cut me short. "It's loadin' quick and killin' a man who don't load faster 'n you."

Pederson interrupted my thoughts. "That man's a freak! Look at his fingers! They had to be chewed off in a brawl!" he said. "Hell, if you get up close, them ain't clean cuts! Them fingers been gnawed on!"

"He don't look to be a fightin' man." Morgan didn't seem to agree with most anyone about anything.

"Don't know what you know about fightin', Morgan," I looked into the face of the short, rotund boy, "but that white man is different. Wouldn't want him against me."

"Hell," Pederson dismissed me. "Hamilton's a damn freak! That's all!"

Strange, Hamilton was without question a person to be watched. But my father had taught me to hold fear for the quiet ones, those who were alone, within themselves, alien to the world about them.

"Stay with Griffin and learn from him," was more like advice coming from Hamilton than an order, creating in my mind more confusion than fear of the man.

Keeping astride Morgan and at musket length behind Griffin, I marched, walking away from our campsite toward the eastern hills. The low clomping and reverberations of feet pounding the earth were steady and mind-numbing sensations. Tapping of metal against leather and of musket stock slapping against empty knapsacks added to the deep thump of shuffling boots to form a hum beneath the voices of soldiers, singing, cursing, laughing, bragging, and complaining that was heard up and down the column. The march was to become a constant in my life, endured and anticipated, the steady rhythm of motion and sound that was like a heartbeat, familiar, predictable, and sadly reassuring.

"Thump, creak, clank, thump, creak, clank, thump, creak, thump, thump, thump, thump," again and again until a trancelike state overcame my boredom, pain, thirst, and hunger. "Thump, thump, thump," pervasive, felt more than heard. The back of the blue-coated soldier before me, hair bunched beneath his blue cap, holding the reservoir of sweat trickling down his neck, and the muzzle of his musket swaying next to a bobbing head was all that existed in sight and motion as I stared straight ahead; "thump, thump, thump," until awakened to consciousness with commands or by the intrusion of distant thunder that I would soon fear to be the roar of cannon. Through the hum came my name, someone calling for me.

"Reed is new to our squad, men...from Angola," Griffin yelled out without turning his head. I met the eyes of the man behind Morgan. He nodded. Again the "thump, creak, clang, thump, thump."

"Is it true we're on our way to Washington tomorrow to finally stop this playactin' crap and begin killin' us a few Secesh?" asked the loudest, most profane soldier, a malcontent named Baldwin.

"I'm warning ya, Baldwin, shut up and keep moving!" Sergeant Hamilton grunted from behind me. "You boys ain't yet trained enough to be soldiers." A few seconds passed.

"I heard we'll be heading there to hook up with the 21st New York." Baldwin, ignoring Hamilton's command, glanced back in his direction.

Encouraged by Hamilton's silence, Morgan yelled out, "I hope we're attached to McClellan. From all that we hear, he's running Rebs the hell out of western Virginny!"

"If McClellan gets a hold of them Rebs, hell, we'll all just walk straight to Richmond," another voice added.

"The hell! You can't count out them damn rabbit killers. They can shoot and fight. If there's enough of them, they might give us some trouble," said someone several paces behind me.

Another, more optimistic, "They might do that, but I'd like to meet one of them slave-chasing cowards. I'd show him a thing!"

Morgan said quietly so only a few could hear, "Slave-chasing cowards, huh? More like slave-fornicatin' cowards."

Baldwin, louder now, responded. "Can you imagine, buying a woman and owning her to do with what you please?"

Laughter came with Morgan's reply, "Shit, ain't you ever heard of marriage, mister?"

"You mean I can whip my wife if she don't do all I tell her?" More laughter.

"You're so ugly, Baldwin, you'd have to whip her just to marry you," Morgan again, followed by sporadic laughing and quiet, indiscernible mumbling and then the familiar "thump, thump, creak, clang," until broken by the muted thud of Hamilton's musket butt slamming into the base of Baldwin's spine. A high-pitched moan caused my head to spin to see Baldwin violently arch upright, dropping the gun, while his hands, now free, spasmodically stabbed in the air as he buckled at the knees. Unstoppable, a cascading number following pushed against those stepping to avoid their fallen comrade.

"Keep moving!" Hamilton screeched and grabbing Baldwin by the hair and pulling him to the side, away from the road, he threatened, "Next time, you'll listen, you dog bastard!"

Soldiers ran along the line attempting to reform, musket and canteen bumping and swinging as they looked to see Hamilton bending over Baldwin, lying to his side, unable to move.

"Goddamn freak is nuts!" Morgan spoke quietly and well beyond where Hamilton remained over his prey.

In a cleared hayfield that had been trampled down to the bare earth by a thousand boots, we halted at the seven-mile turnaround and the long line broke rank and melted away. I stepped only a few feet to settle on the ground next to Griffin. Without a word, I gently guided my boot over the blister that had opened on my left heel.

"He won't do that much more." Griffin looked to the rear where Hamilton remained unseen.

"He might not have to."

"You a smart ass, Reed?"

"No." I eased my sock from the blood that had dried on my foot. "He won't be doing that kind of shit if you listen to what he tells ya."

"I don't see it that way, Reed. Baldwin is just a loud-mouth screw-off, but he didn't deserve what he got from that albino."

"He's a might damn weird. I'll give ya that, but all things are different here, I guess. Things we'll have to get used to."

Griffin took a drink from the canteen and then leaned on his elbows. I watched him carefully nudging his cap over his eyes until he was still. I had said too much to this man who seldom spoke to anyone at all, he who would be at my side when I most needed someone. For what? Who in hell was I defending anyways, and why? That sadistic lunatic, this aberration who would scarcely survive the first clash? Standing out like a beacon of light, Hamilton would be the perfect target, for both Reb and now his own. Pulling my boots on, tearing at the loose flesh, I paused as the pain crept into my leg. Lowering my head, I breathed, "What a dumb bastard I am. Dumb, big-mouth bastard."

February 1862

"Move it! Let's go! Get out of there! We're headed to Virginny! Let's go!" Griffin yelled from outside the tent.

"Oh, no...awww God! And just when I had her clothes off. Oh, why? Why?" Morgan kicked at his blanket. "Get out of my way! I've gotta go!" Pushing his feet into his twisted and flopping pant legs, he hopped on his butt like a frog as he passed through the flap covering the entrance.

"Morning or night, it don't matter with him, does it?" Pederson sat up. "Come on, Reed, better get at it." He then rolled to his knees and crawled through the opening, too lazy or drunk to stand.

As children refusing to grow up in many ways, this life was all a great game of escape for Morgan and Pederson. Drinking, whoring with girls attracted to Pederson's money and Morgan's manners had become a life envied vicariously by some, abhorred by the straight-backed Griffin, and a curiosity for me. Growing up I had loved only two girls and known neither as a woman. My Winnie was gone forever, if her father had his will, and Ellen refused to remain a part of my life. "This war is not of our concern!" she had cried. "It shouldn't matter to you or any of us, James." She pushed my arm away as I had reached to console her. "It just don't matter a bit to me and neither will you if you go." Always the thoughtful one, always too serious, she may be the only one who still saw this war as cheapening the meaning of life. But war itself all still seemed so far away, almost dreamlike, pages from a tale of adventure, no different than swashbuckling pirates or desert sheiks stealing away the giggling girls like those who snuck into Morgan's lair.

Listening to the movement outside the tent, hearing the sound of purpose, I exhaled and felt my shoulders sag. As too often in quiet moments, my thoughts returned to home and my father.

"You don't know what in hell you're about to get into, boy!" he sneered. "Don't come running home or expect me to come and bring you home! You did it, now stay the course!"

The time had come. The routine of camp life that I had once convinced myself to dread was sadly slipping away, to end forever. I needed a new belief, trusting that the worst of the distant war had passed, as the one-armed veteran had said, "It'll be different for you...better...can't get any worse."

In a three-month period of time, clerks, farmers, schoolboys, merchants, and seamen had become soldiers. I too, dressed in new blues, armed with a musket yet to be fired, was a soldier, but a drill-field soldier having earned the gilded and meaningless respect and admiration of those who came to cheer me off to war. Led by a brass band with blaring horns and beating drums, young schoolgirls followed behind, waving, as all eyes turned toward us. Men and boys stood to the side watching admiringly as we paraded by, muskets to our shoulders. Above the flags that flew from the roof of every store, the sky was gray, and a thick fog drifted threateningly over the buildings; still a warmth pervaded us as strangers smiled and yelled, "Godspeed! Good luck!" We slowed our pace trying not to stumble on the heels before us, trying to prolong this march that I hoped would never end. My beautiful Winnie would smile if she could see me as I tightened my jaw and looked into the faces as they blended into another and another and another, young and fair and old men, many who may remember the last time soldiers marched off to war. Beyond, the reverberating of the steam engine heralded our approach to the rail yard. The coal dust-blackened, red-trimmed locomotive, throbbing in anticipation of what was about to occur, emanated a power that would lift us simple boys and in the unforeseeable days ahead lower some home as dead heroes. I knew not what lay ahead. How could any one of us, on this day that I hoped would never end?

The train rolled through central New York, beyond hills covered in pine and oak, past dozens of streams and rivers, beneath a perpetually gray sky releasing snow showers as we neared the Pennsylvania border. Stopping only for water and fuel and greetings with cakes and cookies, nightfall came and still the wind and snow accompanying the bone-jarring rumbling of the ride continued as the steam- and black-smoke-belching iron beast lumbered through the darkness on its path toward Baltimore, a city shielded in gloom, divided, many of its citizens openly providing assistance to the Confederacy.

"People living there don't go out at night; they're under arrest in their homes," Griffin reflected.

"Do you hear if it's safe there now?" Morgan asked, surprisingly concerned.

"There are soldiers...they shoot and kill," Griffin answered.

"It's peculiar, ain't it?" I interjected. "Baltimore, north of Washington and Bull Run just south, surrounded by the enemy."

"That's probably why we're headed there." Morgan shrugged his shoulders. "It might not look good if we have Lincoln being chased out of the capital or being captured by the Rebs, would it?" Again himself, he chuckled.

The morning sun rose brightly over the horizon. White fluffy clouds outlined in peach-colored hues drifted in the blue sky. The rolling hills of Pennsylvania and Maryland leveled out into a great flat landscape broken by fences and small meandering rivers. The troop train gradually slowed as the first houses began to appear on the outskirts of Washington. Small shanties, lean-tos and tents that were no more than blankets held up by irregular and unbalanced poles, appearing in concentrated clusters on both sides of the tracks, soon blended into long, wooden unpainted warehouses with horses and wagons before them and blue-coated soldiers everywhere, a few at first and then more, stationed near the buildings or at intervals along the tracks and upon the rolling plain covered by neatly-lined rows of grayish-white tents. Hundreds of soldiers were columned in marching formation, four or five abreast, stretching into a moving wave of blue, above which rose bayonets gleaming in the early morning sun, vibrating to the staccato beat of drums. At the head of the column, regimental banners, appearing small behind the American flag, unfurled and waved within the blue. In seconds, the drill grounds passed from my sight, disappearing behind the station house and loading docks. I stood, adjusted my pack, lifted the strap of my musket and waited to become a soldier.

Upton's Hill, Virginia
Outside Washington, D.C.

Brick and mortar and wooden supports created the image of a city emerging from the womb of destruction. The white marble Capitol Building itself, sitting as a sentry overlooking its domain below, had cranes and iron beams rising out of its center, giving the aura of supernatural rays emanating from the Holy Grail.

Soldiers by the thousands swarmed, overwhelming the streets and those in civilian clothes. Motion and noise, weaving and throbbing, as buggies, wagons, magnificently-bred horses, heavily-burdened supply wagons pulled by dozens of mules whipped by cursing skinners, and wriggling masses blocked streets and congested all. Negroes, blending within a kaleidoscope of muted hues, appeared and vanished in small clusters, stopping, watching, and swept along as an afterthought.

Crossing a bridge into Virginia and advancing another two miles, we were at the apex of a vast highland. In the valley sweeping before us, a sea of white tents was connected as a continuous train rolling into the blurring shadows where images melted into the colors along the horizon, Upton's Hill, Virginia, somewhere southwest of the capital—"Little New York," where the 21st, 23rd, and 35th regiments rested in anticipation of what might be.

At the top the highest promontory stood silent testimonial to a bygone day; a grand home symbolizing a time lost. On the opposite hillside was the new beginning of what we had become, "Fort Buffalo," a twelve-acre palisade fortress. Beyond the northern end of the fort, at the crest of a small tree-lined rise, bronze and black field artillery stood, wheel-to-wheel, muzzles pointed south. Just below, down the slope of a hill scarred with tree stumps, scattered limbs, matted prairie grass, and pools of muddy and sawdust-coated water, hundreds of soldiers in battle lines, thirty or more across, waited. At the head of the troops, officers sat on horseback, while scattered throughout, sergeants walked. I stood at the crest of Upton's Hill watching the pulsating, machinelike city of blue below. As the noise of the camp rose to sweep over me, I was as if in a trance, staring at the spectacle shrouded in dust and white smoke; the sun glistening off the erect bayonets, shrill commands echoing from the officers, drum beats, and the pounding of boots—the Army of the Potomac.

2 Becoming Killers

August 1862
Bull Run Creek
Manassas, Virginia

We were in a vast sea of men, scattered across this unnamed farmer's field. It had been a hot late-summer day, and darkness had yet to cool the air. Stars twinkled in the night sky. Mosquitoes flew about my face, while crickets delivered their relentless chirp, and fireflies danced in the grass left unoccupied by the soldiers. These ancient sounds and sights of a summer's night were incongruous with the death and suffering brought here this day by those instruments of war that now sat silent on the land.

I slowly exhaled, wanting the aching pain in my back and shoulders to subside. Too weary to light my pipe or boil coffee, I breathed deeply and tried to think of home and Ellen.

To the stutter of a bugle, men were rising to their feet. Pederson stood and brought his musket to his shoulder.

"We're moving out!" Sergeant Hamilton yelled.

"Let's go!" Pederson repeated.

Lifting my weapon, a sickness overcame me. Kneeling, vomiting upon the ground, I wanted to lie down, to allow the overwhelming weariness to blend into dull, encompassing warmth of sleep.

Shaking my head, I drew my sleeve across the wetness on my chin and stood watching the movement surrounding me.

Coarse fiber in the heavy wool blanket had penetrated the sweat beneath it and was biting into my shoulder at every step. Releasing the cord, the blanket slid down my arm and rolled across the ground, unraveling a foot or more. Reaching for it, my hands shaking, I sank to my knees. A sadness rushed upon me, driving my head lower, holding as a dog on all fours.

"God! What have I done?" There was no strength in my arms. My head was heavy and sick. "What have I done?" I can't be sure any of them were hit by my shots. There is no way to know. More than likely, no one was hit. These muskets don't work all that well. Hell, how many times did I miss a rabbit close up at home? Naw, I didn't hurt any one of them. There was no air. Panic crept over me. I couldn't breathe. Just calm down, put your head down. Don't get sick, stop shaking. No one died at my hand today. If someone fell, he needed to die for he was about to take my life. I had a right to shoot him, didn't I? They were all killers, all of them, dirty bastard killers. Weren't they? I didn't hit anyone today. It's okay. My shots surely fell short.

Moisture swelled in my eyes, and in the reflection of flames glowing nearby, I saw tears glistening as one and another dropped to the wrinkled wool. The air in my lungs eased through my throat and sickness crept higher. Images flashed before me—a faceless boy squirming, a gurgling sound coming from his chest, an arm, whole and bloodless wiggling beneath my boot, cries of the wounded, tearing at their clothes to find the hole from where the soaking blood came, screams all around me, flashes, a wall of noise crushing down upon me, suffocating me, drowning me.

I looked up and saw through the growing dusk, shapes and fire surrounding me and there were voices, the familiar. The blanket, unrolled, was covering my shoulders. Did I lift it and place it there? I must have...but I didn't. Wasn't I the only one who would have done so? "A man takes care of himself," my father had said. "Don't be expectin' nothing from nobody! I'd lie down and die before I took a handout and you'll do likewise, boy! Don't you forget it! Do for yourself!"

He stood only a few feet behind me, silent and ghostly. I sensed him more than seeing him. A few minutes passed and then Hamilton was gone, this man with pure white hair showing below his cap, disappearing into the shadows lengthening across the field. I sat alone, among the thousands already here between the turnpike, Sudley Road, and the railroad to the south of us. These massive numbers of men sat here only a few miles from where we had fought today and yet failed to provide reinforcement. Were they fighting elsewhere? I was too tired, too hungry, and maybe too sick to care.

During the night, continuous trains of heavily-burdened ambulances lumbered from the battlefield to a farmhouse where the surgeons had been ordered. From within the two-story, white clapboard house sitting upon the hill among the guns of the battery, I heard anguished screams, punctuating my sleep and boring into my memory.

The morning air was warm for so early in the day. Moisture had collected in large beads on the leaves of the tall grass along the edge of the turnpike. There was no breeze at all, but big pink-edged clouds drifted over the western horizon. In the eastern sky, clouds hung stationary as if dabbed in one great brush stroke. Colonel Rogers, standing alone, silently observing our regiment assembling before him, waited for the arrival of the brigade commander, the hated Marsena Patrick. A retired career officer believing the war to be passing him by as he sat for months in a Washington hotel room begging anyone he knew to help him gain a commission, Patrick was now determined to make a name for himself. Knowing that he could accomplish that end by leading a victorious brigade, nothing would prevent him from doing so. We were harshly disciplined and relentlessly drilled until my hatred of him became so intense as to deny him the satisfaction of breaking me. Angered that his brigade had failed to defeat an inferior force yesterday, he ordered the Twenty-First to take the lead today as punishment for our shortcomings and bringing embarrassment to him.

Coffee, hot and bitter, cut through the yellow sickness that held me in its clutches through the long night. I would eat something later; probably it was better this way, to die on an empty stomach. Maybe I wouldn't puff up and pop like they say a body did in the heat, lying out there while the armies moved away. There was no time for food anyway; he was coming.

Before us, holding sword in his hand, blade resting along the haunch of his mount, Patrick slowly lifted it to where a ray of morning sun peeking over the horizon reflected and flashed as if a spark of fire.

"Men, today you have the opportunity to finish this work you so bravely began yesterday. We can destroy the Confederate army that lies in hiding. The brave boys who now lie beneath this soil," he paused as his horse jerked its head and paced two strides toward our line, "nearly completed the task yesterday. You now owe it to them to finish it today!" He jammed the sword into its scabbard. "You owe it to your loved ones! You owe it to your country! You owe it to God! My men, we return to the battleground of last night. Fight well, and I've no fault to find. Keep well closed up and be prompt to obey orders. Colonel Rogers, lead off by the right flank!" Patrick spurred his horse. It bolted. He pulled on the rein. "We will crush them today!" A long, loud "Hurrah!" erupted as we edged across the turnpike.

Across the green field, marked by boulders and clusters of scrub trees, and dark blotches where fresh graves had been dug the night before, I followed. Near a small rise to the north lay the bodies of a dozen men, grouped together as if resting around a campfire. Beyond the rise, hundreds more bodies were scattered. In the distance, mist rose above the land as the early morning sun lifted the dampness from the earth. On the horizon, trees lined the ridge behind which a thousand eyes watched us, waiting, as we approached step by step. The rattle of metal, dangling and clanging, and the thumping of a thousand boots striking the hard-packed farmland filled the air. Behind us were some fifty to sixty thousand men and before us, an open, rolling green field. Grasshoppers jumped, as my boots bent the weed stalks upon which they had perched. Crickets chirped, and a sparrow flying low, landed on a branch of a small leafless tree forty yards before me, these creatures of nature, unaware of what God's higher order of evolution was about to bestow upon these tranquil fields. I looked again toward the golden-leafed trees on the ridge in the distance.

"Boom! Boom!" Behind and to my right came the hollow thumping of our artillery opening fire, overwhelming all. Instantly the far ridge, peaceful and detached, was afire with silent bursts of flames, leaping and fading behind a swaying wall of white smoke. Then flashing lights came from within the clouding haze. A scream, low and then above my head, pierced my eardrums and shook the earth with a single consuming roar. Unaware of myself, I stood looking behind, where only seconds ago a four-gun battery had been toiling feverishly. It was no more, only smoke and pockets of flame existed where ammunition had once been stacked. Gone were the caissons, the twelve-pounders, the horses and men.

The pounding of Rebel artillery brought our line to a halt. I crouched and then lay to the ground as a wind of dirt and pebbles pelleted against my face. Panting, I pressed against weeds and the cool, damp earth beneath. Sucking in dirt with every breath, I watched an ant traverse between the stalks and over the impediments to stop, clean itself and momentarily ponder me and then disappear within the seclusion of a hole. With my lungs heaving, I fought for more air, thick and wet, unable to quench the desperate panic in my throat. Feeling the earth pulsate as each blast edged closer to me, unlike the ant, I remained exposed, helpless, gasping.

My arms covered my neck and head, pressing to my ears, blacking out the cries surrounding me. The ground, moist from the shade of the tall grass, held my face like a wet pillow. My breath came only with deep convulsions, as I pressed deeper in the grass and loose soil searching for a hole and escape.

As time had no meaning, the pounding became all consuming, taking me from this place to a distant summer night and another terror brought by thunderous clapping above the roof of my bedroom and the slapping of gale-driven rain against the narrow walls surrounding me. The blackness of this soil and its unseen holes would become, as was then, my blanket pulled over my head. There was safety in the darkness beneath the blanket on that summer night just as now with my eyes closed tightly pressing to this earth. My strength was always there within me, within the depths of myself, withdrawn from that which brought pain. And then it slowed. The shelling came only sporadically from beyond the ridge, and then our artillery fell silent. There was stirring and then the screams came from the unseen, cursing, praying to God; all signs that we were safe.

Rising, I saw bodies withering, wounded men crawling, others walking as if awakening from a whiskey-induced sleep, staggering, confused. Pederson was there, five paces to my front, alone, erect, staring at nothing.

"Are you hit?" I yelled. He failed to respond. Slowly, turning, his eyes were of glass, unreal, unfocused, dead eyes of a doll. "Get down, man." There was nothing, only his blank stare. "Don't do this to me. I can't take this." Reaching him, I pulled him to the ground.

Weakly, he crumbled and sat motionless, musket falling softly to his side. "Don't leave me, Pederson!" I lifted my hand and brought it down quickly across the side of his face. "Jesus!" I shook the man. "Will you wake up!" His head snapped backward, a grunt coming from him.

"What's wrong?" he whispered with a look of bewilderment, his hand pressed to the side of his reddened face.

"Here." It was Morgan, seldom far from his friend Pederson, jabbing a whiskey flask toward me. "Give him some of this. It'll help him come back." I took the silver container and placed it to my mouth. Pederson rubbed his cheek and watched me hand the whiskey back to Morgan.

"I think the worst is over," I said.

"No." Morgan held the flask for Pederson. "I don't think it's even started yet. They're forming lines in back of us."

Taking the right flank, our depleted numbers moved on toward the far ridge. Advancing, the pace increased without plan, closer and closer, now faster, swept along by some unearthly hand. Less than three hundred yards from the goal, sucking in deep gulps of air, I heard Colonel Rogers yell, "God be with you, Twenty-First! Forward! Double-quick! Charge!"

Leaping over rocks and clumps of weeds, I was engrossed in an orgy of anticipation, running, screaming. Men fell to the left, behind me and then more. Gun smoke hung in the grove of trees like a great white veil. The faces of the Rebels at the crest of the ridge, blurred, ghostly, the killers in the light, brilliant and gone and then more along a line forever wide.

The echoing of musketry resounded until it was steady and then obscured in the pounding absorption of soft lead into the bark of the sycamores. As the wooden mallet sending fence posts deeper into the hardened pasture floor, the thud of the minié ball equally terrifying in its power, comforted me that it hadn't found my flesh as we now stood and returned fire, again and again and then onward. Men were falling. Wounded before me. I could go no further. Loading, I glanced to see Pederson, his face blackened by the oily smoke that coated my mouth and nose with the stench of sulfur. I could barely swallow. My tongue felt thick and coarse in my mouth.

The second and third lines had now merged into a monolithic mass that pushed forward like an ocean swell rolling to the shore. Among those to the front was Utmeyer, our company's fifteen-year-old flag bearer. With only a holstered side arm, the fool stood urging us onward, waving the banner. At that moment, I saw him lunge forward, violently jerking as a ball entered the back of his head. Dazed at the suddenness of the horror I had witnessed, I stood and watched the flag fall from his hands as he was thrown to the ground. A soldier reaching the fallen Utmeyer stood with flag in hand. His face contorted, he ran up the incline into the path of a rock striking him in the chest. Pushed backward by the force of the blow, he stumbled before regaining his balance and again charged the Rebel line. He reached the crest, and for one brief moment, our flag flew over the Rebel forces.

A two-foot deep ditch at the base of the incline, hidden by weeds and decomposing tree branches, was filling with the dead, wounded, and more seeking shelter from the rain of minié balls pouring from above. Lunging over the bodies, my foot sank between the legs of a soldier, throwing me forward upon his back. At that instant, the lifeless body shook and bolted as a minié ball tore into the top of its skull, missing my face by inches. Grunting, I pulled my leg free, and pushing off from one of the bodies, leaped to the ground beyond the ditch.

Loose soil, moist in the shade of the slope, gave way as I struggled toward the crest. Leading me, a soldier, bent as if resisting a nor'easter, suddenly bolted upright and fell against me.

Instantly, I twisted to let him fall along my side, into the path of another charging up the incline. Both fell backward in a tangle of arms, legs, and musket, rolling onto the dead at the bottom of the ditch.

The Rebels had fallen back into a semi-circle some twenty yards from the ridge. There they regrouped to fire into our broken lines. I lifted my musket. Where was Pederson? Morgan and Griffin? Where was our third line? The Reserves?

"Pull back! Pull back!" Commands came from behind, to my right. Increasing flashing of musketry illuminated the heavy gray smoke hovering above the land. More fell along our line as Rebel reinforcements advanced upon our left. I turned and leaped, down the hill, over the body of the soldier who had carried the banner to the crest, fleeing the charging killers.

A thundering concussion shook the ground as a fiery ball erupted thirty yards from me. Lead filings, nails, snips of wires and rocks tore into those shielding me. I felt nothing. My arms, legs, nothing. Onward I ran, aimlessly. From every direction came the fire of hell. I was trapped! From every direction, I was exposed to grape, explosions so near the onrushing Confederates that both sides suffered the shrapnel. Surrounding me, wounded struggled to extricate themselves from this place that threatened their fragile hold on life. Among them, in the pile of distorted and twisted shapes, was a boy, the left side of his blond hair matted with maroon-colored blood, eyes pleading for help, his silent cries drowned in the deafening tumult. I stood apart as his head slowly reclined and disappeared among the still.

There I remained, desperately breathing. I could go no further, frozen in shame. Angry at the fear that had become me, I raised my musket, but onward they came. From the crest, along a mile front, thousands of Rebel reserves poured down the incline. Our lines had dissolved; confusion became desperation.

"Fall back!" Thickening smoke added to the developing terror of being encircled. Our reserve support was gone. We were trapped! Suddenly he appeared from out of nowhere. With arms waving wildly, face distorted, General Patrick attempted to rally his men. Some stopped, more formed about his horse that was prancing in panic. I was there, leveling my musket, but the mass rush to the rear made it impossible to fire or for the Rebels to hold their positions. The enemy broke as the panic-driven Federals blended into an unstoppable wave. Patrick rode among the men imploring us to turn and face the enemy, but the breakout rolled on unimpeded. Men everywhere poured from the battlefields south and north of the turnpike into the narrow opening of the stone bridge that crossed Bull Run Creek.

Leaving Patrick to our rear, the first of what remained of our regiment reached the bridge and crossing. We proceeded another mile until Colonel Rogers ordered us to form a rear guard. It was growing dark; silver streaks lined the sky lowly on the horizon. Rumbling thunder in the distance, at first confused with the remaining echoes of artillery, sounded in the northeastern sky. The cracking of gunfire, sporadic and dull, concentrated at the bridge crossing, was the only remaining remnant of battle.

"Boom!" An explosion shook the air itself. Flames danced upward into the darkness from the direction of the old stone bridge and the bright glow reflected from the low-hanging clouds. Having blown the bridge to stem the enemy's pursuit, the last of the 35th New York's columns trudged past our lines. Within the hum of boots shuffling on the hard-packed clay road, crickets chirped and mosquitoes buzzed. Above, stars twinkled in the graying sky and the cooling air absorbed the stench of death. The ancient life that had called this land theirs would return as we killers departed to find new battlefields.

December 1862
Near Fredericksburg, Virginia

Griffin sat down next to me.

"If you don't mind the company..." I glanced up to see him remove a pencil from his haversack, just as I folded my letter and placed it alongside the bills inside the envelope—keeping enough for whiskey and tobacco, the rest for Mother and Father. Closing my eyes I could picture Mother's hands holding the letter, a smile upon her face as she read the final two lines of the five-sentence letter, "I hope you are well and warm. Pray that I am home soon."

Griffin helped me drink my dollar's worth of whiskey when finishing the letter to his wife. I don't remember falling asleep, but he was rambling on about some problem his wife was having as I awoke. Attempting to gather my thoughts, I stared into the fire pit where flames sporadically thrust upward from the one remaining charred, crumbled log. As Griffin's words continued, I slowly turned my neck to look at the pile of wood some ten yards to my left. Too tired to care why Griffin hadn't thrown another log on the fire, I stood and stumbled toward my tent.

When the blare of the bugle awakened me, I tried not to move my head. A sick feeling crept through my stomach and I knew I had to move, to get outside of the tent before I puked. Struggling to my feet, I picked up my coat, buttoned it, and, pushing the flap of the tent aside, inhaled the cold air before walking away from the campsite, side pork, the smell of beans cooking. Walking, inhaling the morning air would help to clear my senses, my belly, the pain in my head.

I felt the pounding of hooves. Six riders, coming fast, abruptly pulled up before the colonel's tent. Without dismounting, the lead rider leaned down to speak to two officers. Steam blowing from the nostrils of his animal, the rider rose straight in his saddle, saluted, pulled the reins to the right, and disappeared into the early morning shadows.

Cold air descended upon northern Virginia. Crusts formed over the residue of blackened snow and pools of standing water. The surface of the roads became brittle to the step, posing peril to unsuspecting man or beast. Beneath the cover of ice lay a six-inch deep mass of mud to greet boot or hoof. Temperature by first roll had yet to rise into the twenties, but the sun shone brightly in the cloudless sky. Orders most had anticipated and at the same time dreaded, had come. We were to march upon Fredericksburg, the old city in the path to Richmond.

With bent saplings, hollowed-out trunks, twisted scrub trees, black mud, and brown snow woven among the dead grass and rotting, waterlogged limbs, the Rappahannock was wide, motionless, and formidable. Beyond, a grassy slope, partially covered in snow, rose from the swampy shoreline to meet the stone foundations of warehouses extending for at least two blocks. Above the roofs, red brick and pale-colored buildings formed along parallel streets in tiers rising toward Marye's Heights. The windows of all the buildings were blackened. Behind each, a Rebel sharpshooter. To the far left, on a gentle rise to an extended plain, Confederate soldiers near a new-growth woods waited for our invasion.

It was ten minutes before five. The sun had not yet appeared, when a single cannon blast came from somewhere along Stafford Heights to our rear. A second blast from farther down the ridge, and then as if by a signal, drums and fife sounded. Twenty minutes passed before the music stopped and the warmth from the sun peering over the trees lining the eastern horizon lifted the early morning fog draping the shoreline. Suddenly and without warning, a gigantic roar erupted and then blended into one great unending din. To the right of us, cannons poured shell into the city and the surrounding fields beyond the river. For thirty minutes, the unrelenting noise overwhelmed me. Less than fifty yards from the farthest battery, I crouched down to shield myself from the penetrating, engulfing reverberation.

Between our lines and the river, the cavalry, mounted and lined in rows of four abreast, looked magnificent and foreboding. They stood steady, the troopers, with eyes staring forward, shoulders back, focused upon the open field beyond the river. They would lead the charge. They would be the first to die on this day.

From Stafford Heights, along that ridge, along the treeless crest, cannons were belching flames into the sulfur haze descending from the hillside into the valley below. The resounding thunder rolled across the land, seemingly without end.

I couldn't hear the words that Griffin was speaking. His lips moved, but I heard only a steady, shrill, ringing noise. He pointed his finger toward the direction of two dozen men behind us.

"My God!" I heard Griffin say. "It's coffins that they're making. My God! They're making damn coffins!"

Down the slope toward the river, twenty-five yards from the coffin builders, pontoniers unloaded elongated boatlike structures. Each about twenty feet long and five feet wide at its middle, they appeared similar to the fishing boats launched from the small Italian coastal village south of Angola. The Italian fishermen would take their small boats out a mile and then work their way back to shore, dragging nets behind them, filled with pike, bass, and whitefish. These gray painted pontoons were not fishing boats.

The shelling of the city continued sporadically, concentrated within a five-block area beyond the river's bank and near the road that ran parallel to the river. Flames leaped from windows in the two-story buildings ablaze under the onslaught. Seemingly indifferent to the cannonading, the engineers continued at the water's edge. The pontoons, fastened and planked, would form three bridges to be placed at the bend in the river two miles below the city, and two directly leading into Fredericksburg. We would cross the bridges at the bend in the river and occupy the lowlands.

The big guns were quieted. With a blare of the bugle, the cavalry began to file past us, blue overcoats, gold buttons, black leather saddles, sabers dangling in sheaths at the riders' sides; tall, erect, proud, defiant, they rode in formation toward the river, the first to cross this night. The pounding of hooves upon the wooden planks was a terrible, powerful, frightening sound as hundreds of warriors, swift and lethal, rode astride their animals as if the two were one. Gliding effortlessly, the riders broke into a gallop when reaching the far shore, up the incline toward the road.

As the shadows lengthened in the early evening hours, we stood waiting, watching, on the shore of the Rappahannock. Franklin's Left Grand Division would cross under the cover of early-morning darkness and fog. General Reynolds' I Corps, the extreme left, Doubleday, our division, Colonel Rogers, the brigade, and Captain Layton, regimental commander.

To the steady rhythm of water splashing against the pontoons and boots thumping upon squeaking planks, our army, four abreast, began the crossing. While along the far ridge, behind the cover of oak and scrub pine, Stonewall Jackson sat watching.

It was eight-thirty and Meade's Third Division moved across the Old Richmond Road and up the open fields toward the tracks of the Richmond, Fredericksburg, and Potomac Railroad. He would hit the center of Stonewall Jackson's line, with Gibbon's division on the right, and our division's brigades of Phelps, Gavin, Meredith, and Rogers on the flank. The Center Grand Division, commanded by Joe Hooker, would remain on the opposite side of the river and follow the lead of Franklin. General Sumner, having taken positions within the abandoned city of Fredericksburg, would join the attack with his Right Grand Division, hitting into Longstreet's center.

The thunder from the Rebel artillery positioned on the ridge rolled across the hills with numbing intensity. Vibrations from the dull thumps of shells exploding caused the ground to pulsate under my boots as I pressed my hands around my musket and waited for orders to attack into the great clouds of smoke covering the distant ridge. And still, we waited.

Our artillery, firing from beyond the river continuously since shortly after eight, fell silent. A single enemy battery to our left, firing from that position, was tearing huge gaps into Meade's advancing lines with grape and canister. After delaying for what seemed an eternity, our artillery along Stafford Heights responded. One of the Rebel guns was hit and destroyed. The second was quickly limbered and under heavy fire, raced for cover beyond the ridge.

Meade's forces continued their advance beyond the railroad tracks and were ascending the slope of the ridge when the woods engulfing them erupted in exploding shell. Brilliant red flashes sent white smoke streaking upward, above the tallest branches. Our men stood watching helplessly, anticipating the order to move in support of Meade. We stood, watching, and waiting.

Then it stopped. The fading echoes of the thunderous booms reminded me of what had been occurring. For a moment, only the faint noise of distant musket fire was heard. And then, a numbing shrillness of screams burst from the mouths of men seemingly possessed by madness. From beyond the summit of the ridge, a wave of gray swept downward, ushered onward by nerve-shaking screaming that rolled along the hill with frightening impact.

"Let's go!" A scream, then another, and soon a chorus of demands to support Meade and Gibbon rang out. Aware that Gibbon had been stalled at the tracks and that his brigades were suffering the full force of the Rebel attack, the men of the 21st were yelling for the orders to move forward. As the smoke rolled along the battlefield, the bodies of wounded and dead soldiers were seen scattered upon the hillside. Men walking, bent over at the waist, some crawling, some being carried, dozens of men, hundreds, as if in a dream, oblivious to the confusion all around them, toward the rear, toward our lines. We stood. It was ten o'clock and the Union advance had been halted along the left flank.

At noon, the echoing tones of musket fire rolled down the hillside from where Federal advance lines made their initial push toward the Confederate entrenchment. In less time than forty-five minutes, Union forces had been nearly split in half, their entire center suffering extensive casualties. In spite of such heavy losses, they held their farthest point of advance near the wooded swamp, beyond the railroad tracks. It was from that point, unsupported, Meade's forces launched a second assault upon Stonewall Jackson's right flank. Heavy artillery fire followed the crack of muskets as Rebel batteries concentrated upon men charging across the swampland and up the embankment. Although taking a heavy toll in wounded and killed, the artillery failed to turn the Federals' charge. They had broken through the Confederate defensive line! We stood in amazement watching the flashes of light flaming from the muzzles of Rebel cannon along the distant ridge as smoke, covering the hillside, rolled and obscured the blue-uniformed soldiers charging through the grove of trees south of the railroad tracks. A great "Hurrah" echoed from the throats of our men and spread across the open field.

Meade's forces, breaking across the tracks, were advancing in a three-pronged movement, approaching the defensive wall the Rebels had formed along the ridge. Fighting continued to rage as the two forces stood facing each other across what appeared to be less than a hundred yards of open field. Men near me, their voices pleading desperately, yelled, "Let's go!" We stood watching as smoke engulfed the two armies and slowly obstructed them from our view.

It was shortly after one, and the center of Meade's division had advanced to the level ground that met the peak of the ridge. There, coming face to face with the Rebel artillery, they were met with a great thundering crescendo when the howitzers fired point-blank into the advancing Union soldiers, grape and canister exploding in the center of their lines.

"Dear Jesus!" someone next to me uttered. "Dear Jesus! They're being slaughtered!"

Plumes of white smoke shot upward all along the Union line as dozens of exploding shells scored direct hits upon the Federals. And then, a line of gray-uniformed soldiers appeared along the ridge and moved toward Meade's advance line sending them reeling from the loss of its entire front line, now unable to turn to meet the Rebel charge. Within minutes, it was over; Meade's division had been devastated.

Standing on bent, brittle, and yellowed grass, toes numb from the penetrating cold, pride in what I witnessed shielded the shame that permeated my soul. Before me, long, irregular columns of the remnants of Meade's division made a slow and orderly retreat from the woods and across the open fields toward the campsite from which they had departed only hours before.

The ghost of war haunted me through the long night; campfires across narrow fields that sloped toward the river, dark figures moving in the glow of the distant flames, commands echoing in the night air, neighing of burdened horses, squeaking ambulance wheels squealing under heavy loads, slowly rumbling over loose plank boards spread across the pontoon boats and faintly discernible, but always there, the anguished moaning of the wounded, lying on the sweeping hillside, alone in the cold, damp darkness, crying out for someone to help them. Pressing my fist to my mouth and closing my eyes, I thought of Morgan in the dirt of that distant cornfield, cold and alone. The cries continued.

"Come on, Reed!" Pederson's tone was stern. "Get the hell up!"

"This may be your last day on earth, my good friend," Griffin spoke from where he sat near the fire. "You should enjoy every last minute of it awake." I sat up and squeezed the back of my neck to help reduce a painful knot that had formed there during my sleep.

A light fog shrouded the Rappahannock. Above, the sky was clear, and already the lingering shadows in the valley were receding as the sun slowly edged over the horizon to the east. There were no rations, no fire. We sat, muskets in hand, bayonets fixed, waiting for orders.

"Why are we not moving?" Griffin grumbled. "Were the Rebels pulling back? Why don't we follow them? Why didn't we advance yesterday? Why didn't we go to the aid of Meade's forces?" Each protest inspired the next, as his frustration turned to anger.

Rumors became speculation of what happened the day before. We had not been ordered to advance, Pederson argued, so we would be in position to pursue the retreating Rebel army if it fled along the Old Richmond Road. Pederson learned that Hooker's Center Grand Division, with the exception of Birney's division, was also held out of battle. If he was correct in what he heard, the majority of this newly structured Army of the Potomac had yet to "see the elephant." The confidence that Burnside had instilled in his men was beginning to wane. Another day had passed, another opportunity to crush the Confederate army.

On the field that rose above the Old Richmond Road, and on the slopes of Marye's Heights, an armistice returned soldiers to the battlefield to bury the bodies of their fallen comrades. The only man from the 21st who died in battle yesterday was Corporal Quinton of Company "I." Three others endured wounds, but they would survive to fight another day.

The sight of white flags and burying parties reminded me that we lost only one man. For others, the losses were great. Sumner's

Right Grand Division attacked Longstreet's forces along the hills behind the city. At the foot of the ridge named Marye's Heights, Sumner lost most of his divisions. We learned that Meade's division suffered immense casualties, losing nearly half of its men. Gibbon would not be capable of mustering enough men to fight another day. Birney's division, from Hooker's command, suffered a thousand casualties. Again, an army in rags and on the verge of starvation had stopped us.

Soldiers from Company "I," returning from the burying detail, told of finding Union dead lying naked in the fields, boots, coats, haversacks, and blankets having been taken by the Rebels. They told of Rebels approaching them, introducing themselves and talking of trading while wearing the blue uniforms stolen the night before. The Rebels exchanged news, as they knew it, as well as whiskey and tobacco for Union coffee and rations. Both sides talked of a better day, of the end to the war, and going home.

The bugle called us to rise just before dawn. As soon as the eastern sky lightened into a pale grayness, Jeb Stuart's cannons along Jackson's far left flank again began to send shells toward our lines. This was the day we would advance, Griffin assured me, as he shared his coffee that he had been boiling.

"The Rebs probably were firing artillery only to cover their retreat," he said. "We will end this thing once and for all...I just know it!" Time passed and still we waited for orders. Shortly after nine, they came. Our pickets had been withdrawn, and officers riding along the rows of our pits ordered us to pack everything and to prepare to re-cross the Rappahannock. Under a stillness that was almost dreamlike, the great army formed a massive snakelike column that stretched for miles along the shoreline. Moving at four abreast, we marched across the bridges past limbered artillery and trains of supplies and ordnance, ambulances, graves by the hundreds, and vacant plantations and farms, laid to waste by marauders from Hooker's idled legions to where we bivouacked near the edge of a pine woods.

"Are we retreating?" Pederson, fumbling with his knapsack that he had dropped to the ground, looked up at me.

"I don't think we're retreating," Griffin responded to Pederson's question. "We're probably going to move up river and outflank them."

"We could have done that on the other side of the river." Pederson pushed his knapsack away and sat down. "I don't think Burnside knows what to do."

"He knows what to do," Griffin responded.

"How in hell could he? How in hell do you fight a battle and use less than half of your soldiers?" Pederson retorted angrily. Griffin remained silent. After a minute, he hung his head and began to open his knapsack. I looked at Pederson. He shrugged his shoulders and gently shook his head.

Griffin said little after that. His face showed no expression when I spoke to him. His responses were always a nod of his head or a shrug of his shoulders.

"Is everything all right?" I asked him on that last day I saw him. His lips tightened in a smile that expressed more joy than anger.

"Everything is perfect now," he said quietly. I looked into his eyes. He stared back for a few seconds and his smile broadened. "Thanks, Reed...you've been a friend." He then turned away.

3 Coming Home

April 1863
Acquia Creek, Virginia

Clear ice that had long clung to the shorelines of the Potomac cracked and broke off in chunks, sending ice floes adrift before catching the current and disappearing within the rolling black swells of the river's main channel. Winter gave way to spring, and as the days grew longer and warmer and the earth thawed, my thoughts of battle lessened and memories of what had been blurred by indifference.

May 1863
Leaving Acquia Creek, Virginia

The time had come when the weight pressing upon my heart lifted, when fresh air brushed away doubt that I would ever be freed of this burden. Days yet to be seem never to come, and once past, forgotten seconds. But as the days narrowed to a few, my joy was replaced by a growing fear that some event would occur, some decision made to prevent my leaving this place.

Foreboding filled that portion of my being left vacant by the loss of comrades, my brothers. Griffin, unable to longer endure the loneliness he felt for his family, deserted in the middle of a stormy night. Pederson, no more a friend or companion to anyone, was lost in his grief for the death of Morgan at Antietam. And I searched for relief from the gloom in the memories of what I had left behind in my other life. Memories, real or imagined, became my identity and created what I hoped to become when I again touched the soil of my farm.

Often appearing to me were thoughts and dreams of the dusty lane that led to our house, the lilac bush, fragrant and overgrown, beneath my bedroom window, the rusted plow blade that gave up its winter scales under pressure from the stone in my hand, and my father's nod when he saw the shiny metal surface and bloody blisters peeking forth from beneath the rags wrapped around my hands. But always, there was my mother, her smile, her arms around me, the brightness of her eyes even when filled with tears. In the deepest of dreams, when reality lifted my body, Winnie came to me; delicious, thin body pressed to me, encouraging me to touch her, stroke her. In truth, I had Ellen, and her inner warmth that gave me comfort. She was there for me always. She would be my life.

A narrow center aisle ran the length of the passenger car, dividing the rows of wooden benches. Each section of the seats was undoubtedly designed for three butts in a peaceful world.

"Be damn glad ya got a place to park yer sorry asses!" Hamilton felt obliged to remind us that we were still in the army. "So just press yer sweet cheeks together and get five on each side. If ya don't like it, stand up or get off, but whatever ya do, shut the hell up!"

Stiffly, I pressed into the seat and against the body grudgingly relinquishing precious space. Closing my eyes and feeling the car sway as more came aboard to jostle for a place to sit, I wanted to be away from this place and this moment, to have sleep transport me from the army to a quiet field where there were warm and gentle breezes. Unwilling to smile for fear I would offend the gods of deliverance or exhale completely and let down my guard, I clenched my jaw and thought of nothing.

My head bobbed and jerked as the train struggled to a continuous roll. Confident we had truly departed, I opened my eyes to suspiciously observe tents and columns of men and gray granite buildings slowly passing from view through the side window. The air, held as a solid block in my chest, eased and the blood returned to flow into my fingers slowly releasing from a clenched fist as the locomotive sped past trees and fields and barns and forests and small crossroads—villages blending into a mosaic of northern Pennsylvania.

The curious appeared, a few scattered along the route, waving or standing on roads and platforms watching as we rolled onward. Who were these people who came to wave hankies and pass extended hands, strawberry preserves, pickled watermelon rind, and molasses cookies? The bored? Morbid individuals coming to see the killers?

Maybe I had been too influenced by the bitterness expressed by the newspaper editors. Why should the words of a few writers deny what the public truly believed? Hadn't we been brave and our feats glorious? We defeated Lee at Antietam and South Mountain. We held our own at Second Bull Run. We followed orders at Fredericksburg, orders issued by fools who were no better than butchers themselves. Weren't we heroes entitled to greetings welcoming us home?

May 1863
Buffalo, New York

Then came Buffalo and the confirmation that distance had indeed cleansed our souls and purified our deeds. They came to cheer and make music with horns and hollow fife. Buntings were draped and lies were spoken and with the wave of a hand, I was free from calls to duty and stood in the center of a strange noise.

The press of the crowd turned to bumping and pushing when mothers reached for their sons, wives for their husbands, and children for their fathers. With tears visible on the face of one woman, dressed in a light-blue dress and clutching a white hat that had been pulled from her head, she grasped the hand of Hamilton walking a few feet in front of me and was immediately lost within his embrace. Others near me looked beyond and through me, expressing obligatory smiles of courtesy, of impatience. Within the pulsating throng, I was alone.

"James?" I heard my name being called, not much above that of a whisper. "Welcome home!" It was Ellen. "Oh James…I worried so." Reaching for me, "I couldn't find you! I didn't see you!" Her voice trembled. "I didn't know...where you were."

"It's all right. I'm here. I'm here." Time and motion had stopped. Only Ellen existed. Feeling her heart beating against my chest, inhaling the sweet aroma of flowers radiating from her brown hair, filling my senses while her warm softness eased beneath my fingers, I held her tightly, pressing through her dress and into the gentle sobbing within her. Taking my hand in hers, she led me through the tangle that separated and allowed us to pass. "We need to get away and find a place to talk," I implored.

"No!" Ellen pulled at me. "Over there! My family is waiting over there, near the corner."

Pederson stood near the stage, nodding in my direction. Two young women were at his side.

"Jon, wait there!" I yelled. "Don't go yet!" Ellen's finger slipped from my hand. "Ellen...wait!"

"There they are!" Hearing Ellen, I looked to where she was pointing. Ellen's mother waved to me and then put her hands to her mouth.

"Just a minute, Ellen." I glanced back to the empty space where Pederson stood only seconds before.

"There's my family." Ellen had found my hand again and led me to where her sister, little brother, and father waited. Annie ran toward me. I opened my arms to Ellen's sister just as her small body pushed into me, moving me backward.

"Hi, little girl!" The twelve-year-old looked into my eyes, her laughter fading in that moment, as if the excitement of the day was lost in what she now saw in me. She drew back from me awkwardly.

"We all missed you, James. It's God's blessing that you have returned." Ellen's mother held Annie's shoulder to prevent her from moving further away.

"James!" Her father held out his thick, calloused hand. "You look taller than I remember!"

I smiled and glanced at Ellen. Her dark eyes, sparkling from the wetness of tears, contrasted against a fair complexion and the blush of redness in her cheeks. Brown hair, flowing loosely from beneath a yellow-flowered hat, and intertwined with a wide, white ribbon extending from its rear brim, tumbled against her shoulders, as she stood there, tall, statuesque, desirable.

"Reed!" Pederson was standing a few yards from Ellen's family. "My sisters have come, so I'll be leaving now."

"Yeah, me too." I edged past Ellen's father without a word.

"Your family?" Pederson turned his back as he spoke, looking into the crowd.

"No," I answered. "It's Ellen's family. It's the girl I was telling you about."

"She's very pretty, Reed."

"Yeah," I replied, knowing he hadn't really looked at Ellen's family.

"Were you with your sisters when I saw you?"

"Yeah, my father and mother were not willing to negotiate this mob."

"Mine either."

"Yeah, that's nice." Pederson's face grew stern, ignoring what I had muttered. "I will miss you, Reed."

"Don't you think we'll see each other once in a while?"

"Yeah, I'm sure we will." He reached for me, anxious to bring an end to our conversation.

I squeezed his hand and in that instant a thousand memories, a thousands fears that we had shared flashed before me. It was as if I could smell the sulfur of cannon fire, feel the earth shake beneath exploding shells, hear men screaming, the whine of minié balls passing near me, the echoes of bugles in the distance. He turned and was gone. I stood there, feeling more alone than at any time in my life.

"James! James!" Ellen called. "Are you joining us?"

"Yes…sure…I was just saying goodbye to a friend."

"Oh…who was that? I would like to have met him."

"Yeah. I'm sorry. He was in a hurry, you know, family and all."

Holding on to me, Ellen looked to where Pederson had disappeared into the crowd. She said nothing more about him.

Ellen and I sat together in the Eddys' carriage across from her mother who attempted to avoid my eyes, turning her head whenever I caught her staring at me.

"How is my mother?" I asked shortly after we reached the outskirts of Buffalo. There was a moment of silence before Ellen spoke.

"She has her good days, and then not so good."

"She's not well, James. She has a difficult time holding down any food," her mother interrupted. "I'm very worried for her."

Through the opening in the side of the carriage, I could see trees abruptly appear, and then pass from sight. The New York countryside had awakened from its winter sleep and emerging blades of grass and weeds and rows of early hay growth formed a green hue on the rich black soil. Several puffy, white clouds drifted above in the pale blue sky. Ellen's mother was speaking, but her words were of no more importance to me than an indistinguishable blend of noise. My thoughts were of Mother, of my father, and of Ellen's warmth that I felt through the sleeve of my coat. Uncertain as to what I would find at home, I told Ellen that I wanted to be alone in my first visit with Mother, as the carriage slowed approaching the gate to the driveway.

"I'll come over later tonight, if you don't come by," she promised.

"Please, Ellen, James is right. He needs time alone with his mother." Mrs. Eddy touched Ellen's sleeve.

"Yes, I believe you're right," Ellen said. "But remember, you must come by soon!" I nodded and she climbed back into the carriage. Her father pulled the reins to the left.

"It's right good to see you again, boy, mighty good."

I raised my hand as if to salute before I was aware of what I was doing. Embarrassed, I waved as the carriage idled down the road away from the gate. Turning to face the house, this familiar scene so often in my dreams, the dusty lane, the great looming oak was overshadowed by the chilling warning cast in the darkened windows.

4 Alien Land

May 1863
Angola, New York

My home was as I remembered. Little had changed, as expected, for my father wouldn't have permitted alterations in his design of life for himself, Mother, and me. Fortified with a strong back and meanness of nature, he stood resolute against that which threatened his ways. My volunteering for war had challenged him. He denied my actions and found refuge in the stability of the land that forever remained a constant. It was more his devotion to the land than his dislike of people that drove him from his family. As I stood looking out across warming fields of the New York spring, I knew he was out there somewhere. The planting season had come and with it another reason for being away from dawn to dusk.

The yard was fully enveloped in the shadow of the house and the long grass having yet to awaken in the spring sunlight held its yellow hue. Three robins swooped down, and in the distance a crow was strutting, warning every living creature of its presence. The gentle afternoon breeze cooled as the sun sat over the birch trees in the western woods. My legs felt tired as I approached the steps leading up to the back porch. It had been a long day, made worse by the fact that I hadn't slept while riding the train, and had closed my eyes only an hour or so the night before. At a different time, I would have lain down in the soft grass in the front yard and given in to the childlike sleep of home.

The steps squeaked beneath my weight as I cautiously ascended them. Any second, I expected Mother, laughing, to run and embrace me. But the kitchen door remained closed. Seeing only darkness through its windowpanes, I gently turned the knob. A cold, stale air washed over me as I entered. Upon the table rested a solitary cup. Dishes, along with a black iron pan, were stacked in the sink.

"Hello!" The sound of my voice echoed in the stillness of the room. "It's James...I'm home!"

Resting my knapsack on the table next to a half-filled coffee cup, I stepped to the corner of the room, near the door and carefully propped my big gun against the wall. Turning, I walked through the dining room, toward Mother's bedroom. The door, slightly ajar, squeaked as I guided it. The familiar odor of sickness hung faintly in the air within the room. The outline of a body lay in the disheveled blankets upon the bed. Slowly, quietly, edging closer, I saw her head resting in the deep folds of the feather pillow, her thin, white face enveloped in long coarse, gray-streaked hair.

Beneath high, white cheekbones, her deep, dark eyes sunken in hollow sockets opened.

"Mother...I'm home." Lowering myself to the bed, I gently touched her face, guiding strands of hair away from her eyes.

"Jimmy...my little boy..."

I leaned over her, pressing my lips to her forehead.

"I love you, Mother."

"Jimmy..." Her words faded behind dried, cracked lips. I turned toward the nightstand, seeking a pitcher or glass. There was neither.

"I'll get you something to drink, Mother." In the kitchen, I filled a glass from the pail near the sink and returned to the bedroom.

Holding her head, I watched the water flow down the sides of her mouth and onto the pillow.

"Mother...," I whispered, "are you hungry?"

"Just another drink would be fine."

"Is Father nearby?" I asked, holding the glass to her lips.

"Oh, yes, he takes such good care of me."

"Does he?" I regretted my remark. "Mother, I'm going to fix some soup for you, and then I'm going to clean up this bed a little."

"I'm sorry you had to see me like this. I'm sorry."

"It's wonderful seeing you. I love you, Mother...I love you."

The sun had set by the time I finished boiling the bed sheets. Darkness filled the dining room, and the light coming from Mother's bedroom cast long shadows down the hallway. Father, returning, would see the light in the kitchen window, the same light that cheered me on many a cold, dark night. His immediate response would be of anger, confusion, undoubtedly unconcerned about leaving Mother alone in the darkness, but I mustn't think of him now; too much to do.

Hearing the porch steps squeak, I stiffened my back, anticipating him.

"Well! I see you made it back." I felt the cold air sweep into the kitchen before I heard his words. He hadn't shaved in days. The smell of the cow dung covering his boots permeated the room.

"When did you start bringing your shit-covered boots into the kitchen?"

"I didn't know who was here...being all bright like this."

"It could have been Mother, getting up to fix your dinner." He looked at me for several seconds before turning, opening the door and walking outside.

Needing the whiskey hidden in my dresser drawer, I longingly glanced at the stairs leading to my room, but before I could move, the kitchen door opened. His socks, wet and filthy, left imprints where he walked on the pine floor.

"You've seen your mother then, I take it," he said, pulling a chair away from the table.

"She didn't have any water. Why is she alone like this?"

"I stop in when I can..."

"No!" I yelled. He stopped rubbing his feet to look up at me. "No, you don't! She lies there alone...in her waste until it's too dark for you to be outside!"

"You needn't yell!"

"Why is she left alone like that?"

"I had a lady come by every day, but I couldn't keep that up forever."

"You son of a bitch!"

"Hey! Don't you talk like that in my house! Dressed like that," he waved his arm at me in a gesture of dismissal. "Who the hell do you think you are anyway?"

"She'd have cared for your sorry ass if it had been the other way!"

"I love that woman!"

"You don't love anybody! I wonder if you ever did."

"I didn't have the money! I couldn't afford that kind of help." He dropped his head to look down at his hands still clutching his right foot. "She said it'd be all right if I stopped in throughout the day."

"Why didn't you use the money I sent home?"

"I told you I didn't support your joining the army and told your mother I won't touch blood money."

"So, you'd let her lie there, every day, when all you'd had to do was to use the damn money to help her!" He stood up. He appeared smaller than I remembered. His face was older, darker, different, maybe even sadder than in the past.

"The doctor saw her a while back. He told me she has the cancer and he couldn't do much to help her."

"I'll talk to him tomorrow when I go to town." I turned, picked up the bedding from the table, and walked from the kitchen.

"Good night," I heard him say.

Buffalo, New York

The shoreline drifted by slowly, almost dreamlike, as the heavy-burdened boat lurched through the swells. Smoke from the ferry's chimney coughed in black plumes and then disappeared in the swift breezes. This same boat that had once taken me to the army now carried me to the mustering out. I thought of Ellen and how I hurt her by all that I did, and didn't do. It was easier for my father to take me to the ferry landing than to ask Ellen to do so. Just now, I didn't want to talk about us and our future and endure the worried expressions on the faces of Ellen's family members or the pity they felt for the pathetic Reed boy. There hadn't been time for all of that, and besides, it was better spent caring for family matters. Mother was my concern now. Once the doctor gave me medicine to reduce Mother's pain, I turned my attention to arrangements for her care.

My discharge paper looked very official, the engraved eagle, the dark scrolled ink, the yellowed grain paper. Captain Layton, passing the document to me, broke the momentary spell. He then extended his right hand. "You're a good soldier, Reed. I was proud to serve with you."

"Thank you, sir."

"Reed..." He gripped tightly. "Remember, the war is not over. We'll be needing more men like you to finish the job. You could go back in as a corporal, if you choose. At least think about it."

Corporal Hutchinson told me that Pederson had been mustered out earlier in the afternoon and didn't remember him saying anything. I might find his house, just to say good-bye, but some uneasiness told me not to do so uninvited. Nevertheless, some day soon, we would bump into one another and renew our friendship.

Shadows cast by the tall buildings brought gloom to the wet streets. An old lamplighter dressed in a dark frock coat buttoned to the collar, proudly wearing a tall beaver hat and resting his long pole on his shoulder, indifferently glanced at me as I followed my route to the landing. I paused to watch him work before he turned and, marching beyond the glow of the lamp he lit, disappeared into the darkness.

June 1863
Angola, New York

Standing alone in the field, looking out across the black farmland rolling in a gentle rise to the east, the sunshine of early June was warm against my back. Taking a deep breath, I placed my hand on the top of the brittle, weathered fence post, leaning against it to rest for a few minutes. Two robins sat along the top of the plank board fence a few yards away. A small flock of seagulls were busily pecking for insects in the freshly turned earth beyond the first few rows in the field. Memories of the cornfield at Antietam, Morgan lying in the shadows of the corn—minié balls hissing near my head—the smell of gun powder...Pederson's face darkened with sulfur residue staring into my eyes as I told him of Morgan, came to me.

There was something dreamlike about the corn that morning in fields above Antietam Creek. The sun had not penetrated the rows and a mist seemed to hang in the shadows. Clumps of reddish-brown earth clogged the rows, and flies buzzed about my knees. The familiar smell of corn, the pale green and browning leaves waving in the early morning breezes, all brought back memories of home, of early autumn days running carefree through the rows of giant stalks of corn. But on that day, before me, crouching broad-backed men, blankets to shoulders, long-barreled muskets in hand readied themselves to unleash charges of death.

The air was heavy. I labored in an effort to fill my lungs. The men in front of me, bending low, moved forward. I followed.

"Reed!" Morgan yelled from behind me.

"Morgan! Stay low!" Why did I always feel it necessary to give Morgan advice, even stupid, obvious advice as "stay low." From the beginning, Morgan seemed to be a misfit among aliens. Even more than the others, the war provided him an escape from a home of which he seldom spoke. Comical and disrespectful, he showed no true interest or identity with Griffin's idealism or Pederson's disillusionment. Obsessed with the camp-following whores surrounding us, he drank Pederson-bought whiskey and avoided work.

His toothache had always been there and the whiskey only delayed the pain that increased daily. When it finally became too much to bear, he fell under the knife wielded by a field surgeon. His gaping wound became a greater problem as it refused to heal. Festering, his jawbone swelled so he could no longer eat. He was already dying from gangrene when our army crossed the border into Maryland in pursuit of Robert E. Lee.

The shelling to our rear had ceased and the only noises heard were those of crackling corn stubble and heavy breathing as we pushed forward. "Boom!" A crashing roar of musketry rushing down the tunneled rows deafened me and sucked the air from my lungs. In front of our lead men, less than fifty feet, Rebels, filling every row, fired as we proceeded headlong and blindly toward them. Men screamed as minié balls sliced cornstalks with the efficiency of a knife through rhubarb. I raised my musket, peered down the barrel through the shadows in front of me and squeezed the trigger. Staring into the smoke, trying to sense whether I had found my target, I pulled a cartridge from the box and with trembling fingers jammed it into the barrel. The report of my musket was lost in the explosions that surrounded me. I stepped back, and the second line, moving forward, instantly fired their rounds. Again, the overwhelming roar of hundreds of muskets was as one.

"I'm ready!" Morgan screamed. "Let me go!" He pushed by me and ran forward through the row. I jammed my rod in place, and plugged the nipple, half-cocked the hammer, and followed Morgan.

Morgan had stopped. I moved in front and fired at a gray figure I could now see before me. It slumped to the ground.

"I'm ready." I stepped aside for Morgan to move forward. "I'm ready!" he said again. His mouth, swollen, and distorted, was twisted into a faint smile. "I'm ready," he repeated.

He fired, and I took his forward position. Through the heavy smoke, I saw the outline of a man; he was thirty paces away. The sunlight penetrated the rows now as the top half of many stalks had been cut away by the swipe of bullets. Smoke, heavy and white, filled the rows, and my lungs. I was sucking deeply for air as I struggled to load and level my aim at the chest-high flashes.

"Aim at their knees!" I heard a voice coming from behind me. The roar of musketry was one great continuous noise, broken only by the whine of minié balls near my face. I stepped forward, dropped to one knee, leveled my gun barrel crotch-high and pulled the trigger. Cursing and moaning surrounded me. Men were yelling as they struggled feverishly to load, cock, and fire. My cartridges were only a few, maybe five, I guessed. They too, had to be low on ammunition. They must stop soon, I prayed.

I fired, stood up, and turned to see Morgan slumped over behind me.

"Have you been hit?" I yelled, touching his shoulder. He kept his head down. His cap dropped to the ground. "Where are you hit?" I yelled in his ear. He turned his head to me. Tears were in his eyes.

"I was brave!" He looked up at me. "I was a brave soldier, wasn't I?" he asked.

"Are you hit?"

"I'm just tired, Reed. I'm sick, and I'm so tired."

"Morgan." I reached to touch his head. "Stay down."

"No!" He struggled to rise. "I'm ready!" He began to walk toward the Rebel line.

"No, Morgan! No!" At that moment, he was thrown backward against me. My arm wrapped around him. A liquid, gurgling sound came from his chest. His head bowed forward, his big gun fell to the earth. He began to slip through my arms like a gutted flour sack.

I held him. His body was frail, light, and bony. "Morgan..." He didn't hear me.

His skull exploded. Bone, blood, and hair flew into my face as a second minié ball entered the top of his head.

"Aaaahhhh!" I lowered his body to the ground and quickly pressed my palms to my eyes to clear his blood. Blinking to relieve the burning, I reached for his musket, pointed it down the row and squeezed the trigger. "Die, you rotten son of a bitch! Die!" I dropped the gun, rolled him to the side and removed the few cartridges from his box. I retrieved his cap and placed it over his face. With his loads in my musket, I aimed and fired, over and over again.

"Fall back!" A command came from behind me. "Fall back, Twenty-first! Fall back!" I rose to my knees, and looked at Morgan's body.

"We'll come back for you." My feet were heavy with wet, blood-soaked earth stuck to my soles. I began to run to the rear, stumbling over men lying dead in the corn rows.

I looked above into the blue New York sky and remembered Pederson.

"We'll stay in touch," he had promised. "Hell, I can see us rejoining in a short time. Yeah! I can see us going back to finish the job!"

Pederson hadn't talked much about his family. He did say that he hated his father and didn't look forward to returning to live with him.

"It will be good to see my sisters again," he had said when we drank enough on any particular night. "But I'd just as soon be off to Wisconsin to see Griffin if I could."

Mike Griffin was the oldest of the four of us, the only one married. He had three small children, alone and vulnerable to the threats of a neighbor who stalked their mother. The longer the war dragged on, the less Griffin supported McClellan's delay in pursuing Lee's army and ending it all. Griffin was our leader, the tough one who taught us to be soldiers. When he left during the night, I knew he would not be caught or prevented from reaching his family and killing his lunatic neighbor. He promised to find peace and safety in the isolated forests of Wisconsin, a place we all sought to reach some day.

Soon, I lied to myself, I'd have reason to locate Pederson in Buffalo. Wasn't it just a matter of finding his father's factory? The buzzing of a hornet next to my ear caused me to flinch and swat at the insect. A chill ran down my spine as the whining instantly brought back the memories of a similar sound, a sound that I shall never forget.

Touching the cool soil in the early morning, and feeling the warming sun in the afternoon brought a peace to me I hadn't felt in a long time. The pace of the world had changed dramatically for me. Traveling from the battlefield of Fredericksburg, Virginia, to Acquia Creek and to upper New York was a voyage not only to a different place but also to a different time. A gentle breeze blew and its hollow sound filled my senses and the void within me that grew more intense with each day of silence. I seldom had words for my father while Mother slept most of the time and spoke only through her faint smile, which appeared less frequently with each passing day.

July 1863

She had cancer. The doctor said he could do little for her but help fight the pain she would bear every day.

"Oh, it's not so bad," she said. "We've all been through worse than this." Her sad eyes could not hide her suffering. "I hate to think of the terrible time you had in the war, son. It hurts me to think about it."

At night, staring into the blackness above my bed, I had often heard her cry out in pain. When I went to her, I found my father bending over the bed or sitting on the floor holding her hand. He didn't see me watching or hear me leave.

Ellen came by when she could, to sit, to encourage her to sip water, one spoonful at a time. I watched her brushing Mother's hair, humming as she gently encouraged the bristles through strands flowing to the pillow. It was Ellen that told us of Mother's death.

I heard a muffled whine. Father looked up from where he was washing supper dishes at the kitchen sink. At first, I thought it was the wind until I saw Father drop the dishrag and run to the hallway where Ellen stood. Her mouth was open, tears filling her eyes as she came to me.

"James, she's gone!"

"Mary!" Father screamed as he rushed into the room. "No! No!"

When I reached the doorway, I saw him lift her lifeless body, her arms dangling as he cradled her. Touching my father's shoulder, feeling his body shake in silent protest, I reached for Mother, to feel the warmth of her face for the last time.

Ellen touched my arm as I walked by. There were no words to say. I had nothing to give. The night air was cool against my face. Stars were blinking in the iron-gray sky. Faster, faster, I had to get away! Running down the road, I gasped for air. Pain filled my chest. Having difficulty breathing, I slowed and stumbled to a stop.

"Mother!" I cried out to the heavens. Falling to my knees, I bent over. My body was convulsing in agonizing sobs. "Mommy!"

Heavy, gray clouds streaked with purple, billowing overhead, threatened rain on the morning Mother was buried. For a long time, she had talked about her final resting place next to her mother and father. I told her that I didn't want to hear such things.

"You'll never die, Mother," I had said. "Don't talk about being buried in the ground! I won't ever let that happen to you."

"Some day it will happen, Jimmy. You will have to be brave and help your father. He will need you even more then."

During the days following the burial, I didn't see my father. If he came home at all, I didn't hear him. Neither of us went into her bedroom. It would have been difficult to stand there, among the possessions she so treasured, and absorb the emptiness that her death had brought.

August 1863

It was a dull pain that was not worthy of concern. My father will not hear of the injury or see me walk with a favor. Such stupidity as losing sight of where one of the milkers was feeding was unacceptable to him. My grunting heave to straighten the fencepost had startled the dumb animal and when she bolted, her hoof set heavy on my ankle, pushing it into the soft earth. It was the cushion of the loose soil that prevented a broken bone and the hard whiskey later that dulled the pain and what I hoped, the memory of it all.

A buggy slowed at the gate and turned into our drive. Seeing Ellen's yellow bonnet before recognizing the Eddy carriage, I quickly gulped down the whiskey remaining in the cup and hid it from view under the steps. A sharp pain cut through my ankle when I stood. Angrily, I limped back to the porch. Ellen waved when she spotted me, probably thinking me rude for not coming to meet her, but if so, she didn't show it by the expression on her face.

"Hi there, stranger!" She laughed. "Too tired to meet me, huh?"

"Too lazy and dumb is more like it maybe."

"Well, I can't argue with that." She reached for me.

"It's good to see you. I've missed you." I smiled.

"Well, I'm very happy to hear you say that. What happened?"

"Nothing, just something stupid."

"Is it broken?"

"No, it's fine. Don't much think about it. It'll get better."

She placed her hand to my ankle and gently ran her fingers over the swollen joint. “Poor baby,” she said mockingly.

“That’s what I needed. It feels better already.”

She smiled at my response and then turned to look out toward the barn. “Is your father here?”

“No, I haven’t seen him since the funeral.”

“Really?”

“Yeah.”

“I miss her.”

“Yeah, I do too.”

There were several minutes of silence before Ellen again spoke. “I’ve missed you too.”

“I’m sorry, Ellen.”

“Yeah. I know you’ve been going through a bad time right now.” She paused. “That’s why I’ve stayed away from you, too.”

“Well, it hasn’t been fair to you,” I said.

After a few moments, she asked, “Why do you think that?”

“What?”

“That you haven’t been fair to me?”

“I wrote to you. I mean...”

“Oh, James, do you think you owe me something because we wrote to one another?”

“No! I’m sorry, I didn’t mean it that way.”

“Why then, because I took some care for your mother?”

“Don’t do this, Ellen.”

“I’m sorry. I didn’t want this to be ugly.”

“What do you mean?”

“I’m sorry. I know you need time.”

“I don’t know what I need. Maybe I should think of what you need.”

“I have what I need. You’re home safe and sound. My prayers have been answered.”

"Ellen!" I clasped her hand and looked into her eyes. I wanted to tell her how much I loved her, how much I missed her, how much I needed her, but the words stayed in my throat.

Crickets chirping and the cry of a barn swallow filled the night air. From the western ridges toward the lake shores, the setting sun cast a purple and maroon glow along the horizon. Fireflies danced in the darkness of the side yard.

"It was bad, wasn't it?"

"What do you mean?" I asked.

"You know. The fighting and all."

"It seems like it didn't really happen at all sometimes." I took a deep breath.

"Why do you think that is? I would think it would be impossible to think about much of anything else."

"Maybe you're right. I try not to think of it. Maybe that's what I mean."

"Were you afraid?"

I shook my head. "Sure, everyone is afraid, all of the time." There was silence for a few seconds before my rambling memories became words. "One always thinks of death...of those who have died...of those who would die in the next battle. It doesn't do any good to think about it!"

"Thank God it's over for you!"

"Yeah...maybe it is," I said.

"Maybe?" she blurted out. "Do you read about the war at all?" she asked.

"No. I only hear some talk in town."

"At the tavern?"

"Yeah, there, and other places."

"It all seems so terrible. Like there is no end to it all."

"It seems like it, doesn't it?"

"All the time you were in the army, I read of all the battles where so many men died, and nothing seemed to come of it but more battles and more senseless killing." My hand fumbled with my swollen ankle. "I don't know of many people that care about this war," she said cautiously. "I mean what you did was wonderful and brave, but does it matter so much to have those Southern states leave the Union? Who needs them? I've never been there. I don't plan to go there. I never see a Southern person. Daddy doesn't sell anything there. They don't have anything I ever would need. Let them be!"

"Do a lot of people feel that way?" I finally asked.

"I don't know. Some agree that slavery is wrong and those poor people should be free."

"What do you think about it?" I asked.

"I think God will punish those wicked people who chain up others. But, I don't know if so many men should die trying to stop slavery; that's all I know. I didn't want this to happen. I wanted this to be a night when we would talk about us...but listen to me!"

"I'm sorry." Taking her hands that she had cradled in her lap, I bent to kiss them.

She pulled free and threw her arms around my neck. I held her tightly. Seconds passed and then minutes. Releasing my hold, I leaned back and then found Ellen's lips. She pressed into me. Her mouth opened. I was lost in the kiss that was long and deep. Ellen's hands gently stroked my cheek. My hand touched the firmness of her breast. A low murmur came from deep within her as our lips met. She leaned back and I pressed into her body. My leg came over her small frame. Her legs parted as I slowly raised myself from her.

"What is it?"

"Not like this," I whispered.

"What's the matter?" Ellen sat upright, pushing down her skirt to cover her exposed knee.

"Not here. Not on my porch with my father out there. He could see us," I stammered. "You deserve better than this." We sat for a few minutes staring silently out across the fields.

"Can we see each other tomorrow?" she finally asked.

"Oh, sure!"

She stood and then patted her skirt down around her legs. "I must be going now," she said awkwardly. Rising, I held my arms out to her. "No, that's not necessary." She moved down the steps. I tried to follow her. "I'll be all right—you don't need to help me," she said as she walked toward her buggy. Without turning to say good-bye, she pulled the reins and the buggy rolled out of sight.

September 1863

The heat of this first Friday in September seemed less oppressive than any previous summer day. My shirt was still dry even though I had been out in the field since before ten, and with the drier air my breathing seemed to come easier. It should have been obvious from the signs around me that the humidity had lessened. For the last several days, my boots remained dry as I walked through the thick weeds along the roadside, and no longer could I see drops of any early morning dew on the grass. Maybe being away from this land for those two years made me forget the signs of nature or perhaps my eyes chose not to see that which surrounded me.

"James!" my father yelled. Pulling the team to a stop, he sat there, hunched over on the bench seat, arms resting on his knees. I waved to him as I walked to the fence alongside the road. "How's it going with the plowing?" he asked.

"Not too many weeds along that stretch any more. I'll finish it before two."

"It looks pretty good!" he said without looking at me. "I've got this load to take in for Halgren and then I'll be back around sunset."

"Yeah, I'll be here." I leaned against the fence post.

"By the way," he now looked in my direction, "if Godsen from the bank comes by, tell him I'll see him at the end of the week."

"Do you want me to talk to him about something?"

"No! He's hard to talk to. I'll take care of it."

"Is there some problem with the bank?"

"Nothing I haven't seen for all the years I've had this place."

"Is it money you need?"

"I told you that I would talk to him!"

"I've got my money that I sent home. It's still there!"

"It's not your problem, I told you!" With that, he pulled the reins abruptly and snapped them across the rumps of Buck and the big black plow horse I had named Lucy Diamond. With a high-pitched groan from the iron wheels, the heavily loaded wagon heaved forward, stopped, and lurching again, strained along the rutted path. Listening to the breezes stir, I silently watched as my father faded within the red dust that billowed upward.

5

Strangers Evermore

October 1863
Angola, New York

Standing opposite the store, reading the sign that blended with all that was familiar, it was as if I hadn't left here at all. Brass-gilded letters protruded from the surface of the sign's red facing that extended above the main entrance for three quarters of the entire storefront, "McFarland and Son Mercantile." The two newly-ascribed words, "and Son," were incongruous with all that I had desired for Winnie and me. She was to have been my bride, live on my land and bear my sons. McFarland's sign prophesized a legacy which erased me from Winnie's future and deflated my memories to no more than wistful dreams.

Her lips touched my neck and I felt the warmth of her breath and heard her whisper. "James, we shouldn't."

"Margaret!" Marshall McFarland's voice boomed through the thin walls of the storeroom.

"Oh, my god, he thinks Mother is back here!" Winnie pulled away from me. "He will find us!"

"Be quiet!" I fumbled in the darkness to find her mouth. "He won't come in here, just be still."

"Margaret, I'm leaving soon! You'll need to come up front!" McFarland's voice became muffled as he walked away and faded beneath the panting of Winnie's labored breathing.

"It'll be all right," I whispered, releasing her arm from my grasp. Light easing into the storeroom through cracks at the doorjambs painted the paleness of her neck, the white of her eyes, her teeth. I touched her face and then opened the door. "He's up front now, Winnie. Just stay here until you hear me yell. I'll draw them all to the front." Winnie put her hands to her mouth to stifle a giggle as I closed the door and adjusted the front of my pants.

"Hello, Mr. Rajek!" I raised my voice when I saw the bank owner enter through the front door of the store.

"What?" Startled, the portly man abruptly stepped backward.

"Hello, Mr. Rajek!" When I yelled at him louder than before, his forehead wrinkled and he anxiously turned from side to side.

"What in hell is all the noise, Colin?" McFarland came from his office behind the register.

"I have no idea what is wrong with this boy here." The banker looked relieved. "Him screaming like a drunken dock hand."

"Reed!" McFarland's jaw was clenched. "Keep busy while I'm gone. If you've got time to scare the holy moleys out of Mr. Rajek, maybe your services aren't needed!" I lowered my head and began to retreat to the rear.

"I was working in the storeroom. I'll just finish what I started."

McFarland lost interest in me by the time the words were out of my mouth.

"You ready, Marshall? I'm in a bit of a hurry." Rajek impatiently tapped his cane to the floor.

"Yes. Margaret, I'm leaving!" Without waiting for a response from his wife, McFarland held open the front door and as the banker passed, he asked, "How is Harold today?"

"He's better every day." Rajek smiled. "Had a vigorous walk yesterday and will probably join us tonight for the recital Mrs. Rajek is planning."

"I'll look forward to seeing the lad."

"I just hope he doesn't pick up anything from all those people coming, that's all."

"You can never be too safe, but he's a strong boy that Harold, mighty good young man!" McFarland didn't look back at me as he closed the door.

Marshall McFarland seldom looked at me or noticed me in any fashion. Had he not enjoyed the morality of his payday lecture, he never would repeat it word for word once a month.

"Reed!" He held onto the pay envelope as I reached to take it. "I hope you save this money. What I'm paying you is very generous for what little good you do my business, but I'm generous to a fault. No one ever helped me, but just look around to see proof of how hard work and thrift can result in success. You put this money in Mr. Rajek's bank and you'll wind up a whole lot better off than your father. Let me tell you!"

He scoffed the day I told him I had volunteered for the army.

"Oh, don't worry about me, Reed, I can get anybody to stock shelves and clean the waste. The way business is today with all this talk of war, I was about to let you go anyways. But the army is for fools, boy!" Winnie stood behind the counter, glaring at her father as he spoke. "There's no money to be made other than the initial bounty and that'll probably go to your father's loan at the bank. I'd like to take advantage of all this patriotic hubbub by waving Old Glory and selling to the army, but can't much stomach it. However! If I had some damn cattle, I'd be in a good selling position all right! The generals, those scoundrels, they make the money, but not you, Reed, not you."

Entering the store, I stepped aside for two ladies hurriedly brushing by me, each carrying a wrapped bundle. Pausing, I inhaled the familiar mixtures of cinnamon, nutmeg, coffee, and exotic perfumes from the East wafting from within. Looking for Winnie standing behind the counter as I had remembered, I saw only the glass showcase, shelves stacked with velvet-covered hat boxes, colored thread on display bobs, rolls of cloth, and glass jars lining the entire wall. She wasn't here.

Without anyone noticing, I slowly walked to the rear of the store. The door to the storage room was propped open. Jammed inside the long, narrow room were red-painted iron plows, two black stoves with brass handles and a cutting machine that was unfamiliar to me. Bending down to inspect the wheeled device that appeared to have too many belts and not nearly enough blades, I heard Marshall McFarland's voice. "So, the war hero has finally found time to pay his respects, huh?"

"Hello, Mr. McFarland."

"You've gained a little weight in the army, I see."

"Clothes don't fit too well anymore. Probably I'm a bit bigger in some places."

"You here to buy that there Phillips mower? It's the best they make, but I suspect it might be more than your father could afford right now."

"No. I'm not here to buy. I came to ask about a job. I could use a job, if you're hiring."

"I don't know if I need anyone to clean up right now."

"No! I was looking for a clerk job, if you had a need for one."

"A salesman? Don't have time to train a new salesman," he said. "You can however, stop by now and again to see if I need any clean-up chores to do." Turning to face the noise coming from the front of the store, he said, "That's all I can do for you right now." Walking away, he added, "We're all proud of you."

He didn't see me pass by him and leave the store.

Through a dust-covered window, I saw a light coming from the back room of Little Phil's livery. The evening air had turned colder. Warm inland breezes changed direction in late afternoon to bring a cold wind blowing in from the lake. It was approaching that time of night when Phil's "regulars" came by to drink someone else's whiskey and cheat at cards. This was the third time I had seen Little Phil since my return and the third time that everyone drank from my bottle. We talked of matters beyond our control—sex, weather, racing stock, and the killing in war.

The three men sitting at Little Phil's worn oak table knew little of sex and nothing of killing a man. They were secure in their opinions, never having to prove them. Little Phil's limp would prevent him from walking very far, and Ed Sacket, nearly sixty, was too bent over to do much good at all any more. Gabe Paulson, in his mid-forties and capable of marching, had been afflicted by the shakes in his left arm since his lung collapsed from the blow of a horse's hoof slamming into his chest when he was fifteen. His heart had stopped beating for a while and when he had awakened from his weeklong coma, he had the shakes so bad it was like he had fallen into the icy waters of the lake in the middle of February. The tremors lasted for the most part of a month before finally stopping.

Gabe stood up when I entered the room. "Hey, Reed!" he yelled. "We didn't expect you tonight."

"Why is that?" I asked, setting the bottle on the table.

"No reason I guess...didn't see you earlier that's all." He pushed his empty glass across the table, using his right hand. "Pour me a shot, will ya?"

"About to play some poker?" I asked.

"Just wastin' time mostly," Little Phil answered.

"Me too." I grabbed an empty wooden box, placed it at the table, and sat down.

"You in town to pick up something?" Little Phil watched me.

"No...just came in to buy a bottle and see if anyone was in town."

Ed picked up three cups from the counter next to the washbasin and set one in front of me and another before Little Phil. He carefully poured the amber liquid until each cup was half filled.

"You're a good man, Reed!" he said, placing the bottle on the center of the table.

"Let's drink to Jim's safe return!" Gabe held up his glass.

"No! No!" Little Phil interrupted. "We did that the last two times, for God's sakes! Let's drink to all those dead Rebs he put in the ground!"

"Hey! Hey!" Ed yelled out. "To the dead Rebs!" I took a gulp from my cup and sat back while the hours passed slowly.

A chill in the night air seemed even greater in contrast to the warmth I felt touching the loose flesh on Buck's muscular neck. Having mounted, I patted and nudged him away from the rail down the street to the front of McFarland's store. It was the quiet time of night. A few horses stood tied to the hitching rails along the opposite side of the street. With the exception of McFarland's Mercantile, the shop windows along Main Street were darkened.

"Come on!" I said quietly, edging closer to the front of the store. Gently reining in Buck, I sat peering through the glass storefront. The door to the office stood ajar enough for me to see a lone figure moving about within the office. I sat there for a few minutes before recognizing Marshall McFarland. A smile came to me when I became aware that I had clenched my teeth. I relaxed the tension in my jaw and pulled the reins. Buck's head moved to the side as he stepped toward the middle of the street. In less than a few steps he had broken into a deliberate trot. Within a few minutes we reached the countryside. The few lights that I had seen along the streets of

Angola were disappearing into the darkness that now engulfed my world.

November 1863

Looking above the buildings to the white smoke rising from the chimneys, I was oblivious to the people around me or the few wagons passing by.

"Reed! Reed!" I looked to the shadows beneath an awning. My eyes adjusting, I saw Ellen's father standing with another man. "James!" he called my name. "Stop for a minute!"

"Whoa!" I pulled the reins and forced the brake.

"Colin," Mr. Eddy turned to Harold Rajek's father standing to his side, "this is the war hero I've been telling about." Stoically, the round banker looked at me. "James, say hello to our bank president, Mr. Rajek." I nodded and Ellen's father continued, "James is a war hero, Colin! Fought at Antietam and Bull Run. Saw a lot of action too." Hearing no response from Rajek, a few moments of awkward silence passed before I turned to climb back onto my wagon.

"Give my best to Harold."

"Oh, you know my son Harold?"

"Yes sir, we attended school together." I pulled the brake that I had just released.

"Well then, you must come by." He handed me a card he had taken from his vest pocket. "Harold follows the exploits of the Army of the Potomac with great interest. He would enjoy hearing your stories."

"I will do that, Mr. Rajek, matter of fact, it will be a distinct pleasure."

"Good then! It's done. Both Harold and Winifred will enjoy your tales."

"So long, Mr. Eddy," I waved to him. "Tell Ellen hello for me."

This was my second attempt since my return to get past the front door of the Rajek mansion.

"Mr. Rajek is not receiving guests today," was the response on my previous visit, but prospects of touching Winnie one more time were favorable with Rajek's card in hand. Closing the iron gate at the end of the walkway, and looking to each window in vain hope Winnie might be there, I approached the formidable oaken door. The smooth surface of the brass knocker felt fluid to the touch when it slipped from my fingers to fall against its shiny base plate. Immediately, the door opened and Winnie stood before me.

An aura of blue surrounded her as the bright light of the reflecting sunlight shone upon the dress that clung to her chest and cascaded to the floor. Her eyes, round and warm, stared into mine. She stepped forward. Her hair, tied tightly upon her head, held the morning light as I had seen in a hundred dreams. Lips, full and red, contrasted against her teeth that were visible in her slightly opened mouth. Slowly, her lips parted and I saw the pink of her tongue, and then, she spoke.

"James, I've missed you." She moved closer to me and extended her arms. I reached out as her hand grasped the sleeves of my coat.

"Winnie."

"Come in, Mr. Reed!" Words, cold and firm, came from behind Winnie, from a figure standing in the shadows of the entryway.

"Winifred, my dear, let the man enter!" The white-faced Mrs. Rajek closed the door. "Please follow me, Mr. Reed."

The short, broad figure of Mrs. Rajek proceeded down the hallway. Alone momentarily, Winnie approached me, her figure silhouetted against the glass panel bordering the vestibule. Within seconds, my vision adjusted to the dim light and I could see the smile on her face. She held her hand out to me. We touched. Her delicate fingers entangled with mine. The embrace of her skin was warm and soft.

"Mr. Reed! If you please! This way!" Mrs. Rajek's command filled the hallway and echoed off the walls. Winnie pulled away from me. "Please make yourself comfortable in this chair, Mr. Reed." The old woman pointed to a high back, maroon-colored velvet chair. A lamp on a table near the fireplace illuminated the room. Faint, narrow beams of sunlight struggled through the tiny space where the heavy, dark drapes folded against the walls. "Mr. Reed, Harold is unable to see you today. I will repeat what I said on the previous occasion, he will contact you." Her mouth continued to move, but I had stopped listening. There was only Winnie, her skin stark in contrast to the dark brown eyes staring at me. "Mr. Reed!" A high-pitched shrill penetrated my consciousness. I looked to Mrs. Rajek. "Mr. Reed! Will there be anything else I can help you with?"

"What the...," I blurted out. "What is it?"

"I beg your pardon! What do you mean, Mr. Reed? What is it, indeed!"

"What?"

"Good-day, Mr. Reed!" Mrs. Rajek stood. With her hands folded at her waist, she abruptly walked toward the hallway.

"What?" I again asked, as the short, broad figure rapidly brushed by me.

"Indeed!" I heard her say as she disappeared through the doorway into the shadows.

Winnie leaned closer. "I think of you often, James."

"Why, you're never from my thoughts, Winnie. Is this proper for me to be so?" I whispered.

"I don't know," she said softly. "But, I am pleased."

A coughing noise came from Mrs. Rajek. I pressed against the back of the chair, pushing off to rise and go to Winnie. Quickly returning, Mrs. Rajek filled the narrowing space between me and her daughter-in-law. "Harold needs your attention, dear," the old lady said calmly and then, jaw firmly set, turned to me. "Thank you for paying your respects, Mr. Reed. We will inform Harold that you were by again to visit with him. I'm certain his spirits would have lifted in hearing of your accounts of the war." Her words trailed after her as she again walked to the front door. "You will be notified as to when he will receive guests." She released the door knob and stepped to the side. "Until then!"

"Thank you, Winnie." I reached for her. "Extend my best wishes to Harold."

"I will," she squeezed my hand. "He will be pleased. We are all pleased, James."

"Good-bye!" Mrs. Rajek touched my shoulder. I released Winnie's hand and passed by Mrs. Rajek.

"Bitch!" I said close to her face before walking into the bright sunlight flooding the porch. The door closed with a loud thud and its knocker bounced against the brass plate once and again before falling to rest in silence.

A narrow strand of silver against a dark, gun-barrel gray sky was the last remnant of a cold sun disappearing beyond the wooded ridge that bordered the great lake. I could not remember a Thanksgiving Day sky that was not oppressively overcast. There were no defined clouds or cracks of blue sky, only a solid mass contributing to the stark bleakness that descended upon the land. The trees, fields, roads, and buildings, painted in hues of black on a nondescript tapestry, added to the foreboding gloom.

I reined in the stallion pulling the Eddys' carriage and let the big animal stand in the wild oats that grew alongside the roadbed. We sat watching the horse lower his head and shake, causing the leather straps and metal rigging on the harness to rattle and squeak beneath the strain. Steam, spouting from wide nostrils, drifted into the air as his tail swished to brush his right flank, involuntarily, contentedly.

"You have a lot on your mind, don't you, James?" Ellen spoke for the first time since leaving the Eddy dinner table for our ride.

"Why do you ask that?"

"You know that I talked to my father when we were washing the dishes."

"Yes," I answered, "and?"

"He told me that you may have decided something about the army and our future."

"I don't know if that's true."

"Have you decided to volunteer again?" I ignored her question. "I think you just answered me," she said after a few seconds. "It should have been clear from the beginning. I thought it might have been me at first. Maybe I didn't measure up to the girls you had while in the army."

"Oh, Ellen!"

"No! No! That's all right. I'm not mad at you or anything like that."

"Ellen! I never..."

"I don't want to talk about it! I don't want to know about the whores."

"But, there's nothing!"

"I don't want lies. I just don't want to talk about that now!"

"I'm not in the habit of lying to anyone."

"You're not lying to me as much as you are to yourself."

"Ellen, what do you mean by that?"

"You don't have to keep saying my name. I know you're talking to me. You have been troubled by something ever since you came home. I thought it was your mother's sickness and her loss, but it's even more than that...isn't it?"

"I have no idea what you mean, troubled?"

"I thought it might have been your childhood crush on Winnie McFarland. Even though she's married now."

"What?"

"But then, I began to believe it was more than that. I was fearful that it was the war. I had prayed that it was because of Winnie and not the damn war. I'm sorry for saying that. What must you think of me cursing like that and slobbering like I promised myself I wouldn't do!" She breathed deeply and continued, "I prayed that you would come back alive, and be the same boy that I had always loved. You came back, but I'm not sure who you are now." Removing the knitted, white mittens she wore, she quickly, impatiently, wiped her hand across her eyes.

"Ellen."

"No, it's all right. I'm sorry. I didn't want to do this," her voice wavered. "I will wait for you, James. I will wait for you to finish what you started and then, come home to me."

"Ellen, I love you."

"I know I love you, but you need more time to know if you love me enough."

I put my arms around her. Pulling her to me, I could hear her gentle sobbing, feel her body tremble against mine.

"Ellen," I closed my eyes and held her tightly to me. "Ellen..."

6
At Peace in War

December 1863
Outside Buffalo, New York

Lines, emanating from the gaping hole in the upper right corner of the window, streaked across the glass pane, as would rays from a rising sun. Through the grime-covered window of the train car, I stared blankly at the sectioned fields that appeared and disappeared with mind-numbing consistency. Heat coming from the potbelly wood burner at the far end of the car was reduced to ineffectiveness by the time it drifted to where I sat. Body heat of the passengers warmed the air more than the over-burdened relic that belched more smoke than heat. Sweet, pungent odors of cow dung, unwashed men, coal oil, and tobacco juice spit upon the hay- and dirt-covered floor hung heavily near the ceiling of the car. I remained still, trying to will myself to the deep sleep of dreams.

"What makes you want to join the cavalry?" Colonel Raulston had asked, looking down at the sheet of paper before him. "I see from what you wrote that you were at Antietam and Second Bull Run."

I didn't know if he wanted an answer or if he was only thinking out loud. His fingers fidgeted with the letter in his grip, while he looked at what I had written. "I have kept track of some of the men in the

Twenty-First. You did New York proud. I need men like you," he finally uttered. "Men who have seen the elephant." Raising his head, he looked into my eyes. "I need men who can teach these dumb farm boys and no-account-vagrants some military discipline. I really don't give a damn if they shoot themselves. I just don't want them shooting me by accident." His chair leg squeaked as he stood. "I will count upon you to assist in the training of our volunteer cavalry, Reed. We will fare better this time." He extended his hand to me. "Meade will profit from what he learned at Gettysburg. He will push the Rebels, and Grant won't lose, I assure you of that!"

I opened my eyes and then closed them again. Muffled conversation and the rumble of iron wheels clicking against the rails lulled me back to sleep, to dreams of home, Ellen, and those memories in the deep recesses of my mind that I once prayed never to recall.

January 1864
Winter Training Camp
Auburn, New York

It hadn't returned, that feeling which deserted me when stepping from the Buffalo-bound train and touching home soil in May. The freedom so long cherished, but once achieved, had cast me adrift in an unbounded ocean, without restraint and purpose. There existed for me no land, harbor, nothing that held meaning for me as far as I could sense from horizon to horizon. Without direction or destination, I found this very freedom beginning to suffocate my spirit. But always looming from beyond the sea of frozen fields and leafless woods of my upper New York home there had been the glorious tales, this siren calling me back that extended from every tongue and printed word; praises for this civil war that defined our country, a conflict that would forever forge our nation's destiny, a fulfillment greater than the insanity of it all. I had to believe that with re-enlistment, maybe the touch of the uniform to be issued to me at Auburn or the feel of the cold steel gun pressed to my hand would rekindle that spirit that had once made me whole.

Struggling to push doubt from my thoughts, I leaned back in my seat and, as the troop train carrying volunteers to winter quarters squeaked to a stop, looked into the faces of these men, some veterans of early battles, many joining for the first time, to see if they too questioned the wisdom of the decisions made. Maybe as I, they knew for whatever reasons how foolish we all had been. But perhaps, they might feel better, more assured in what they had chosen to do if they too had heard the one-armed veteran, in what seems like a lifetime ago, tell another group of wide-eyed, scared-as-hell volunteers, "God has given you the right to wipe out them heathen bastards, to destroy their homes, ravage their land and women and be heroes fer adoin' it!"

His words had lost their meaning for me as I watched the dying within the 21st New York mount. But as yet, the boys of the 24th New York, on this train speeding toward the eastern battlefields, still believe in God's righteousness. Winning battles will confirm their trust because in the end, victory and only victory ensures God's favor.

May 1864
Camp Stoneman
Outside Washington, D.C.

Standing, looking out upon a panorama of tents sweeping across miles of cleared fields bordered to the south and east by woods of pine and poplar, I watched heavy smoke crawl from makeshift chimneys attached to the rear of each tent and roll along rows that blended into one continuous line until fading into the distant haze.

Motion framed in time portrayed drills and routine, preparation and delay, anticipation and monotony. Each day I was reminded that war meant procrastination and more dashed hopes for engagement and conclusion. The column of supply wagons sitting day after day were symbols of what we had become; heavily burdened for action with wheels resting to hubs in the soft mud of early thaw, an army in waiting.

We of the newly-organized 24th New York had become drill-field soldiers following several months of tedium, eventually receiving orders to do the improbable. On the eventful day of May 5, 1864, in the early morning hours we crossed the river that had separated the armies of the North and South.

Gentle, early morning breezes teased the flags flying from poles mounted in front of the four tents housing the divisional commander and his aides. Sloping downhill away from the tents, the treeless land had been worn bare by the pounding of boots. From the bottom of the gentle incline, the sound of beating drums rose upward to drown out the muted clicking of the flags hitting against the cords holding them to wooden poles. Colonel Raulston stood at the entrance to his tent, looking toward the pulsating mass of men dressed in blue, blanketing the vast farm fields. Columns in coordinated motion, swaying to and fro, drums beating, flags flying, caissons rolling, teamsters screaming and whipping their mules, the sounds and sights of the largest, most powerful army ever to assemble on American soil, and I, a part of the 24th New York, Second Brigade, First Division of the IX Corps, but a ripple in this enormous sea of men that like a tidal rising and then flowing against a distant shoreline began to move upon Lee's Virginia.

May–June 1864
Wilderness Campaign
Spotsylvania Court House, Virginia

I anticipated this tour of duty to be different; greater armies led by determined men, purposeful and unmerciful. There was no longer hesitation as I had witnessed earlier under McClellan, Hooker, and Burnside. The new leaders, Grant and Meade, had two hundred thousand men and unending trains of supplies. As fragile and crumbling outbuildings vulnerable in the path of a tornado, Lee's Confederate resistance will be futile. The winds of the Union onslaught may stall temporarily and slightly alter course, but their divinely guided destruction and devastation will ultimately lay waste to all the land.

They came quickly, the battles, or rather they never did cease completely following the crossing of the Rapidan. We lost too many men in the tangled mire of the Wilderness, the impenetrable "Bloody Angle" of Spotsylvania, the mud marches along the Ny River, and the mind-numbing bloodbath at Cold Harbor.

June 1864
Cold Harbor, Virginia

Raising the pike to my chest, I plunged it into the ungiving earth with a jolt that abruptly halted the triangular blade but not my hands from sliding several more inches downward. The woolen sock that I had wrapped around the iron stiletto to protect my hand from its razor sharp edges tore with the pressure of each jab, increasingly exposing my skin. Pausing to ease the ache in my shoulders and to assess the progress of deepening the trench, I opened my hands to see the lines of blood trickle across my palms.

"Stupid shit!" I hissed. I was foolish to cripple my hands and weaken the grip I needed to load and fire my carbine. The trench appeared to be deep enough. "I'm done...to hell with it." Moving into the narrow opening and wedging myself below the mound of packed dirt, I smiled. "This is good. If they're going to get me, it won't be with a minié ball." Thinking I was losing my mind, I glanced to see if anyone nearby heard me talking to myself. Seeing no one, "It'll have to be a shell landing right atop me, but then," I smiled, "it won't matter a bit how deep I dig the damn thing."

Sucking in a deep breath and then letting my chest sag, I looked to the small fire behind me and loosened the string holding my cup.

The faint aroma of coffee drifting over me had caught my attention. Digging had become an obsession with me, more important than boiling coffee or eating hardtack, but I knew it wouldn't be wise to become weakened or tired. Maybe the smell of coffee and the blood on my hands told me to stop. Just maybe it was time to beg for coffee and watch the other poor, scared, obsessed bastards dig a while.

Peeking over the lip of the hole, toward the Confederate lines, I watched the many shades of green leaves flutter in the gentle breeze that I hoped would not change direction and bring upon me the smell of rotting flesh. There was no noise in the wind, only stillness between sporadic cracking of the distant reports from skirmishers and sharpshooters. Carefully scanning the field where we fought yesterday, I saw no one, not even the bodies of the thousands that fell there—as many as three thousand in a span of five minutes. Those who survived the killing-field did so by frantically clawing into the earth to shield themselves from the incessant fire while others found shelter behind the bodies of dead comrades. The wounded yelled for hours during the night until their cries grew weaker and then were no more. I rejected these men, their pleadings for help, ignoring their bleeding, their pain, their thirst, praying for the silence that came.

"We're going to need volunteers!" the major begged. "I can't order this detail. You're gonna have to want to help them out there get buried."

I lowered my head and looked at my palms. There was no way I could help dig graves with these wounds. I kept my head down as the major talked, running my fingers across the cuts to release more blood. With little or no movement, the direction of the breezes must have changed as the stench from the decomposing bodies crept heavily over me. I lifted my bloodied hands and pressed my sleeve to my face blocking the putrid odors and knew that in the darkness, the bold, wild pigs the size of dogs would sneak from the woods and uproot the shallow graves to be dug by the detail I watched moving out.

Without coffee in my cup or having the energy to rise to my feet, I surrendered to an insidious weariness, a foreboding, a sense of resignation. We were so close to ending it all. Didn't all evidence indicate there existed merely a matter of weeks, even days before the beleaguered Rebels quit? Couldn't I then return home and have this be soon forgotten? The end was within sight! I didn't want to die for the lack of an inch more of soil packed above me, not with the end of the war so close. To die now would be a waste beyond measure. Shaking my head and coming to my knees, I wrapped the sock around the blade of the pike and, lifting it to my chest, felt the flesh of my palms split open as I brought it down violently against the boot-packed clay floor of the trench.

7 Enemies Among Us

June 1864
Petersburg, Virginia

"We're done here, Reed." The major was sardonic. He didn't have to say more, for I had become accustomed to charging into impenetrable defenses, losing men, and then slinking away. But he said something that caused me to hesitate. "Get 'em headed up, we're going south."

What did he mean? We hadn't won this battle. Hell, Bobby Lee was still hunkered down over there! Then it hit me. What had I been hearing about this man who led us now, this stout little man who soldiered like a mole plowing a field. Just keep going, don't matter how tired I be or how thick the soil, just keep agoing! Just keep moving to Richmond, going around Lee, just keeping going south.

"Think them damn fools will ever give it up?" Moccero said little to me, and this question now showed how desperate he was for a companion or some kind of answer that made sense out of what we were doing.

Gino Moccero, a dockworker, laughed when he picked up his sword. That was to be expected, for he mocked every detail of army life. Made sergeant when he dragged Colonel Raulston's wounded nephew to safety behind the shelter of a tree, he refused to lead anyone or follow orders of which he disagreed. He and I seldom spoke to each other. Moccero was a brawler. His fists solved most problems with men he knew he could beat. With me, he wasn't sure.

"I don't think so." Feeling uneasy out of my trench, my thoughts were distracted. "We took too much from them and we're on their land, near their women and children. They want us dead...wouldn't you if it was the other way around?"

"No," he quickly responded. "None of this shit's worth dying for. Hell, if I was them fools and saw all of what we got to throw at 'em, I'd quit and go home."

"You'd be shot dead by your boys or us if ya did."

"Yeah, maybe, but if I lived in Richmond, I wouldn't be down here in this place defending it."

"What about Petersburg to the south, where we're headed? What about defending a city like that?"

"Size don't mean shit." He seemed to be angry with me. "I wouldn't die for the damn place. I'd say, let the blue-bellies have it, I'm going home."

"Yeah, that's smart, give up the one city that is still supplying Richmond with food and arms. The one route keeping their capital alive and the Rebel army on the battlefield."

"I wouldn't care, Reed. I'd go back to Richmond, rent me a darkie and head off to some place where there ain't no damn soldiers."

"Rent...what in hell are you talking about?"

"Well, Ol' Abe says they can't be bought anymore but maybe he wouldn't mind much if I just rented a blackie for a while."

"You're a dumb ass, Moccero. I'm surprised you're still in this man's army and ain't off hiding somewhere."

"We'll see, Reed, which of us is the first to go off hiding." Moccero stood tall and lifted his carbine to his shoulder. "I hope you're the one guy who catches me hiding somewhere." He grinned. "I'd like that, Reed. Just you and me alone..."

Our supply trains had left Cold Harbor on the ninth of June; ambulance and munitions wagons followed the next day. During the night hours, the artillery had been hitched to the caissons and by daylight disappeared to the rear. We pulled back from the line during the late afternoon hours of the eleventh and, on the following day, were on the road moving in an easterly direction away from Cold Harbor and then south toward Petersburg and a face-off that was to become a siege.

July 1864

The days passed and continuing my incessant digging, packing, and wedging whatever I found into a dirt wall, my fortification grew more complex and superfluous. A sawmill four miles from the front lines produced lumber enough to secure nearby redans and intensify redoubts to withstand direct artillery hits. If I was to ignore the high pitch wail of incoming shells or their ground-shaking explosions, my fear of cannoning had passed, becoming little more than a nuisance. That, no longer a problem, I was forced to deal with what others thought to be of concern: the Rebel cavalry.

"They're trying to break out." Major Richards kicked at the green log that had rolled from the stack above the embers. "We're getting reports the Reb cavalry are probing all along the front." His voice sounded coarse and gravelly, more tired than sick. "Your men did well here, Reed." He looked at the redoubt that was not unlike a dozen others he had seen his regiment construct. "They know they can't get through all this stuff, so they sneak around until they find a gap in our defense and they call out a brigade to pound into it. If they can get behind these redoubts, they can do a lot of damage."

"Are there such gaps?" I asked, crouched near the pit, stroking the blue flames struggling to stay alive beneath the two logs just cut from a thirty-foot elder.

"Hell, yes! My god, we're talking about a fifty-mile front. They're bound to find some openings."

"We need more men then?"

"Yeah, but we won't be getting them for a while, too many other places where they're needed more."

"So what happens?"

"That's why I came by, Reed."

"What? Not to hang out with me and have some whiskey?"

"I'll drink your whiskey all right, but I'll also assign you duty you won't much like. I want you to get with Sergeant Hemming. Each will head a patrol in your sector looking for Rebs and any deserters out there." He pulled back and tried to stand taller. "Let us know if you find any sign of cavalry," he continued. "But if you find any deserters, do whatever in hell you please. They ain't much good to anybody anyhow." Without another word, he turned and walked away.

"Don't want the whiskey then, huh, sir?" I said quietly, pushing the log away from the flames. "Shit!" I stood. "God damn luck!"

"This is the most worthless piece of a crap a soldier could use." Dick Hemming, a skinny, six foot-four gunsmith from Buffalo, held the straight-edged saber in his hand, smiling, shaking his head impatiently. He had taught me to use the carbine, to clean it, to load it while prone upon the ground and sight it. "It just gets in the way. Hell, we don't even use the bayonet, how will anyone ever use this?" Hemming was a serious soldier, disappointed that he had failed to get a battlefield promotion. Now resigned to the reality of remaining a sergeant, he withdrew into the distraction of his Sharps. It was his love, his woman, the one thing he knew better than anything else, his comfort. A gun to him was all that mattered. He had no use for the saber the major had given to each of us.

"They'll just get in the way," Hemming grumbled as he yanked at the belt, struggling to move the scabbard to the rump side of his hip. "They make too much noise and, hell, look, the damn thing nearly drags on the ground."

Moccero, coming near the fire, laughed and said, "It will make you look like an officer, you fool."

"And how in holy hell will that help any?" Hemming turned to Moccero.

"The Rebs might listen to us better," Moccero answered. "And if we get captured, they might treat ya differently if they think ye're an officer. If nothing else, use it as a tool."

"A tool, my ass!" Hemming scoffed.

"I'm talking about poking bodies, you skinny freak! No one wants to reach down and touch something dead about to explode from rot!" Moccero glared at Hemming. "The sword is a better choice than is a god damn boot or gun." He paused and then reached for his haversack, having no intention of leading a patrol or joining up with one. "The blade wipes clean and doesn't hold the smell as does leather and you don't want your sweet little gun there smelling like shit, do ya?" He turned to walk away. "If ya see any dark meat out there, let me know."

"Moccero!" I interjected. "You're in the wrong army, like I said. No better than any of those Johnnys over there!"

"Me! What about you, Reed?" Moccero scoffed. "Listen to you, you ain't got no reason for being here!" He laughed derisively. "Hell! You got no friends here. You don't talk to nobody. You don't listen to nobody. Why are you here? Don't ya have a home to go to? Hell fool! Get a black vixen and find some fun. That's what them little darkies is for. Try 'em, fool!"

"You're on the wrong side, Moccero." A grin crossed my face. Hemming looked up and set his sword to the ground and then edged between the Italian and myself. "I'll keep that in mind when the shooting starts again," I said.

"What are you talkin' about, Reed?" Moccero stepped toward me.

"You figure it out. You got all the answers for everything." Staring into Moccero's eyes, I spoke calmly. "Just lettin' ya know, dog, that you don't mean nothin' to me. Take that for what it's worth."

Hearing only the rustle of the tall, brittle grass rubbing against my trouser legs, I led my small detail away from the stand of pine across the clearing. The incline of the railroad bed was cleared of grass and only scattered clumps of milkweed protruded from the hard-packed clay of the embankment. Climbing to stand on the cracked and weathered ties, I looked down the tracks to see the iron rails draw together in the distance and become one dark line stretching out of view beyond the trees that engulfed them. A gentle breeze attempting to stir the hot, humid air brought with it a slight odor of sulfur mixed with the familiar smell of oil.

I turned from the tracks to look into the woods some hundred yards to the south. "That's where we'll look first. Try to stay off the tracks," I spoke quietly. "If we get separated from one another, remember to fire your pistol only if you should spot a Rebel patrol. The pistol fire will bring our cavalry." Looking into their faces, I searched for some sign of fear or doubt. "Are there any questions?" Hearing none, I continued, "If you find any of our soldiers out there, put your carbine to them and order them to return to their company immediately! Should the sorry bastards not listen to you, then shoot 'em."

"You mean that, Sarge?" One of them, Jason Gale, spoke.

"If they don't listen, then figure them to be deserters."

"What if they're not deserting?"

"Maybe they won't always be deserting but if they refuse to follow your orders, then think of them as bummers, as planning to steal from locals."

"It might be hard for us to do that, Sarge, if you know what I mean." Gale had taken it upon himself to speak for the others.

"Don't turn your back on them, that's all I'm telling you, Gale. If they're out here this far, treat 'em as deserters, god damn it!" I turned to look toward the south. "Divide up into three teams and spread out. It's twenty minutes before noon. We'll go as far as we can but meet back here at three."

"What about you, Sarge?" Gale asked.

"Don't worry about me. If you need something, I should be able to hear you yell."

As the men proceeded slowly down the embankment and through the tall grass, I remembered something. "Boys!" The men stopped. "Any contraband out there, just let 'em be. A lot of 'em are following these tracks. All they know is that they go north." I looked toward the woods. "You may find some there. If you do, just pay 'em no mind. They're scared and hungry...and pretty damn smart to get this far without being caught by a Reb patrol." Gale nodded and led the others toward the woods.

Rays of sunlight warm against my dark coat brought sweat to the back of my neck and attracted a horsefly too quick to catch. Resting for a moment alongside a dying chestnut, I glanced up at the leaves overhead and was blinded by the intense glare streaming through the branches. I walked from the shade into a narrow clearing.

Standing still in the tall grass, I drew in my breath and held it. There was a noise. It was faint, maybe some distance away. In the silence about me, every sound became acute, even the noise of the gentle breeze an impediment to what I strained to hear. My heart throbbed against my chest. I heard it again. Something out there, faint and distant, caused a chilling sensation, an inexplicable foreboding to sweep over me.

It came from nearby, in this very clearing, the whine of a hungry dog or the cry of a small, trapped animal. After a few short, cautious steps I stopped and turned my good ear in the direction of the muffled sound. Slowly, I pushed through the thick weeds, searching for the unforeseen that may lie in my path; a few yards more, and then saw a dark object, moving close to the ground. I lifted my carbine and walked past the low-hanging branch of a solitary tree, standing like a scarecrow in the open field. Now, I could see it. There in the grass were two people, the one on top of the other, a blue-bloused soldier, pants to knees, his huge body braced between bony legs, back arched, head raised, sweat coating the back of his neck, and pinkish-white ass moving up and down in rapid motion. Above the deep groaning of the humping man, I heard a high-pitched whimpering and saw thin brown arms extending to the side, pushing against the face of the rapist in a futile attempt to stop the assault.

"Enough!" I yelled. "For God's sake, enough!"

The child's eyes were dark, wide, and terror-filled. The side of her face was swollen, her left eye bleeding. Closer, I again yelled, "Stop it! Enough, I said!" I pushed my carbine's strap to my shoulder, and then unsheathed the saber as the man's face turned to look up at me. It was Moccero!

"Almost done," he gasped, continuing to thrust his hips against the child. "You get her next, Reed." As he uttered my name with a loud grunt, the flat edge of my blade met the front of his exposed, protruding forehead, jolting his head. Blood oozed from the red line as he rolled off the child, and placing his hand to his head, glared at me.

"What in hell?" His jaws were clenched as he reached for the trousers still bunched at his knees. "You bastard!" He grunted, raising himself, pulling at his pants to cover his blood-covered crotch. "I will kill you for that, Reed!" He bent to retrieve his Army Colt that had fallen a few feet from where he stood. "You had this comin' a long time!"

Those words were the final he uttered on this earth. The blade of my saber sunk in the bone immediately above the left ear. The downward momentum of the blow forced my body to twist away from Moccero. Quickly turning, I pulled back the blade, embedded with pieces of brown hair and small white and pink chunks of flesh in the coating of thick crimson fluid, and watched his body slump to the ground and settle peacefully in the matted grass.

The child had risen to her feet, her body trembling, air entering her lungs in great protests. With shaking hands, she pushed at her dress as if to cover herself again and again with the same cloth before moving away from me. Carefully, she watched me. I remained still, not wanting to add to her terror. She took another step, and then another, her stride lengthened, but she flinched. Her hands dug into her lower stomach; bending forward, pressing into her crotch, she stumbled on through the grass.

I looked down to Moccero's still body at my feet. Raising my boot, I pushed to roll him over. Laying the blade on his chest, I slowly drew one side across his shirt and then the other. The child, who had reached the edge of the clearing, stood in the shade of the trees. I saw her look back at me, and then disappear into the woods.

Moccero was a soldier, he can't be found looking like this, I thought, as I tucked his pistol in my waistband and then pulled his trousers to cover him. Now, he will be mistaken for a war hero defending our freedom, killed by a Rebel patrol and not for the pathetic creature that he had become.

8 Captured

July 1864
Petersburg, Virginia

Hunkering down behind breastworks, bombproofs, and increasingly extending abatis, I was becoming desperate, seeing each day drip by in an ocean of unending boredom. Home and memories of Ellen, with me every minute, had become my obsession, driving me deeper into anger and sadness, waiting for word of a breakthrough that would end the war and take me away from here. It finally came with the rumor of a great and terrible bomb.

Beginning with the last few days of June, a regiment of Pennsylvania miners were working to undermine a Rebel fortress that stood at the crest of a hill rising a hundred feet above our position. For over a month, they had been tunneling into the side of Cemetery Hill, a burial site since colonial days, and the tallest rise along a ridge that ran north and south and commanded a view of the city of Petersburg north of us. To reach the Rebel fort, we would be forced to climb an exposed incline that rose from its base in a sunken hollow. Had the officers considered such a suicidal advance against the fortress, they would have gone without me among them.

A tunnel, supposedly no bigger than the size of a man crawling on hands and knees, ran underground for over two hundred yards, branching off into a "Y" pattern for an additional fifteen yards beneath the salient upon which the fort stood. Two tons of gunpowder had been packed into the farthest reaches of the tunnel.

"We're going before daybreak," Colonel Raulston said. "You'll know when to advance." He ordered us to remain in position throughout the night. "No fires, no food, sleep as best you can." There was little sleep as I lay thinking of death and what it would steal from me. I shared the bottle passed around and sought seclusion within memories and the whiskey.

It was near four o'clock and through the faint glow of the early sky I saw before me the black monolith emerge from its darkened cloak. Along the eastern horizon, the hills and trees silhouetted against the lighter shades of gray outlined the unsuspecting Confederate fort and contrasted with the gentle rolling line of the ridge on which it stood. The fort was less than a hundred yards to my right and through the pale light I saw the pathway through our tangled defensive barrier, as narrow as it might be, to be the opening through which I would lead the men when the order came.

Air violently pushed through a narrow opening as if by some gigantic force was followed by a rumbling noise from deep within the earth, widespread and muted, of such moment I dare not imagine. In one great eruption, the ground itself opened up, releasing a turbulent pressure that rolled across my face and shook my body, continuing to intensify, engulfing my senses. A brilliant white light shot upward from within the earth, instantaneous and terrifying as a second explosion swept over me. The noise, deafening and consuming, pressed against my chest and stole the breath from my lungs. The flash had melted into a reddish blur of fire leaping along the ground in pulsating bursts, catapulting a hundred feet into the gray morning air.

The earth moved as a powerful and abrupt jolt was followed by a series of rumblings causing the ground to tremble and then shift.

Particles of rock, dirt, and splintered wood rained down upon my head. Lifting my arm to shield my eyes, I squinted to see a column of blackness rising into the sky from the billowing mass of white smoke where once stood the Rebel fort. Unable to breathe, I desperately inhaled sulfur-laden air thickened with dust, particles of earth and rock.

Cannon fire from the roadway to my right heralded orders to advance. Bursting forth from out of the haze, I was swept along with a wave funneled through an opening in the breastworks. Battle banners flew above the mass advancing toward the gaping hole from which clouds of smoke pushed upright in overlapping columns—cathedral-like pillars in the sky.

I was beyond the walls of the trenches and approaching the abatis. Through the straight poles that jutted out like quills of a deranged porcupine, I saw ahead the men of the 50th Pennsylvania, spread about the open field, many having fallen under a hail of Rebel gunfire. Trapped by a crossfire of infantry to their left and batteries of Rebel artillery to the right, they had only the smoldering crater for shelter. Rushing headlong into the abyss, they flooded the hole, a vast pit surrounded by our enemy. Caught as an animal in a snare, they were defenseless against the firing from above. The slaughter had begun.

"Halt! Turn back!" My voice was lost in the din. "Fall back!" I screamed. "Retreat!"

"Fall back in order!" Hearing the voice of Major Richards, I turned my head. The men who had been standing at my shoulder were no longer to be seen. Glancing backward, I saw dozens of men, dead upon the field.

"Retreat!" I yelled. "For God's sake, retreat!"

Running, gasping, saliva dripping from my mouth as if I were a mad dog, I reached our abatis. Struggling, straining, I crawled up the log wall and fell behind its protection. We had failed.

The "Battle of the Crater," as was called the senseless slaughter of obedient men, simply reminded me of the tragedy of leadership. Grant had forgotten the lessons of futile frontal charges against an entrenched enemy learned at the "Bloody Angle" and Cold Harbor. In the future, I would remember.

August 1864

Reinforcements arrived daily, new recruits to replace those who were lost or wounded. I was grateful that I had survived the battle, but each passing day reminded me that nothing had changed. The siege was to continue and still we were held at bay, unable and unwilling to penetrate the Rebel defenses, and as we were able to receive supplies, so too were the Rebels. Nothing would change as long as both sides remained strong, and by early August when the expanding Confederate entrenchments reached as far as the Weldon-Richmond Railroad, it looked to prolong the holdout. On the sixteenth of the month, action finally came with orders for our regiment to move out and support the withdrawal of two divisions of the X Corps attempting to extricate themselves from a failed attempt to take back control of the Weldon rail line.

The sounds of artillery fire grew increasingly louder with each step taken. I saw smoke floating above the line of trees a mile to the front and knew, within the hour we would be in it. Closer, I found the first of the ambulances coming from the front, blocking our advance.

"Fall out!" I repeated the command that I heard along the column. "Let 'em pass!" And for the next hour, I stood and watched until the last of the long train rolled by.

"We can move now! Let's do it!" I echoed the orders, "Let's go!" Slowly we approached the extreme left flank of the X Corps. Behind me, I heard the tell-tale pounding of beating hooves. Coming hard, they looked majestic, tall in the saddle, leaning forward, the powerful giants below them breathing, snorting, swinging their muscled necks, the dark riders galloped around us to the left, hoping to draw the attention of the Confederates in the area and divert their fire away from the retreating Federals. I stood to the side, despondent. That was to be me up there on those horses, riding, feeling the wind on my face, the pressure in my chest and the powerful beast beneath me. Me! Up there! Damn it! Standing here is exactly what I didn't want, would never want again! I was no more than a pathetic grunt deceived again by liars who recruited me.

"You'll be mounted soon...just a bit short of good horse flesh right now." Lying bastards!

They were to ride around us, and we were to follow a direct line through the wooded hills to the south and east and expose ourselves to the right flank of the enemy. Reaching the woods, I found them to provide some shade from the intense rays of the August sun, but they were thickly overgrown with spruce, elm, oak, and tangled weeds and briar so dense as to inflame my anger and self-pity with each step.

The woods ended near the ridge of a gently sloping hill. Down the far incline, the land, clear of trees, was covered in prairie grass waving gently in the afternoon breezes. At the bottom of the hill lay the tracks of the Weldon Railroad. Beyond the tracks were more woods and somewhere in the depth of them, the Rebels waited.

Standing quietly in the shadows I watched Confederates ease from out of the far tree line. Mounted officers rode among them, talking loud enough for us to hear their voices and laughter. I smiled that they too could still find humor in these obscene circumstances. With death hovering over me every day, was I too finding morbid humor in dying or was I just losing my fear of it? I pressed my carbine to my chest and felt a bead of sweat trickle down the back of my neck as I watched, listening as the sounds from the enemy drifted upward in the warm breezes.

It was half past three and the afternoon sun was now positioned to cast rays of light into the tree line at the edge of the woods. Below us, the unsuspecting Confederate guard unit toiling in the boredom of duty was in full view of their harbingers of death. I raised my carbine to my shoulder, as did every soldier along the line. Steadying my sight on the soldier I had selected below, I waited to kill him.

"Aim high, men!" Colonel Raulston's voice rang out. "Aim for their heads! Fire!"

A sudden thunderlike clap erupted, reverberating among the tall trees, echoing out into the valley below. Within the enclosure of the woods among the deafening noise, smoke rising into the air was being trapped beneath the umbrella of the overhanging branches.

"Double quick!" The order echoed along the line. "Forward! Forward!"

A great "Hurrah" came from within the woods as we surged into the clearing, rushing down the hillside, upon the fleeing Confederate soldiers. The heads and shoulders of the soldiers bobbing before me momentarily obscured my view of the Rebel defenders. Above the charging lines, banners of the 46th New York, 50th Pennsylvania, and 20th Michigan emblazoned in full glory, unfurled in the wind stirred by the downhill rush. Sunlight, reflecting on brass standards and hand-rubbed steel bayonets, created flashes of brilliant light, sights, and sounds that I hoped would overwhelm the enemy and drive them away into the shelter of the nearby woods.

Crossing the roadbed, I clomped onward; arms churning, heart pounding, mouth agape with the primordial scream of an ancient beast in pursuit of his quarry. Through the tall grass, I leaped and strained to push forward. Onward I ran, bursting through the narrow stand of trees to fall upon them. They hadn't run away. There they stood in line of battle. We had come upon the right flank of the Confederate army.

Our smaller force had the advantage of position and surprise and the enemy began to break apart, some turning, most moving to the left, crumbling before my eyes.Behind, to my left, our caissons had stopped and the first of the batteries began to pound the Rebels. They held fast and returned fire. We stopped and formed lines just before the first shells struck the open field a hundred yards to the north. Those following, in rapid succession, landed near the bottom of the sloping hillside we had descended. Exploding shells, sending earth and smoke shooting upwards in blackened pillars, fell directly in the path of our following ordnance trains. The agonizing cries of maimed and terrorized mules filled the silence between each blast of exploding shell. I stared at the ridge upon hearing a sound more electrifying than any explosion, the cries of screaming men. The Rebel yell, concentrated and shrill in the first instance, began to grow until a resounding bansheelike wail overwhelmed all other noise. The ridge came alive with a flood of gray colors washing down upon the level field.

"Hold the line!" I screamed, leaping over mounds of wild prairie grass, running toward a dozen or so men from Company "M." "Hold the line!" I lifted my carbine above my head, waving to the men who were peeling away in the face of the Rebel advance.

The charging Rebel lines swelled outward, every second edging closer. I leveled my carbine at the chest of an advancing Rebel, but could not pull the trigger. Movement and noise, chaos consumed me as my own soldiers ran, obstructing my view of the enemy. Men screamed, muskets discharged, and shells exploding some fifty yards to the flank shook the ground.

"Fall back!" The sound of my words was lost amidst the din of musket and cannon fire. "Fall back!" I muttered to myself. Kneeling, trembling with an anticipation of some great calamity about to descend upon me, I took aim at a figure approaching. The soldier before me, in my sights, was no more than twenty yards away. Pressing my finger to the trigger, I hesitated. The 24th New York was dissolving around me. Some had fallen but many were fleeing to the rear without carbines or bedrolls. I lowered my weapon, turned it, and with both hands, lifted it above my head in surrender.

The carbine was pulled violently from my hands.

"Sit down!" Light-colored bunches of hair puffed downlike from the sides of his forage cap; face blackened by dirt and gunpowder, the Rebel soldier glared at me through reddened, narrow eyes. "Get down!" Drawing gulps of air, he was a young man having earned the leathered skin of the old. Convinced that I would feel the black pike pointed at my head, I hesitated and lowered myself to the ground. Feeling a deep-boned weariness descend upon me, I let my head sag to my chest, trying to release the fear frozen within me. My eyes closed; I could only hear the pounding of boots as the Rebels ran past me and the gasping of men laboriously sucking air through their mouths. Feeling the movement of air sweep over me as dozens, multiple-dozens of men brushed by me in their pursuit of the fleeing Federals, I squeezed my closed eyelids together in an attempt to deny the reality of the moment. I wanted this to be a dream, a chaotic vision floating within a cloud in the subconscious, between the state of human exhaustion and one's struggle to remain awake and coherent. With resignation, I opened my eyes to stare into the faces of those men standing over me—my captors.

9 Libby Prison

August 1864
Libby Prison
Richmond, Virginia

We were massed within a great circle, some with arms raised, others dazed, many defiantly looking for relief and rescue parties to be returning from the woods where the last of the retreating Federals faded.

"Damn it," I whispered, angry with myself for casting aside my Army Colt following my last patrol duty. Even the sword, had I kept it, might help me overcome a rider and steal his horse, but the gun could get me a hostage, I reasoned. Stupid fool I am for not having either.

The firing of artillery lessened and then ceased. In the distance, somewhere beyond the far ridge, musket fire continued, and then, that too was no more. The soldiers left to guard us spoke few words. When the one who appeared to be in charge issued a command, he motioned with the barrel of his musket.

"Hey, Billy Blue!" A regiment passing by the circle of prisoners took little notice of us except for one young buck. "Got your asses in a jam, huh? You weak-kneed women-killers. You be damned!"

"Kiss my ass, Johnny! Your wife did already!"

A soldier holding his blood-soaked sleeve, stood only a few feet from me, cursing the wife of the Rebel. Immediately, a surge heaved inward as the offended Confederate lunged for his antagonist. In that moment when the bayonet penetrated the side of the wounded Federal, fear among the many succumbed to rage and the blue mass recoiled, bulging outward as a hundred muskets leveled.

"Boom, boom, boom!" The deafening roar quelled all movement as dozens of advancing Federals fell into those pushed backward by the force of bodies collapsing against them.

"Hold your fire!" An officer, mounted, lashed his horse in a desperate effort to disengage his dusty veterans. The roan snorted and strained as it bolted backward. "Whoa!" The officer jerked at the reins. "At ease!" he yelled. "Lower your weapons!"

Mournful cries came from men upon the ground. Several of the wounded were sitting upright, others kneeling over those stretched out before them.

"These men need help!" Again the officer yelled, "Bring up the ambulances for these men!" He pulled the roan to the left. "Fall into line!" He waved his saber in front of the squad of soldiers still pointing their weapons at our men. "Move out!" The Rebel infantry began to move, many in the long passing columns turning their heads to observe the fallen.

Forced away from the wounded, we were led four across, to follow a widened trail that cut through the woods in a northeasterly direction toward where I imagined Petersburg to be located. I saw a tangle of abatis stretching on a gentle rise in irregular overlapping patterns and beyond lay the formidable earthen entrenchments of felled trees stacked a half-dozen high with mud and rock wedged between them: the target of General Grant's maneuvering.

Upon that same rise to the west, rows of tents in perfect straight-lined formations and a cookhouse, its fieldstone chimney blackened by heavy use, stood between buildings extending in a north-south direction. Near the buildings, dozens of ambulances sat in a straight line. In a corral to the side, mules and horses were lazily nosing the dirt and snorting as they probed for remnants of hay.

Reaching a clearing beyond the buildings, we came to a halt. Rebel soldiers standing at intervals of twenty yards from one another had formed an arc encircling as many as a hundred Federals sitting upon the ground, observing the approach of our column. Guided within the circle, I squatted, shielded from the guards' view, to look beyond the corral to the tree line, to rest, wait for nightfall, and escape.

Campfires by the hundreds quilted the landscape as the darkness deepened and the shadows in the tree line grew more intense. Flames seen earlier through the oven doors had now subsided and flickered out along with my hope of receiving rations. I glanced upward at the clouds that hung heavy in the starless night. Soon more of the campfires would die and the resulting blackness would be my chance for escape.

It was only a tiny glow, not much more than the flicker of a firefly, growing in size as it approached. A flaming torch held high in the air lighted the features of the soldier nearing a sentry some thirty yards from the edge of the arc. He lowered the torch to the ground and slowly, a larger, brighter flame climbed into the air. Hidden from my view in the darkness, the guards had constructed a pyramid of tree limbs. At the base of the stacked wood, dead grass ignited, sending flames slithering up the branches to stretch high into the night sky. Within a matter of minutes, dozens of such stacks had been set ablaze and the stench of coal oil drifted over the prisoners. The open space between our men and the nearest guard glowed as if the noonday sun beamed from a cloudless sky. Resigned to my captivity for this night, I lay back and closed my eyes.

In the eastern sky, the grayness had diminished and with the morning light came musket fire from the south.

"To your feet! Now!" The prisoners began to rise like a great blanket unrolling before me. Four riders on horseback, each with drawn sword, sat mounted in the clearing to my right. With a wave of his sword, one of the riders motioned for the prisoners to follow him. Crossing a small stream and proceeding a quarter-mile from Rebel encampment, we came to a rail spur where a rumbling engine and six dilapidated boxcars awaited us.

Waves of dust particles drifted through beams of sunlight streaming into the darkness of the car through cracks that separated the warped roof boards. Compressed into one solid mass of humanity, I listened to the groan of the iron wheels and the pronounced thud of the door slamming shut.

The train teetered as it rambled through the rail yards and began to roll at an increasingly steady pace. I reached to my side and let my fingers rest on the cool surface of my canteen. A drink of water would help clear my head of the stench of urine that pervaded the car but I dared not risk that others might see me. Darkness and the steady, pulsating rhythm of the train brought on a drowsiness. My head slumped and with my chin resting on my chest, I thought of a distant place—fields, green with corn in early summer, birds chirping, gentle breezes stirring the leaves, sun warm upon my face.

Morning came and went and the train continued on methodically until I heard the name "Richmond." Then suddenly without warning, the entire mass of human cargo shifted to the left and then to the right in quick, violent thrusts as the train lurched to a stop. A clanking noise of iron against steel, followed by a shrill squeak and from the far wall, light burst in upon the men as the car door was pushed fully open.

"Come out of there!" a voice commanded. "Slowly! Slowly!"

Mounted cavalry lined the route we followed through the rail yard. Shuffling along, six abreast, the columns snaked through the tangle of tracks, water towers, crates, caissons, and artillery pieces, broken and rusted. Empty wagons were parked along the sides of warehouses in rows of six to our left and a dozen to the right side of the tracks. Beyond the yards, we turned down an ancient cobblestone street lined with black water puddles where stones had once been.

Dominating the block of long, rectangular buildings was a solitary structure of great size. The building was whitewashed from its base to a height reaching the second story. Above the white paint, black and brown brick and mortar covered the upper three stories. Wide cobblestone streets surrounded this structure with its blackened windows outlining all four sides of the building. A large open yard was opposite the building where dozens of men and a few small boys stood observing our approach. Several more men sat on the curb, arms resting on their knees, staring in our direction. Above them, along the upper reaches of this side of the building, emblazoned in bold gray letters, chipped and faded by abuse of the elements, the words "Libby and Sons, Ship Chandlers and Grocers of Richmond, Virginia" proclaimed the prison we were to enter. Here in this old warehouse on Cary Street with Canal bordering it on the side of the James River, the Rebels were to hide us away from the citizens in their homes to the northwest. A distinctive tone of a tolling church bell, coming from somewhere up the hill behind the warehouses, penetrated the thumping beat of boots against stone. Listening to the delicate notes, I looked above the black wooden door that was the entrance to the prison to see figures of men within the shadows of the iron-barred windows at the second floor.

The entranceway had been cleared of prisoners as I was forced into the building's darkened interior, which was illuminated by light shining through the opened door into the anteroom. The smell of the unwashed, of sickness, of human waste wafted over me.

"Get in there! Clear a path!" Angry words came from officers in the street, followed by the crack of a revolver, then another. Men to my rear began to push and shove their way through the opening, into the safety of the walled room.

"Welcome to Libby, you poor bastards!" Ignoring the sarcasm of the guards, I pushed against those in front of me, stumbling over others in the enclosure.

Glancing back over my shoulder, I saw the last of the prisoners step inside the room just as an air-sucking thud echoed off the walls when the heavy metal door slammed shut. Adjusting to the pale grayness unfolding before me, I saw the prisoners, hundreds standing and sitting, all blending into a nightmarish tapestry.

"Where are you from?" He wore no shirt, his big head tilted back to speak to me. "Can you spare any food?" he continued, without waiting for an answer to his first question.

"What makes you think I have any?"

"You have that," the man nodded to my haversack. "If you got food in there, you best share it before we take it from you." My haversack was empty as was my canteen but I held on tight to them in reaction to his challenge. At that moment a light flashed into the room as the iron-framed door creaked open. Words, commands came from a small unit of Rebel guards who were guiding prisoners out through the doorway.

"Hide yer stuff or they'll git it like he told ya." Ignoring those words I crouched to the floor to better shield myself from view of the threatening eyes.

There was too little time to find water before the guards ordered me to get into a line that led out a doorway opposite the main entrance. Slowly, I followed the others from the building into the cooler night air. Darkness had descended and the glow from a street lamp cast light upon a brown canvas awning, beneath which sat two Confederate officers.

"What is this?" I whispered to a man in front of me. "What are they doing?"

"No talking!" A guard stepped toward me.

"Do you have any money on you?" one of the officers asked when I finally reached the table.

"No," I lied.

"I asked you a question and I expect the truth to come out of your stupid mouth. Now, put what you got here!" I reached into my pocket and removed two coins and a rolled-up note.

"There it is." I laid the money on the table.

"Take off your belt!"

The canteen made a dull, hollow noise as I dropped it upon the tabletop. "That too!" He pointed toward my haversack. As I removed it and the cord attached to my cartridge box, I saw him unwrap a folded piece of paper hidden beneath my greenback.

"You don't need that." I reached for Ellen's letter, but not before he pulled it back.

"I'll rip up the goddamn thing if you try that again!" He crumpled the letter in his hand, and then raised it as if to throw it upon the ground.

'No!" I lurched forward, grabbing his raised arm and squeezing it tightly. Quickly turning my head toward the movement behind me, I saw a black object and then felt a numbness sweep over me. There was darkness, sleep, noises, flashes of motion, and then sleep. Someone was lifting me. There came more noise but no words, and then darkness and blurred figures followed by pain, sharp numbing pain at the back of my head.

"Stay still. You'll be right in a little bit."

"What?" I tried to focus on who was speaking. The pain blinded me. Closing my eyes, I reached for the back of my head.

"No!" someone cautioned. "Stay still! It will soon pass!" A coolness touched my face, my lips. "Drink this." I swallowed the water and looked into the eyes of the soldier, this angel of mercy. "You went too far, my friend," he said, extending his hand toward me. "This must be from someone dear to you." He pressed the wrinkled paper into my hand.

The sickness passing, I slowly lifted my head to feel the bulge protruding at the base of my skull. Through hair rigid and matted, warm blood oozed onto my fingers.

"Don't let that trouble you none," he said. "I'll help wash it out." I pressed my palm against the open wound, sending a sharp pain through my head. Becoming faint, I lowered my head and continued to hold my hand against the gash in my scalp.

"One of them use their musket on me?"

"Yeah," he paused. "Didn't go down easy. Remember grabbing his musket?"

"No."

"He had to wrestle it away. Then he jumped and beat ya down before ya let go."

"I'm sorry I did that."

"Yeah, maybe," he said quietly. "In all the goings on, the officer dropped your letter while he tried to get out of the way. That's when I got it, all right."

"Thanks..."

"Yeah," he responded. "Ya know," he stood to his feet, "you're either dumb or brave. I'm not sure which."

I watched him walk away as I carefully drew my hand from the wound and then looked at the yellow, crumpled paper resting on my legs. Thinking of his parting words, I knew Ellen not to doubt which I was, dumb or brave.

Drinking the water remaining, I turned to the side and rested my head against my arm. Even though the minuscule glow from the three gas lamps along the far wall provided little illumination in the vastness of the room, I closed my eyes tightly, forcing my fingers into them in a futile attempt to drive out the pain and dull the bright flashes of light.

Sleep, interrupted and brief, came in spans of minutes. The pain, constantly throbbing, refused to release me from its grip, and the heat seemingly increased as the night grew longer. The shirt I wore was heavy with sweat and my feet burned within my boots. Bodies pressing against one another in the heavy humidity of a Virginia autumn made the air itself overwhelmingly oppressive. Rolling from back to side, searching for an escape from the pain and the heat of this inferno, my fingers found the edge of the folded letter and slowly caressed it.

Morning came and with it shadows of men awakening, rising and walking to the pump room at the rear of the room.

"You must have a thick head, soldier." He was looking at me, the man who spoke, sitting between two others lying upon the floor. "When they dragged you in yesterday, I would bet ya'd be dead by midnight." I closed my eyes, unwilling to release the numbness given by sleep. "Ya got a bad cut back there."

"Yeah, I forget about it when I'm sleeping."

"We're with the 13th Indiana, the X Corps," he said, trying to awaken me. "Captured on the thirtieth of July."

"At the Crater?" I asked.

"Yep, ya know about it?" He leaned forward, anxiously looking for my response.

"I'm with the 24th New York, the IX Corps."

"Well hell, ya say! Ya went into that hole after the explosion?"

"Didn't go in..." My words faded as the man continued to stare at me. I needed to tell him we were ready to do more that day and didn't let them down. I wanted to explain.

"Name is Hill, from Indiana." One of the men lying down sat up and held out his hand to me. "Ye're talking to Charley Benson and that boy there is his nephew Jeremy. We come from outside of Terre Haute on the Wabash."

"James Reed, western New York."

"Not too far from Indiana," Hill replied. "Ya just got here. Ya must know what's happening out there!"

"Just rumors, is all I know."

"Hell! We don't want to hear that!" the younger Benson spoke. "The longer the army sits on its ass, the longer we rot!"

"Is there talk of an exchange here?"

"Every day we hear crap," Jeremy snapped at me. "But we're still up to our ass here!"

"Some officers got exchanged," the older Benson interrupted. "It could happen. It don't do them no good to keep us here. Anyways," he added, "don't the Johnnys need soldiers even more than we do?"

"Grant canceled all paroles!" Hill responded. "So, don't get yer hopes up."

"Some officers got exchanged?" I wanted this sign of hope to be real.

"We were told so." The older Benson was becoming impatient. "We hear stuff, but ain't sure."

"Well, if they're taking men out of here, it might be a good sign."

"Hard to say," Hill spoke quietly, glancing over his shoulder as if about to reveal some great mystery. "There is talk they might be sending 'em to hell-holes deeper south."

"Don't go believe them lying bastards no matter what," Jeremy blurted out.

"Shut up!" The older Benson grabbed his nephew by the arm, but Jeremy yanked it from his grasp.

"I ain't puttin' up with this shit much longer!" Jeremy stood, turned, and walked away.

"Ya need to rope that little calf," Hill spoke quietly.

"Maybe, just maybe he's right," Benson responded. "If more be like him," nodding his head in the direction to which Jeremy departed, "maybe we just rise up and take the guards."

"Stupid bastard!" Hill spoke with clenched jaws. "Talking like lunatics!" He nodded his head toward the rear. "All they have to do is turn off that damn pump, lock the doors and we'd all be dead in three days and not a ball wasted on a one of us." The older Benson had walked away before Hill finished his words.

It was either late at night or early in the morning of the fifth or sixth day, as time was no longer measured by light or darkness. Awakened by heat and vermin, and men pacing throughout the long room in search of relief, I heard sounds from out there, from the city beyond the wall, a distant squeal of a wagon wheel, a lamplighter's reassurances, and muffled words coming from the guards. My feelings of inadequacy, of weakness, suddenly overwhelmed me. My delusions of walking the cobblestone streets, sitting on a bench and watching people move about freely, of feeling the breeze against my face were absorbed in the reality within this place. I slowly stood to my feet and remained still as the room swayed. Gradually, taking one step at a time, I walked toward the pump room. They were there, Hill and the Bensons, watching me, none of them saying anything.

The pump room was vacant this late at night and I sat until the pain lessened and the dizziness cleared. To return to my space and slip into a sleep was all that seemed important. Anyways, it was all that I could do. There was no strength within me to stop to watch the Bensons bending over a body on the floor. Seeing me behind them, they looked up and quickly pulled their hands back. The sickness was returning and I had to quickly find my space. As I turned back, I saw them again lean over the curled-up figure.

"Reed! Reed!"

"What?" I opened my eyes to see a blur of colors swirl above me.

"What'd ya see?" It was Jeremy Benson.

"What?"

"Wake up, damn it to hell!" His hand lashed across my face, jolting me awake. Rolling to my side, I drove my fist into him and came to my knees to clutch his head as he slumped forward. With one hand on the lower jaw and my other behind his ear, I twisted as to bring down a yearling colt.

"I'll break your neck if you ever do that again, dog!"

"No!" he whispered, "Please, no!" I knew the uncle and Hill were somewhere nearby and would be on me soon. Pushing his head to the floor, I came to my feet to look into the darkness for a sign of them.

"Why'd ya do that, Reed?" He lifted himself and held his hands to his stomach.

"What do you want, you crazy bastard?"

"Nothin', just to tell ya he was dead before we got to him."

"Who you talking about?"

"The one we were gettin' the boots from!"

"You stupid fool! Get away from me! I don't care what you lunatics do!"

"We can help you, Reed!" he stammered. "We get things and I know where there's a tunnel too!"

"Get away from me, Benson! And do it now!"

Awakening to noises about me, I lay there to wish away the swirling motion. Of more pressing concern to me than the sickness was getting water. Rations of cornbread and pork came each day, but not water. It was scarce, coming only from a single pump and only when it was primed at its source somewhere beyond the western walls at the far end of the building. The water flowing in trickles provided little to drink and even less of an overflow to reach the troughs that would clear the shit, which spilled onto the floor to seep through the planks into the basement chamber below where hundreds more men were imprisoned.

Without water, there was no cooling from the heat or relief for my dry throat, cracked lips, and dreams of madness. Sickness increased all around me and death swept the room. It was during the night hours when I could smell it among the mixture of pungent odors that hung in the air, and watch it as it happened. He walked slowly, this nameless soldier, bent at the waist, reaching toward the wall for support, shuffling along on his hourly vigil to the pump room. He made no sound as he slumped to the floor, his head disappearing behind the mass of bodies silhouetted against the shadows cast by the lamp's glow, like all of the others too weak to rise to his feet. I closed my eyes and hoped for sleep and denial.

"I said, you!" I was awakened to see the guard's menacing glare focused on someone behind me. Turning, I saw the thin boy named Tom Krebs standing there. A loner, separated from those of his 50th Pennsylvania, he had become a slave-boy to the guards, their target of ridicule. "Help drag them out of here and be quick about it!" The guard waved his musket to help clear a path for Krebs and a second soldier to follow. I watched the two struggle with their burden until fading within the bright glare of the early morning sun shining in through the doorway.

"Got the cramps yet?" Lifting my head, I saw Krebs.

"No! Damn it, man, I didn't see you standing there."

"Glad to hear it! That's good." Ignoring what I had said he smiled uncomfortably. "We may be the lucky ones who don't git the fever!" I didn't acknowledge his remarks. "I heard news about the war." He lowered his voice although everyone nearby heard him. "They were talkin' about Sherman in Georgia," he smiled. "They're right worried!" He leaned closer to me. "This here war won't go on much longer! They is taking a whoppin' real bad! Hell! Everywhere!"

"Except here, I guess."

"It won't go on," he continued. "They'll give up and we'll be paroled right soon. You mark my words!"

Rumors as he had expressed had been disheartening. At first they inspired hope, uplifting and then all too quickly dashed. But these words from the cowardly Krebs meant more to me. Having earned the trust of the guards, he had access to information as had no other prisoner. The question was how much of it was true and how much based upon his fear. Fear was an integral part of Krebs' character and had to influence his interpretation of what was happening outside of the building. Were the Rebel soldiers digging trenches along the foundation of the prison? Did he truly see ordnance wagons being unloaded when he dragged a body out into the yard? Were small kegs of what he believed to be gunpowder placed to the side of the trench at intervals of ten yards and later covered over with freshly packed soil? His warning of the gunpowder meant more to me than the hollow words of a pending parole.

It was faint, from somewhere in the distance, the melodic chiming of a solitary bell rising above the persistent dull groaning existing within the room. During the quiet times, day or night, I heard many noises; bells from boats passing on the James, clanging of train cars coupling together, iron wheels tapping as cars passed over gaps in the rails, and whistles from factories nearby; sounds of life in a world that no longer existed for me. By some devilish act, I had been buried in a darkened hell where all rules of civility were denied or ignored. Lying here now, beyond comprehension of reality, my senses had fallen victim to a horrible nightmare from which I could not awaken. Only those sounds coming from beyond the walls assured me that I hadn't died. There was life out there, within my grasp, if I just endured a while longer.

Sleep, long and precious, will release me and set me free from this dog-tired weariness. Even while standing in the midst of others, I felt as if I could close my eyes and slump into deep sleep. But when finally coming, it lasted only a brief time, maybe minutes. Be it for the pain in my back, the ever-present itching of the vermin crawling in my hair, the pain in my belly or the gnawing hunger, I was awakened again and again. Ever so brief, it was an elixir, a sweet medicine that brought relief. It blurred my senses, took away the pain and allowed a few minutes to exist without loneliness, to be with Ellen, to touch, to hold, to kiss her lips, and drift together in the coolness of evening.

There was a flash along the wall. I blinked as its bright light penetrated my eyes and blurred the images in the colorless haze within the room. Through the open doorway came shadows in staccato-like rhythm blocking the sunlight. In rapid succession, figures filled the opening to the outside world and then blended in among the throng of prisoners.

"Get back! Get back!" Commands were coming from my left and right. The crowd surged toward me, away from the doorway.

"Boom! Boom!" Reports of musket fire engulfed the room and echoed from the walls.

"Get back!" Grunting, gasping, men pushed against immovable bodies, struggling to escape the gunfire.

"No! Stop shooting!" I yelled. Arms and fists lashed out as prisoners in near panic swarmed through the living impediments.

"Move away! Get back!" Men were being trampled in the melee, unable to rise from beneath the feet of the onrushing mob.

Sweeping in through the doorway, a column of Confederates formed against the wall, bayonets jutting above the heads of the pulsating mass of prisoners. Amidst the wailing and cursing, a voice rose above it all.

"Halt! Damn it! Halt!" The protests quieted. "If you persist, you will be shot!" A man in a dark suit of clothes stood between two guards. "We will take roll!" he yelled. "There will be no mistakes. All living and dead will be accounted for!" His brief pause encouraged scattered talk among the prisoners. "You sorry bastards!" He yelled louder to drown out the voices in the room. "All that attempted to escape were found and killed! Anyone of you who helped them will face the same fate!" His face was reddened. "All of you," his voice sounded a shrill whistle, "will suffer for your silence. When your stomachs cry out in hunger, maybe you will talk to the guards!" He turned and along with the column, faded into the enclosure of sunlight. With a deep thud, the door closed and again shadows descended.

Threats of whippings or fewer rations meant less to me than the excitement born of hope that I had not before felt. Beginning with my first day there had been talk of escaping. The talk, prior to today, that had been hopeful but subdued, almost melancholy in tone, had changed. Men were now speaking in emotionally charged voices, challenging others who may disagree. There was an intemperance in their manner, a sense of hope for their future. I even heard laughter.

"Don't know if they're lying about those who died," Krebs' words sounded distant, as if he was talking to himself. "They might have killed 'em all. Don't know what it means."

"What are you rambling on about?" I asked.

"Don't know if I believe 'em." He looked into my eyes. "They say they caught a bunch of prisoners trying to escape south of the James River, clear of Richmond. Some of them were headed south toward Grant's line near Petersburg. The rest went east toward the coast where the Federal fleet is."

"What did they say about catching them?"

"Some were caught up to by hounds south of here," he answered. "They'll be brought back."

"Do you believe it?"

"Hell, no!" someone spoke from behind me. I turned. "Maybe they're telling you what they want us to believe!" It was the voice of Jeremy Benson. "Them officers are too damn smart for those Johnnys! Hell! Look how many got away!"

"Over a hundred," Krebs said confidently.

"They got out through the fireplace closet like I always suspected, didn't they?" Benson's voice reflected the excitement shown on his grinning face. Krebs pulled back in silence. I stood to my feet, turned, and left Benson waving his arms in the air while Krebs lay upon his blanket, his arm covering his eyes.

"Sarge!" Krebs poked my shoulder. "I got something for you." He extended his arm; something was hidden in his clutched fist. "Take it!" he whispered. "It won't hurt you, it's safe." He pressed a chunk of white pork into my hand and then reached inside of his shirt. "Here," he said, retrieving a biscuit-size piece of yellow cornbread. "Don't let it be seen!"

"How much longer will they do this?" I asked as I hid the meat under the waist of my blouse.

"They don't have much themselves anymore," Krebs answered. "They're doing the best they can."

"We're dying, for God's sake! I wouldn't treat a dog like those bastards are treating us!" I put the cornbread in my mouth.

I heard less talk of escape with each passing day, and the new prisoners brought confirmation of Confederate resolve, of Grant's intransigence and the shallowness of Sherman's conquests in Georgia, Alabama, and Mississippi. Battlefield successes meant little to me if they were not transferred into immediate release from this place. Victory was without meaning if I failed to survive Libby.

October 1864

The night air had cooled and sleep came with less difficulty. No longer did sweat soak my shirt collar and attract the sucking insects that crawled about the floor.

"Something has happened," Krebs spoke absentmindedly, looking not in my direction but rather toward the corner of the room made light by the early morning sun beaming in through the opened door. "Regular army out there...in good numbers."

"What?" I sat up. "Another escape?"

"Don't know," Krebs answered. "They're doing something. I can't believe they would blow up this place and kill us all!"

"No!" I shot back as Krebs stood and stumbled over the legs of men sprawled upon the floor. "They won't do that."

At that moment four Rebel soldiers appeared in the doorway, muskets pointed toward the floor. Following behind them was the man in the black suit.

"I have news that will please all of us!" he yelled. "President of the Confederate States of America, The Honorable Jefferson Davis, has proposed that many of you will be paroled to civilian life!"

"Hurrah!" The eruption from hundreds of voices burst out across the room, drowning out those who had cursed the sound of Davis' name.

"The names of prisoners will be read!" the commandant yelled again. "Those men will be given instructions as to what to do. If you follow those instructions, you will assist our efforts to expedite the president's orders!"

There was little order as we filed into columns clutching whatever possessions any of us managed to steal or preserve while here. Hearing my name read or failing to hear it read meant nothing to me or anyone else, because every man who could walk or crawl had already taken a place in line. All but Krebs, who had been pulled out by the guards. I saw him watching me, standing alone at the far wall. His face was expressionless. Only his eyes followed as I passed through the main door. I dared to do nothing that would diminish the hope hanging over me like a fragile veil.

The glow of the lamps illuminated the narrow streets and entrances to the shops and markets along our route to the train depot. Few people walked the streets but many peered at us from darkened windows as we were prodded by nervous guards. Nearing the depot, I heard the whistle of the steam engine grow louder in the echoes of iron squeezing and straining against itself. The increasingly strong smell of coal smoke confirmed that we were leaving this terrible place. My chest felt as if it would explode as I struggled to hold back the emotion that swelled within my body.

"Thank God! Sweet mother of God, thank you!"

Within sight of the train that would deliver me to freedom, I paused, wishing for time to take flight and carry me away. Minutes slipped by until the blare of a single bugle pushed the column of prisoners toward the ramp where smoke trailing from the train that had pulled away only minutes before, hung in the air and dimmed the lamps along the loading dock. A cavalry company rode along the far tracks, slowly moving in the direction from which we had come. A second company remained in line between the loading dock and the waiting train looking old and feeble in the dim light shining from lamps along the depot wall. The boxcars were an assorted collection from a dozen different rail lines and the engine seemingly too small and fragile to pull itself.

Shuffling through the straw scattered about the car's floor, I found a wall space to lean into and slouched down to hear the sharp reports of couplings clanking together as the nine boxcars, aged, discolored, and bulging with men heaved toward the pitch-blackness at the southwestern end of the rail yards. As the train increased its speed, a feeling of euphoria swept over me, peeling away the mental images of that room which was falling farther behind.

Through cracks in the brittle side walls of the car, lurching and swaying and rumbling slowly into the night, I saw signs of heavy troop concentration, campfires dotting the darkness beyond the tree lines bordering the tracks and along the hillsides. In anticipation of passing through the front-line entrenchments of Lee's army and then stopping for disembarkation, I felt the engine straining as its speed increased. Onward we rolled, in a westerly direction.

Daybreak came and with it the realization that we were not headed for the Federal lines but rather deeper into the South. I wanted to beat my fists against the walls, to rock the car, teeter the rotted structure until it tipped over, broke apart and freed me.

"Danville!" someone to the front of me yelled as the train squealed to a stop.

"Danville?" I asked. "Where are we?"

Peering through the splintered wood siding, I saw soldiers along the side of the track, and then heard shouting coming from outside. The car stilled as the door slid open for air to wash cool over me and release the foul smell trapped within, then tilted as the weight of the men shifted toward the opening and on to the gangplank leading down to a rock-strewn roadbed.

"There's water in there!" A guard pointed to the corral opposite the tracks. "Git it if ya want!"

Steadying their muskets to shoulders, they stood fearful of us ragged wretches descending the ramps. Wearing the nondescript homespun of local militia, their leader spit a brown run of tobacco juice onto the ground, some of the trailings pasted on his right boot. He then spoke, "Water's over there!" He nodded and shifted the plug to his other cheek. "Git it if ya do."

Running to a partially-filled cow tank, I tripped when someone fell against my legs. "Damn it," I muttered to myself, glancing back to see the man who had collapsed to the ground reach out to grab at the legs of the prisoners running past him. I pushed and pulled at any obstacle blocking me from the water trough until only two men and five more paces denied me water. Those struggling to reach the basin trampled those who fell. One man who had either jumped in or been pushed, stood crotch-deep in the middle of the trough, a dazed look on his face, water dripping from his gray beard. Ignoring the old man, I lowered my face into the water.

We reached Greenville where another train awaited to take us deeper into the South and farther from Federal lines. Loaded into a boxcar emblazoned with faded white letters, "North Carolina RR," peeling from its weathered exterior, I sat, bent over, leaning against the back of another prisoner, feeling the train roll and shake as it labored along the tracks. I dug my boot heel into the soft wood of the car's floor. Holding fast to the firm resistance of the body behind me, I closed my eyes and let my fingers find the edge of Ellen's letter as cold air seeped in between cracks in the wall, drying the sweat beneath my collar and sending chills through my body. Wrapping my arms around my chest, I bowed my head and prayed for sleep to take me to Ellen's arms.

My eyes opened upon feeling the shifting pressure as the train slowed and hearing someone cry out, "Salisbury!"

10
Entering Salisbury

November 1864
Confederate Prisoner of War Camp
Salisbury, North Carolina

The train jerked to a stop, throwing me against a man hunched over to my side. Grunting but failing to raise his head, he along with many stirred only at the sound of the door. Through the opening, I saw a great earthen wall extending forty feet up the sides of the gorge into which we had descended. A torch-lit staircase at the end of the unloading ramp led upward where darkened figures looked down upon the ascending columns of prisoners.

Inhaling the strong odor of oil and burning wood, I placed my right foot on the first step and with a tightness in my hip began to climb. A hand pressed to the small of my back steadily lifted me to the next step.

"Thanks," I whispered through clenched teeth, without looking back to see who had helped me. Beneath the weight of each step I heard the cracking and popping of the beams supporting the staircase until finally reaching the ground-level platform to see a massive wall on the opposite side of the crevice. Bathed in the light of burning torches and oil lamps hanging from poles, a great black specter in the form of a ten-foot high fence extending into the night loomed before me.

Standing as sentries before the fence, two buildings, one wrapped in darkness, but lights shining from every window of the second cast a bright glow illuminating the surrounding yard to reveal a thirty-foot high pole to which clung a large Rebel flag. The inviting ambiance created by the candlelight was incongruous with the foreboding of the ominous barrier to its rear.

Pushed along, inching closer to the lighted house, an image began to emerge in my senses. As if I had been swept up to look down from above, the two upper windows situated in relation to the three on the first floor gave the appearance of glowing holes in the human skull of death itself. Behind, loomed Salisbury Prison.

We approached a wide, iron gate, the only opening in the great dark wall of plank boards reinforced with log beams. Along the top of the wall, guards peered as we entered through the gate and into the enclosed yard. Flaming torches at the top of the wall shone light on the faces of hundreds staring, silently watching as we walked by them. There was no recognition, no reception of brethren. I could go on no further. Lowering myself to the earth, to blend into the security of anonymity, surrendering to the exhaustion of my soul, I heard the clanging of the gate closing behind me.

A few feet from the edge of the road I found a space in which I crouched. Everything was spinning. I lowered my head and then felt the pressure of another body against me. I remained still, fighting the sickness creeping from within. In this place, now huddled together as one, I would again use others to survive and hold back the fear.

Figures began to take shape in the dusky light of dawn. My head had cleared. The swirling had stopped and in the distance I saw a group of men, prisoners guiding a two-mule wagon. My senses were suddenly awakened to what was unfolding before me; the dead squad was collecting bodies!

"Oh, God!" I whispered. What I had been denying was taking shape before me. There was to be no exchange or parole. We had been delivered to Salisbury to die.

"Reed!" Startled, I looked into the face of a man I didn't recognize. "I thought that was you," he said. "I'm Kalmbach, Company "C"...the 24th...you know me, don't ya?"

"Kalmbach?"

"Reed, we thought you were dead, killed by that bastard at Libby." He came closer. "Come on, man, what the hell is wrong?"

"Oh! Thank God!" I sighed.

"Come on, get up!" he urged. "We need to find a better place than this...some water." I followed him.

"You best stay back!" A short, thin man, a large bent nose dominating his drawn face, spoke as we approached him. I reached Kalmbach who had come to a stop. "There's nothing here's any business of yours."

"Just looking for some help." Kalmbach was not deterred. "Need water, that's all." My attention had turned from the little man to the half-dozen to his rear. They remained seated, unconcerned. "Just water!" Kalmbach raised his voice so that the others could hear him.

"You two," the little man took a step closer to us. He glanced at me and then turned his eyes back toward the threat before him. "Move on! That's what I'm telling ya!" Placing my hand on Kalmbach's shoulder, I guided him toward me.

"We don't need trouble," I spoke quietly. He stiffened as if to resist my hand, before looking at me and then slowly turning.

"We're gonna need some help," Kalmbach, a stockily-built man, a whole head shorter than me but with arms muscled by work, spoke so only I could hear his words.

"Yeah, but not from them," I cautioned.

In the growing light of the rising sun, the magnitude of the prison was unveiled to me. Within an area half the size of a forty-acre corn-field, thousands of men were huddled together. Everywhere I looked I could see them, standing, crouching, lying upon the ground as if suspended in a Breughel painting of hell itself. Above it all stood a stately four-story red brick factory building that dominated the entire right quadrant of the grounds. Three rectangular one-story buildings were to the east of a red clay-packed road that extended from the front gate to the wall at the far end of the stockade. Smaller wooden-frame shacks sat adjacent to the far rear wall. Strewn over the vast open field of mud, between the outbuildings and the overpowering presence of the four-storied factory, were hundreds of two-man shelter tents. Near the road, two barren oaks absent of autumn hue, stood in testimony to the ravages of desperation.

"Wait!" Kalmbach yelled from behind me. "We have to find water!" I continued walking onward through an opening in the prisoners sitting upon the ground, toward the north end of the stockade. Glancing back over my shoulder, I saw that a dozen or more men had joined Kalmbach and following me, had drawn the attention of the guns pointed down upon us from the wall above.

Imposing in its vulnerability, the wall was built of weathered, unpainted plank boards that extended vertically to a height of a yard above a tall man's head. Standing on a walkway near its crest were Rebel guards, two together and another two, ten yards to the right and left, their eyes fixed upon me. I stopped walking.

"What's the matter?" Kalmbach asked as he reached my side. I turned back to the men following to look into their faces for the first time.

"Hughes?" I questioned, staring at the man closest to me. "My god! Hughes! Where'd you come from?" John Hughes from my Company "M" stood with the others, those I had feared to be lost.

"From Libby, with you!"

"Sorry, Sarge," Kalmbach volunteered. "I thought you saw them with me before now. There's seven of us, all told. With you, we're eight."

Panes of glass covering the darkened windows reflected the sunlight, blinding me to what might be behind them. At the base of the old factory, prisoners crowding to take advantage of the windbreak numbered in the hundreds, crouching down in rows three and four deep along the two sides of the building. As our group approached, several of the prisoners quickly rose to their feet, staring defiantly at us. I had seen that look before, in the eyes of captured Rebels. As then, these Federals also had the look of "ghost warriors." Absent of epaulettes, brass buttons, or fine cloth, these men too, held the fire of strong will, ignited by adversity and fanned by the instinct for survival.

"Will you help us find water?" I looked to the man nearest me.

"A well...," he pointed absent-mindedly. "Ain't none here."

I clenched my fist, wanting to drive it into the man's face, to quell the hunger in my gut and the anger deeper inside. "Any food?" I took a deep breath.

"No! We have nothing here!" He retreated between the two men standing behind him.

"Where then?" I raised my voice.

"Water's there...that way." Having turned, the man nodded his head toward where he had been pointing.

I backed up and, placing my hand upon Kalmbach's shoulder, prodded him to leave. Slowly, hesitantly each man fell in as the dozen or so of those we had collected wound through the stockade, passed the prisoners, momentarily glancing at us before instinctively turning their heads to avoid our searching eyes.

"Why?" Kalmbach whispered to me. "Why are they doing this? They act like they're afraid of us, that we're the damn enemy or something." Ignoring his words, I looked to the guards staring down from the top of the wall.

"There's a well!" one of my men shouted. Behind us, in the direction of the front gate, through the opening in a group of men, two poles projected above the heads of the cluster of men gathered there. A rope hung from a crossbeam. A well! Already the men were upon it.

"Wait!" I grabbed Hughes' arm. "The guy said it was in that direction!"

"It's water, ain't it, Sarge?" He yanked his arm away from my grasp. "It can't be no worse than the piss at Libby!" He began to run in a desperate attempt to reach the others. I followed.

Had I not seen the well posts, I would not have known how close the well was to us. Why didn't the soldier tell of its location? Was the water at another well fit to drink but not this here? Was he trying to save the water from this well for his own? My thoughts wandered as I stood waiting to drink from the cup. So desperate in need of water to drink, I could no longer collect enough spit to swallow. My tongue felt thick, rough. To think about it now caused me to gag, to gasp for air, to shake my head to clear the confusion, the dizziness that clouded my mind.

The guards had turned away from us. We were no threat to them, standing in line waiting to drink. The ground surrounding the well was an open area, ten foot wide. Extending along the far side of the clearing was a three-foot wide trench nearly two feet deep. No one was within five feet of its entire length.

"We're to stay clear of that ditch?" I asked the soldier standing in front of me.

"What?" He appeared dazed, distracted.

"That ditch?" He failed to respond or look where I was pointing.

"Please," he said. "Water."

"What is it?" I reached to support the man who swayed as if he was about to collapse.

"Please...," was his only word.

"Just hold on." I tried to support him. "We'll get there." His arms hung at his sides. "Here," I placed my hands on his shoulders. "Sit down." He had no substance to his body. His blouse, filthy and with a pungent odor, concealed protruding bones beneath it. "Water!" I yelled. "Help with some water!"

"It won't do him no good," someone said.

"What?" I asked angrily.

"It's stink-water." He nodded his head toward the well in front of us. "You can wash a bit with it, but it can't be drunk none." I looked down at the man lying at my feet. Bending, I placed my hand under his head and gently lifted it. His yellowed eyes opened and pleadingly looked into mine. Wrinkles formed deep crevices in the loose skin across his forehead. His cheeks, gaunt and sunken, were covered with the faint hair of a young boy, a boy of sixteen at the most.

"I'll get water," I whispered. "Hold on." Looking away, I yelled, "Where can we get him some goddamn water?"

"That way." The man behind me pointed. "I'll help ya." I placed my left hand under the legs of the fallen boy and my right under his back to lift him.

"Show me the way." I gulped air into my throat as a sharp pain tore across my shoulders, causing a tingling sensation that traveled like a lightning bolt down my spine.

"Let me help!" Kalmbach guided the young soldier from my arms. Standing him to his feet, we positioned his arms on our shoulders.

"It won't do much good," the man following warned. "This one's from Andersonville. Won't last long here."

"What?" I asked. "What do you mean?"

"A trainload came in about two weeks ago from some hellhole in Georgia, all of 'em near dead."

"Why'd they come here?" I asked.

"I don't know, maybe it's because Sherman's army has got almost all of Georgia by now." He quickly added, "It sure as hell ain't because they'll be helped here."

"I'll show you the hospital," the man continued. "But that's as far as I go."

"Anything to help," Kalmbach snapped. "It might be better than dying out here, don't ya think?"

"No, sir!" the man responded. "There is the hospital." He had stopped and was pointing toward a small brick house. "He'll sure enough die in there."

We stood as the soldier disappeared within the faceless crowd. A faint noise, a squeal similar to the sound of a terrified rabbit, or that of a stranded kitten's meow, came from the boy. His head rolled and fell to rest upon Kalmbach's shoulder as we proceeded to the building. I shook my head to clear the nauseous feeling that had again crept over me.

Wearing clean butternut uniforms and standing with musket butts to the ground, bayonets rising up, silver-gray against the backdrop of the single-story brick hospital, they were the young home-guard militia, four of them, each positioned at a corner of the fifty-foot-long building some ten yards from the nearest prisoner. It was into this clearing we carried the boy.

"Halt!" The guard to my right had leveled his musket, pointing it at my chest. To my left, I saw that the other guard had also pointed his gun at us. Above me, I detected rapid movement of men along the parapet, and stopped.

"This man needs help!" I pleaded. "He needs water!"

"Put him there and get back!" the guard ordered.

"He needs help, for God's sake!" My shoulders slumped, a feeling of bewilderment pressed upon me. "We don't need to put him in the mud!" The sound of a musket hammer clicking to full cock made me look up. Kalmbach began to lower the boy to the ground.

"Move away!" Without looking at the guard yelling the command, I released my hold and stepped back.

"Stay there!" Another command, this coming from within the open doorway of the hospital. Glancing toward the building, I saw a man wearing a Union-issued cotton blouse with blood stains covering the sleeves and the front of the garment.

"Don't leave him for me to carry. If he's alive, bring him here!" He nodded his head.

Shuffling sideways, we guided the limp frame of the boy through the doorway. With what little weight there was to his body, Kalmbach now absorbed the majority of it. I merely held his blouse, fearful that any grip on his arm might cause it to break. My breathing labored, I was suddenly aware of a pungent, heavy-sweet smell of death flowing from the darkened interior of the room. Turning from the stench, a feeling of revulsion overwhelmed me as I released the boy and bent over in violent gagging. Deep in my stomach, a tightness wrenched forth bitter, yellow phlegm.

Within the shadows, I saw figures lying side by side in the straw-littered dirt. At the opposite end of the long room, two aides, each wearing a rag covering mouth and nose, were lifting a body from the floor. Holding on to the outstretched arms and legs, the two swung the dead man in the air. A dull, hollow thud sounded as the body fell onto another that lay at the base of the wall.

"The dead squad," I whispered, watching the workers who had now turned their attention to another upon the floor, an old man, bearded with long, gray hair flowing from his head. With feeble, determined gestures, he moved his hands while twisting his upper body. He was naked from the waist down, and his right leg amputated and bandaged at mid-thigh was black from the lower edge of the red-stained cloth up to his crotch. Pleadingly, his low, wailing utterance, "I'm alive, I'm alive," was lost in the anguished moans of others, all desperate to be released from the agony of slow death, from pain so deep and persistent that only opened-mouth cries brought momentary relief from its misery.

"Put 'em there!" The steward jabbed toward an open space between two men to our left. Apparently asleep, the men remained still as I kicked small piles of loose straw into the space. Kalmbach gently placed the boy's head on the straw and then looked at me.

"They're not sleeping," he whispered. "They're dead!" Looking into the face of the man at my feet I saw him to be a tall man with bushy eyebrows and heavy black hair. His broad Greek-like nose dominated his high cheek-boned face. I was inexplicably drawn to him. Leaning down, I quickly jerked my head away.

"Oh! Dear God!" I blurted. The skin on his face moved! Lice crawling on his face were coming from his mouth and nose. Without thought, I stabbed at his face, rubbing across his skin, forcing his mouth closed. Slapping my hand against my leg, I stood and turned before a deep gagging came from within my throat. Reaching for the wall, I stumbled to the doorway and into the light of day.

"We need to find us a well." Kalmbach placed his hand on my shoulder. Several of the men from Libby who had been waiting for us followed a few paces to our rear.

He saw me first. As my eyes swept along the crowd, he was looking at me; the man who had been standing in front of me at the well was now approaching. Kalmbach, realizing that I had stopped, turned.

"I knew I'd seen you before," he spoke as he neared. "It took me a while, but I'm good with faces. For some reason I remembered yours," he smiled. "It was at Spotsylvania Court House." I stared at him, hoping to recognize something. "You were in the New York regiment on our left."

"Yeah," I said hesitantly.

"I was in the 24th Michigan. We passed by your brigade when we pulled out. You were digging in. Some of our boys yelled to you."

"I remember something like that."

"My boys like yelling." He held out his hand to me. "Damn waste of time as far as I'm concerned."

I had no recollection of this event occurring but whatever happened, it mattered only that I had made a connection with this soldier who held some ground.

"Were you with Gibbon, the II Corps?" Kalmbach asked.

"Yup, that's who we be all right!"

"We're with the IX Corps, 24th New York," I said. "You saw the thick of it at Spotsylvania and were hurt pretty bad."

"We lost a lot of good men, but we all did." He turned his head as if he were looking for someone. "Here," he pointed toward the men standing nearby, "come sit with us." Taking a few steps back, he crouched and motioned for us to sit down. "Where did ya get captured?"

"Outside of Petersburg," I answered, "trying to hold the Weldon Railroad." I paused. "And you?"

"North Anna...got cut off from the others in that damn swamp. We took a road we shouldn't have. Hell! That's why I recall your face," he smiled. "You stood away from your men with your carbine pointed at us as we passed by. It was as if you were telling us to stop and wait for daylight to come. I remembered your face because of that."

"Where did they take you?"

"Richmond," he answered. "You?"

"Richmond too, at Libby."

He acknowledged what I had said with a nod and then turned toward Kalmbach. "You all from Libby today?"

"Yeah," Kalmbach answered. "How long you been here?"

"We were taken from Belle Island outside of Richmond on the first of October." He glanced at the men sitting on the ground behind him. "Got here about a week ago. Thought at first we were heading for the coast somewhere for exchange. Couldn't tell riding in the train. We stopped so damn much to get on different trains. The gauges are all different down here; can't imagine how they git along." He shrugged his shoulders. "Didn't take us long to figure something else was happening."

"What is this place?" I asked.

"Whatever it was, it's now a holding pen for every prisoner of war being held in Virginia."

"We saw the inside of that place." Kalmbach lifted his hand to point toward the hospital building. "It's worse than any field hospital I ever saw."

"That one might just be better than the rest here," the man interrupted. "Every building you see in this stockade is now being used as a hospital."

"That three-story building too?" I nodded my head in the direction of the front gate.

"Don't rightly know." He paused. "At one time they held their own people in there, those who didn't abide by the new ideas of the Confederacy, people still loyal to the flag. Later they began to add Federal officers on the lower floors, leaving the top for muggers, a bad lot from what tell."

"Are they still there?" I asked.

"No, not now. They gotta be out here with us."

"Is that why so many turned away from us when we tried to get help?" Kalmbach looked at the man.

"Maybe, but all I know is a man does what he must to stay alive." He looked over my shoulder toward those behind me. "Ya help those you can, but ya gotta stay alive too." Staring at me for a few seconds, he let me know he had finished his talk with us.

"Before I go," I tried to remain calm, "can you at least tell me how to get tents?"

"There ain't no more and we ain't got room fer ya."

"Are there any somewhere?"

"No," he replied. "At first they gave a couple of dozen to each hundred, but now no more."

"We got shit!" Kalmbach pushed to the front. "We can't live without shelter dressed like this!" His voice became louder. "Some ain't even got shoes!"

"They gave some blankets earlier." The Michigan man glared at Kalmbach. "I can't help ya. Ye're gonna have to do what the rest do and take from the dead."

"Go to hell!" Kalmbach barked.

"If you can't stomach it, someone else will."

"Good lord!" I shook my head.

"You ain't got much of a choice." He shifted his eyes to me and then to the sky above. "The rains will be coming soon. It's already cold."

"They can't keep us here!" I said anxiously, looking at the guards on the parapets. "There's too many of us! Those walls are not strong enough..."

"None of us are what we were," the man spoke as my words faded. "I don't know how many could make it." He glanced toward the western end of the stockade. "That six-pounder down there could do a lot of damage at this range."

"It won't get much better from what you tell us." I stood.

"We gotta wait for the right time." He turned to face me. Holding out his hand, he smiled. "My name is Ardell Dooley, from Detroit, Michigan."

Clasping his hand, I responded, "I'm a Great Lakes boy too. Erie County in western New York. James Reed's my name. This fellow is Kalmbach." Kalmbach nodded. The men to my rear appeared indifferent, sick, weary, seeking some degree of comfort and finding little in Dooley's words. I wanted to give identity to these lost faces, some substance to their humanity. "We're all from the 24th

New York!" I spoke loud enough to gain their attention. Pointing to the soldier nearest me, I introduced Sam Taffner and then Shilton, Hughes, Dan Halleck, and Coroat. "That's Lenny Baker over there." I pointed to the only man lying upon the ground. "He's not doing too well right now."

"Gentlemen," Dooley nodded his head. "As time passes," he turned to me, "your boys will meet the others from my regiment." At that moment, he caught the eye of a man standing a short distance away. "That's Chuck Willard there, Dan Bombassa sitting there and Tom Burness. Give a wave to some soldiers from New York!" he yelled.

"Hey," the man introduced as Burness had a smile on his face. "There are some of your buddies not too far from here, from the IX Corps too!" A couple of the men seated near him attempted to conceal the grins on their faces.

"Who's he talkin' about?" I asked Dooley.

"Not sure," he responded. "Burness is always full of shit."

"Are there more from the 24th New York there?" Kalmbach asked.

"No, he probably means the colored boys from the 30th New York."

"Teleferro's division," I responded.

"Yeah," Dooley nodded.

"You were at Gettysburg, I hear tell," Sam Taffner interjected, ignoring Dooley's talk of the blacks.

"Yeah...and paid a heavy price for it too." Dooley's mood was somber. "Eight of ten failed to report after the second day." He looked at Taffner. "By the time we joined you in the Wilderness, there were only a few left in the regiment who had even been at Gettysburg."

We spoke of battles and dying, of Gettysburg, the Wilderness and Spotsylvania before I said, "Now look at us..." Several seconds passed in silence. Taffner brought us back to the reality of the moment.

"Do I have to dump on the ground in front of every one too?"

"Best not," Dooley answered. "The sinks are at the far south end of the stockade." He pointed. "Just follow your nose."

"Hold up, Taffner!" I stood to my feet. "We'll all go." I looked to Dooley. "Thanks for your help. Right now we need to get water and a place to rest."

The sink consisted of two, one-hundred-foot-long ditches dug along the southern angle of the prison. They were carved into the red clay extending beneath the wooden wall to empty into a small creek some thirty yards from the prison. Taffner was the first to join the dozens of prisoners squatting over the ditch. For lack of a roof overhead, little had changed from the pump room at Libby.

At the center of the stockade, the land rose upward from which all surrounding ground descended. The high point was composed of iron-hard, clay-imbedded soil, and as the terrain sloped downward, its surface gradually turned from soft to mud near the wall-bordering deadline ditch and two small hospitals at the eastern edge of the stockade. In the red clay of the slope, holes had the appearance of graves. Initially, I imagined they had been prepared to receive the dead from the adjacent hospitals, but in that same instance, I saw a man's head, shoulders; men, moving about within the tomblike cocoons. Two, three, maybe more, pressed within each, shelters for hundreds. It was here where we were to lie. Here, our desperate claim to civility.

On the high side of the two hospital buildings, Halleck had found an open space some ten yards long and half that wide.

"Sarge." He held his arms, extended wide. "We can take this."

"We still need tents!" Kalmbach said as he looked back over his shoulder toward those a short distance away.

"We've got no food, for God's sake," I snapped. "How in hell can we expect tents?" The pain in my stomach that had been sharp and distinct now subsided. It was still there, but it had dulled, diffused, and become an extension of my being. My arms, legs, and chest had assumed the weakness, an aching that was impairing my walking, and my thinking. I wanted to fall upon the ground, to escape the pain through sleep. Lowering my head, I bent to the ground.

"Are you sick?" Kalmbach leaned over and touched my shoulder.

"I need water." My eyes remained closed. The cold earth gave into the pressure of my fingers as I leaned forward, slowly allowing myself to sink into the security of rest.

"Hang on, Sarge!" he said boldly. My eyes opened. "We'll get some...somehow..." His fingers dug into the muscle of my shoulder.

Hughes, Coroat, and Dan Halleck, sitting only a few feet from me, were talking about slaves.

"What the hell are they talking about?" I looked up at Kalmbach.

"Nothing important," Kalmbach answered. "Hughes likes to hear himself talk."

The three men were looking in the direction of the group of Negro soldiers sitting on the ground between the hospital and the parcel of land we had claimed.

"Is it about them?"

"Yeah, I guess so."

"Where did they come from?" I stood to my feet. A wave of sickness came over me. My eyes were struggling to focus on the men.

"They were here before us, don't ya think?" Kalmbach's eyes were fixed upon me. "Probably why nobody took this stretch."

"I'm going to ask them for food." I touched the sleeve of his shirt as I stepped by him.

"You're gonna do what?" he asked incredulously.

"They would have been fed last of all." Ignoring Kalmbach's concern, I walked toward the Negroes. "They would know best about hunger." I continued on.

"Sarge," Hughes asked, "is everything all right?" Refusing to respond, I tried to be inconspicuous to the blacks who had yet to notice me approaching. A few began to look up. No one moved, when suddenly, to my left, one of them stood, only a few yards from me. The eyes of many were looking at me. I stopped. He remained motionless, staring into my face.

The fatigue blouse he wore was torn, and one sleeve, no more than strings of cloth, failed to conceal a heavy-muscled arm. He was a powerfully built man, much taller than me. His broad chest, thick neck, and skin blacker than any Negro I had ever seen, presented a formidable presence. His eyes were little more than narrow slits, concealing seemingly lifeless coals.

"We need help," I said.

"Don't want trouble." His voice had a deep resonance.

"I'm not here for any trouble." Fearing a move that might appear aggressive, I remained posed in an awkward stance. The dull pain that gripped my lower back all morning suddenly shot downward, into my hip and right leg. Unable to withstand the pain, I shifted my weight to my left leg. Instantly, the big man stepped backward. His hands came up to his chest in a defensive posture. "We're hungry, probably starving," I continued. "Haven't had anything to eat or drink in days."

"We got no food," he spoke after a few seconds of silence. "We got nothing! We hungry too."

"Can you at least tell us what to do?" I took a step toward him, attempting to reduce the tension that existed between us.

"Why ya come here?" His hands rose higher. Three other men came to his side.

"I thought you would know, that's all." I turned to walk away.

"Who is you?" he spoke.

Stopping, I answered. "My name is Reed. I'm a sergeant in Company 'M,' 24th New York Cavalry." He failed to respond. "Who are you with?" I asked.

"Ya know!"

"Why, should I?" He remained still. "Were you with Teleferro under Burnside?"

"I thought ya knew." His voice was raspy, low.

"Yeah, but only because of what I was told."

"Talk of 'nigger' soldiers?"

"I didn't hear no more than what I said."

"Ya know Teleferro's division?" he asked.

"We were there with you at Petersburg, at the Crater." As I spoke, more Negroes edged closer. With Hughes at my side and Kalmbach behind him, a dozen or more men had now encircled us.

"Welch, Sergeant Joshua Welch, 30th United States Colored Troops. All here," he raised his hand, pointing to the men behind him, "we New York boys, most New York City." He paused and took a breath, nervously looking at the parapets on the near wall. "Captured at the Crater, then off to Richmond and then here two days ago. Had nothing here."

"Have you tried the guards?"

"Them?" He raised his head as if he were to laugh. "They'd soon shoot us like dogs. Why ya think we here, behind buildings, away from the wall?" The two buildings he spoke of provided a barrier between his men lying on the ground and the Rebel guards on the parapet. Only when walking several yards beyond the last building could the guards see the few soldiers from Welch's regiment who were unable to squeeze close enough to the buildings. "I know there," he pointed to a wooden lean-to between the hospital buildings and the deadline along the wall, "prisoners get food."

"That a commissary?" I took a few steps to the side for a better view of the building.

"It's where they give passes fer food," he answered. "That one and another at the front."

"Passes?" I stepped closer to Welch.

"Paper...like greenbacks, fer food. Only sergeant majors or higher gits 'em...only white sergeant majors." He shook his head. "Only whites."

"How do you get the pass?"

"We don't!" His jaws clenched. The long cords of neck muscles tightened. "Dey be none fer nigger-soldiers."

"We need to get those passes." I grabbed Kalmbach's arm. "Come with me. The rest of you stay here." Kalmbach followed. "Dooley might know."

Kalmbach didn't respond to my words. The look on his face was that of resignation and despair. "Only slavers would have such a back-ass way of giving rations," he muttered. "Trying to give order to this insanity."

The Rebel guard stood hunched over, a man worn by age and weather. His beard was a darker gray than his uniform and hung loosely on the chest of his sack coat. Reddened eyes peered out from deep-set sockets, shaded by heavy eyebrows. Watching me approach, he seemed to be ignoring me until I closed within ten feet of him. In a jerking motion, he raised his musket from its rest and fumbled with it awkwardly.

"Halt!" His voice had the shrill pitch of the aged. "You don't come closer!"

Stopping, I held my hands above my head and without looking directly at the guard on the parapet behind the old man, sucked in a breath of air and spoke slowly, "I just got here and was told to get a pass for rations. Can you help me?"

"Hell!" He appeared more frightened than agitated. "Why do you come to me, Yankee?" The barrel of his musket moved up and down in his insecure grip.

"Then who do I go to?" Again, slowly, calmly, I spoke. The old man paused for a minute. The loose skin on his face was deeply furrowed. His eyes darted from side to side before stopping, fixing upon something to his left. Turning slightly, I could see a second sentry nodding his head in approval—his musket also pointed at me.

"Go to that soup house and ask!" the old man spoke, motioning the muzzle of his weapon to the right. "Now git!"

Two guards stood at the entrance to the windowless, crudely constructed out-building. Light from lamps or the glow cast by cook stoves emanated from cracks in the warped siding boards that had separated from one another. Warm air drifted from within the building through the opened doorway. A faint, familiar aroma of cut grain greeted me as I neared the guards. They too were older men, both wearing the brown-colored, homespun uniforms of the reserve guard and holding Federal-issue Springfields. Neither lowered his musket upon us as we approached.

"Will you help me?" There was no response from the guards. "I was told that you could help me with passes for rations."

"Go away from here! Go to the water gate to see the quartermaster tomorrow, early." He gestured for us to move away.

Kalmbach gently touching my arm began to tug at me while I remained still, looking into the deep-set eyes of the old guard. Gripping my arm tightly, Kalmbach urged me to move. "We'll find the water gate," he said. "Let's go!"

Using their fingers and sticks found near a barkless oak, the Negroes were digging L-shaped holes in the soft mud. Lying in the open fields at Cold Harbor, pinned down by the hail of bullets, men dug shelter holes with bayonets and spoons to escape pending death. Fighting under Grant and Meade at Spotsylvania and Petersburg had forced all of us to be dirt-diggers. Here watching the Negroes from the 30th New York toiling, I realized that use of that skill would again save our lives.

"Any luck?" Hughes, who had been working alongside the Negroes helping to stack the excavated mud into a twelve-inch lip at the top of a hole being dug, stood to my side. "From the look on your face, I suspect you found nothing." His shoulders sagged as he exhaled loudly. "You do know some of those boys won't make it through the week." He looked in the direction of the building near which were huddled the blacks. "They got to get rations soon."

"None of us will make it for much longer. The sons of bitches should shoot us rather than this!" I had no reassurance for my men, only futile emotion that I could not retract. "We will find the water gate and return with food," I tried to repair the damage caused by my words. "I'm sure it's near the front gate. I'll find it and get the rations."

"No!" Welch's voice came from below, from out of a hole a few yards away. I then saw his head emerge at ground level, above the packed-down dirt lip. "Don't go there without a pass." He strained to extract himself from the hole. "Sergeant majors, it's only dem dat git the paper!"

"How in the name of all that's holy can we get this food?" Hughes pleaded. "I don't give a tinker's damn for this paper talk!"

"In da morning dey count dead and give paper to the sergeant majors for all dat's alive." Welch spoke calmly, as if ignoring Hughes.

"You can do that for us, Reed," Kalmbach said. "You can get paper for us and the coloreds!" I nodded. Welch looked at me for a few seconds and then lowered himself into the hole.

Through an occasional parting in the billowing purple and white clouds that stretched from horizon to horizon, the late afternoon sun warmed my shoulders and head. A steady breeze began to blow when the sun faded behind the pine trees on the ridge to the west and the air turned colder and the ground upon which we sat, surrendered what little warmth it had absorbed. Pressing my knees to my chest, I wrapped my arms around them to keep the warmth of my body from escaping with the air flowing into the hole from above. Without a word, Hughes, the last to enter, pressed against me, Taffner behind him and then Coroat. Remembering the Negroes saying to lie together like spoons in a drawer, I pressed my face to the cold wall and my back to the chest of Hughes. Sleep would give escape from the hunger and the stabbing pain that cut through my spine and hip. We were silent, huddled together, as dogs in the wild.

Voices resonated in the distance. The sounds of guards yelling commands to one another gradually faded. Darkness finally descended and the wind sent gusts of cold air through the opening of our hole. Bending my body into a tighter fetal position, I listened to the sounds carried by the wind. There were voices again, muffled and indiscernible. "Crack!" I flinched at the sudden charge of musket fire. Hughes moaned and pulled his arm away from my shoulder. I tried to change position but was wedged in by the pressure of the body and dirt wall. I strained to hear what was happening. Then another shot, again nearby. A cry, someone had been hit by the second volley, someone near to us, near to the hole sheltering Kalmbach, Baker, Halleck, and Shilton. Struggling to extricate myself, I rolled over and strained to pull free. Hughes opened his eyes.

"What is it, Sarge?"

"Stay down! Someone's shooting." Haltingly, inch by inch, I raised my head above the rim to see Kalmbach peering from his hole.

"Where'd they come from?" I whispered loudly as I crawled toward him.

"Above...not sure. Anyone hit?"

"I think they were shooting at the Negroes. Sounded bad." There was no moonlight. The clouds that had threatened rain for the last few days still hung in the sky. The buildings were darkened. There was no light visible in the vast stockade, only a glow coming from beyond the front gate, near the headquarters of the guards. To the north beyond the wall and the pine trees along the ridge, the lights of Salisbury reflected from the low-lying clouds. The darkness within the compound prevented me from seeing the guards on the wall. I listened, but heard only the sounds of footsteps along the parapet, boards squeaking under the weight of the sentries.

"Any luck?" came a voice in the distance.

"The second shot, maybe. Thought I heard a squeal."

"Like a pig squeal?" Then laughter.

"Yeah, like an old black boar!" More laughter—then mumbled talk that I could not make out—more steps, squeaking boards, and then silence.

There were shapes of men moving in the shadows of the hospital building. Sounds of moaning, dull and low, came from that direction. Standing and moving, slowly, methodically, taking one step and then another, until I was close enough to discern the shapes before me. As my eyes adjusted, I saw the shelter mounds and their black entrance holes.

"Git down!" A deep, raspy whisper came from somewhere in the darkness. Dropping to my knees, I began to crawl. Panting heavily from weakness or fear, I struggled awkwardly past the first mound before seeing a man lying on the ground. It was Welch. "A man's hit bad," he whispered, motioning to me.

"Can we get him to the hospital?"

"You be a fool, Reed!" Barely above a whisper, his words vibrated like distant thunder, muffled and somber. "We'd best die with our own."

"Can I do anything?"

"No!" he answered. I didn't know what to say to Welch. "We put water on da wound," he continued. "More fer us than fer his hurtin'."

"Crack!" Again musket fire came from the scaffolding, echoing across the compound before quickly fading. An uneasy stillness hung over the prison camp. If the bullet had found its target, its victim gave no indication. I could see no movement.

Lying exposed to the wind, my torn shirt offered little protection from the cold along the wet, clay surface of the ground. Trembling from the chill that swept my body, I whispered, "I can't help here. I'm returning to my men."

"Wait!" Welch said abruptly. "They be shootin' more. Keep down!" I pressed to the ground and hoped the minutes would pass quickly. My breathing, the only sound I could hear, had slowed. Trembling from the cold that surrounded me, I curled my legs up to my chest and hugging them, sucked in deep, sustained breaths and let the moist heat from my breath warm my face.

"New guards!" Welsh's voice startled me. To escape the hunger and cold, my mind had sought refuge in the fading colors and sounds of shallow sleep.

"What?"

"Them boys is gone. Them home guards up there now," Welch answered.

"How does that matter?"

"Them old ones don't shoot." A few seconds passed before Welch spoke again. "You stay if'n you want." Unable to feel the pain beneath the numbness in my feet, I grasped them with my hands, squeezing, in a desperate attempt to create warmth. Beneath the paper-thin leather of my boots, my toes were thick and numb. Terror swept over me as the memory of Jim Truesdill flashed in my mind. He was eight years old, red hair, freckles on his face and arms, lying still in his bed, fingers black and rigid. His father always beat Jim. It didn't matter for what reason. There were always swollen lips, blue and purple blotches on his neck and cheeks. No one ever said anything about it. Jim was afraid to go home that night he ran away, something he often had done before. When they found him the next morning, near the garden fence where many times we had dug for potatoes, he was wearing only flannel drawers. He had left his house to escape his dad and fallen asleep in the snow. His mom thought him dead when they carried him into their kitchen. Jim screamed when his dad poured hot water on his reddened feet and hands. The doctor cut off three of his fingers and his right foot. Jim didn't return to school. I never dug for potatoes on his farm after that day.

"I'll get warm," I whispered, crawling in the direction of Welch's voice. "Then I'll go back."

Inching down through the hole and against the wall of his mound, I pressed alongside of Welch. Still warm where he had lain, he tried to move to give me more room. Fearful for the numbness in my feet, I raised my knees against Welch's back. My feet pressed into his thighs. Within minutes, I felt a tingling in my toes and then a dull pain as warming blood flowed into them.

"You be right soon," Welch whispered assuredly, seemingly aware of my struggle.

"It's the young ones that do the shooting, huh?"

"Yeah," Welch answered. "Only dem."

"Why? Why them?"

"Don't matter much, does it? Hate and killin' don't know age."

"Just at night?"

"Day too." Welch paused and adjusted his big body that seemed much too large for a space as small as this hole.

"Dey be killin' us all." The words came from one of the men in front of Welch. "But dem will surely die if dey be trying."

As soldiers, fear was a part of our lives, not just before battle, but all of the time, every minute of every day. Bushwhackers could hit anyone without warning, or ordnance could ignite accidentally. Death surrounded our every move. Didn't I too know what Welch and his men feared? Their suffering was no greater than mine or anyone else in uniform, Blue or Gray. That's what war means. Everyone fears the same and dies the same. Negroes have no monopoly on any of that. They had only an excuse that set them apart.

"We stayed away from the sinks," Welch interrupted my rambling thoughts. "Used the ground hereabouts and be shot at!" he sighed deeply. "Der commander, man named Gee told the guards to treat us like the white boys. There to be no difference."

"But they don't, do they?"

"Don't much matter none. Just sayin' it matters."

"What?"

"We die no difference here or out there, don't much care. We won already."

"Welch, I don't follow you."

"The Rebs say we no different den da whites. We be the same. We wear the same blues, killed the Rebs and die like soldiers. We be the same now."

"You think so?"

"The Rebs think so. My men think so and look at you...here with us. You must think so too."

"Like you say, don't much matter. We'll all die here."

"Maybe so, but it matter to me. Havin' dis blue clothes, ragged as dey be, sure do give us somethin' to be won. We free men, dyin' fer our freedom! It matters!"

"Well, you're not free now," I said. "None of us are."

"Dey have our bodies, dat's all."

I thought of the meaning of this big man's words, but I knew of nothing more to say and began struggling to extricate myself from the small space between Welch and the dirt wall.

"I will do what I can to get rations for us in the morning...I promise you."

The air was cold and damp. A faint glow appeared as a narrow slit in the gun-barrel gray sky just above the eastern wall of the stockade. Directly overhead, heavy, low clouds threatened rain. Pain shot through my knees and hips as I stepped quickly to stay abreast of the hundreds of men walking toward the southern end of the compound. The beat of a solitary drum resulted in more men rising to their feet, while others, emerging from holes in the ground, joined the throng moving forward. Nearing the water gate, dozens of prisoners had stopped, pressing against one another.

"Reed!" I jerked around to see who had yelled my name. At that instant, a hand clasped my arm. Dooley's face was reddened. He was gasping for breath. "I've been trying to stop ya!" he panted.

"Why?" I asked. "What's wrong?"

"Get out of here! There are no rations here."

"What are you saying, Dooley?"

"Ya don't get rations here!" He attempted to compose himself. "Just follow the damn rules or there'll be nothing." He began to walk away. "Come with me. You're assigned to our brigade." Hearing Dooley's words failed to reassure me that I would get any food this day. Dozens of men were passing by where the two of us stood. All of these men will soon be taking food that might have gone to my men.

"Hold on!" I grabbed Dooley's arm. "What do you mean?"

"Just tell them you're a sergeant assigned to Sergeant Major Philip Crown."

"Who? How?"

"Do as I say!" Dooley, holding tight to my arm, turned me and began pushing me toward the water gate.

In a clearing, ten yards from the edge of the crowd of men, between the deadline and the wall, four prisoners stood by themselves. Two armed guards escorted a Rebel officer toward the four prisoners. The officer was dressed in the uniform of regular army; a North Carolina epaulette was sewn to the shoulder of his woolen coat. For a few minutes he spoke to the four men before handing each a small bundle of papers. Turning, he departed through the gate. The four stepped across the deadline ditch before the guards followed their officer.

"Now!" Dooley spoke quietly, his mouth only inches from my ear. "Go over and tell Crown, the one with the black beard. Tell him you're Sergeant Reed with the 24th New York and the colored troops. Tell him there's a hundred in all!"

"There ain't that many!"

"Just go and do it!" Dooley put his hand against my back and gently pushed me forward.

Weaving lines formed alongside of the cookhouse at the eastern end of the stockade, close to the shelter holes dug by the colored troops. A cool breeze had begun to blow over the west wall and bring the stench of the sinks directly upon the area surrounding the cookhouse, overwhelming the sweet smell of warm cornbread.

"Mess!" A Rebel guard, leaning back on the box on which he was seated, cupped his hands to his mouth and yelled. The four lines to my left, nearly one hundred men in each, began to advance toward the tables. They moved slowly, shuffling, staggering, many walking only with the support of another, all covered with the dirt of the unwashed, bearded, with scrubby hair crusted and matted to their heads. A few men turned to look at me, their faces thin and drawn, eyes darting from me to the guards and then to tables where the cornbread had been stacked. The loaves, baked in four-quartered tins and separated by the cook into eight sections, were given out in one-section rations with a piece of salted pork to each prisoner.

The sergeant major at the head of the line placed his bundle of coupons on the table and stepped aside. A Rebel guard seated on a keg behind the table pushed the paper into a wooden box sitting on the ground at his feet before the line was allowed to move forward. The first man in line yelled "One!" and with both hands held out in front of him, received his bread and pork. Within two steps of the table, the prisoner had already stuffed the cornbread into his mouth while tightly squeezing the pork in clutched hands.

"Hurry up!" was the only order given me when I announced my number to the guard standing at the corner of the cookhouse. The others followed, with Welch leading his colored troops. Upon finally reaching the table, Welch told five of his soldiers, too sick to stand, to get to their feet if they wanted any food.

"This will not happen again." The guard sitting on the box stood to his feet. "Niggers too lazy to walk or stand won't be fed!" Without a word, Welch held his blouse away from his body to form a crude pouch into which sections of bread and several pieces of pork were placed. A look of defiance reflected in the faces of the Negroes passing by the table. Only a few lowered their eyes in the presence of the guards as they took the bread and pork before turning.

The light cast by the flickering of small fires outlined the mounds of dirt surrounding the shelter holes of the 30th New York. Hughes and Kalmbach, following the advice of Welch's men, had been searching the grounds for scraps to burn but reported very little available. A breeze continued to blow into the compound and from appearance of the heavy clouded sky, rain was fast approaching. Each of my men, with the exception of Kalmbach who had yet to return from his hunt for wood, looked toward the fires of the blacks. Heat from the flames was of less appeal than the aroma of pork cooking in their pits. Having saved my pork ration, I rolled it between my fingers and thumb and thought to ask Welch for use of his fire, but looking into the faces of my men and seeing the hunger in their eyes, I held my hand to shield my mouth from view and slipped the chunk of meat into it.

The pork had the taste of metal. Looking at my hands, I could see the filth that had built up on them. Whatever had touched my hands must have given the meat a foul and bitter taste, but smelling my fingers, I knew the pungent odor had come from the pork. I closed my eyes and attempted to erase the smells from my memory.

Unable to chew the foul-tasting meat any longer, I swallowed the chunk whole.

"Dead!" A distant muffled voice that became increasingly louder rolled across the compound. "Give up your dead!" Two men walked along the side of a dilapidated wagon and two more followed to the rear of the slow-moving vehicle. The driver, head slumped to his chest, his right hand holding a four-foot long metal pole with a gaff-like hook at its end, lackadaisically watched his team plod, step by step. The two swayback horses, graying and old, strained visibly to move the empty wagon through the yard's soft clay, their heads hanging low, oblivious to the thousands of men surrounding them.

"Dead! Bring the dead!" A slow migration swelled toward the road, depositing what they carried until those rigid and still lined its length from gate to sinks. Face down and naked, they lay amidst indifference, no more important than a source for clothes or boots and no less than a memory. I too will learn to accept the sight of the dead squad as they perform their ritualistic dance.

Working in pairs, the squad detail lifted one of the fallen, and struggling to reach the tailgate of the wagon, swung the body up into the bed, one holding the feet, the other, the outstretched hands. The driver, turning upon hearing it fall into the wagon, slammed the end hook of his bar into the neck of the body. Giving a quick jerking motion, it was impaled under the jawbone and then, slowly, forcefully dragged to the front of the wagon to be stacked as cordwood. As carp spawning in the shallows of a river's bottom, arms and legs wiggled when the wheels of the wagon jolted along the rutted path leading through the open water gate to freedom within the fields beyond the walls of this place.

11
Pit of Hell

November 1864
Salisbury Prison
Salisbury, North Carolina

Withering purple clouds absorbed into a solid gray mass that descended over the land, and a biting wind blowing steadily from the east and south brought a pervasive mist that had become rain. Knowing the sick to suffer this night without warmth of a fire, I looked to Welch's encampment to see the fragile trails of smoke drifting from but a few holes. The cold rain and blowing wind, having intensified, had driven the guards from the parapets. Crawling out like a rat from its hole, a black emerged and quickly ran behind the building at the road. Then another appeared, and soon more, all ignoring the blinding rain that forced my retreat within the cold darkness of my mound.

The wet clay of the floor pressed into me. I lowered my head and looked at my hands, to the dirt embedded into the cracks in my skin, and my fingernails, raised by the pressure of the dried blood caked beneath them. I couldn't feel my fingers as I attempted to straighten them. Shaking my head, I swallowed to clear my throat and lowered my face to the earth. Was it day or night? Was that the sound of rain sweeping across the rooftop of our farmhouse, blown by gales off the Great Lake? Lying in my bed listening to the rain, I found comfort in the warm air drifting through the vents from the kitchen below, carrying the aroma of Mother's bread cooling on the stove. Where was Hughes? Hadn't he gone in search of wood some time ago? I was tired and the world around me became smaller. There was only my breathing and my heart beating its rhythm, soothing me and bringing sleep.

Sounds of men yelling, penetrating those of the rain striking the mud roof, awakened me. Lying still, I felt something in my skin, a tingling, crawling sensation. They were biting! It wasn't the noise that had awakened me, but the lice. Creeping into my clothing and then into the crevices of my body, they bit so viciously I wanted to scream out in agony, to slap at my skin, to stop them from eating me alive.

Water was striking me in the face, droplets seeping through openings in the roof. The rain was falling heavily, rain that would wash the vermin from my hair and cleanse my skin. I had to move to escape the lice. More water came in through the cracks above. The roof will crumble before I crawl out. We should have listened to the blacks on strengthening the roof and elongating tunnels. We should have patted the mud more firmly, found more branches. I could have worked longer, dug more dirt. My mind was racing, thoughts were blurring, memories returning and fading. Did I hear Ellen's voice calling to me from the porch? Had she come to visit, to lay her hands upon my forehead, to soothe me with her warmth? I must rise up, to go to her. She must know that I'm here!

"Ellen! I'm home!"

I felt the wind against my face and the rain beat upon me as I sat in the mud, confused, looking toward the main gate, to something that had drawn my attention. They were moving, hundreds walking toward I knew not what, cheering. Was it freedom? What did it mean? Was it finished? I too ran, to the main well, less than one hundred feet from the front gate when I heard musket fire coming from the parapets. Guards along the walkway began firing into the gathering throng of prisoners. Without warning, four more sentries began shooting. The prisoners closest to the gate turned and frantically pushed against others, desperately attempting to flee.

More shots rang out from the parapet. A path before me opened; a clearing permitting an escape. Grabbing and pushing, I began running to the side, away from the push to my rear. Forcing my legs to move up and down, the pain with each step ripped through my ankles and knees. I couldn't stop, I had to push onward, to ignore the pain, only a few more steps. Men in front of me slowed. I stumbled. A hand clutched my arm and lifted me. I felt the firmness of a brick wall press against my shoulder. Gasping, I looked into the face of Ardell Dooley.

"The sons of bitches! Shooting helpless men like that!" Dooley's eyes were fixed upon the main gate and the figures perched to the left and right along the scaffolding.

"What is happening, for God's sake?" I pleaded.

"They have no control of their men!" Dooley spoke through clenched jaws. "No one should shoot into defenseless men like that!"

"But why'd it happen?" I asked.

"With all of us here...we are too many! They can't stop these many. They're scared of us! The dumb bastards thought we were rushing the front gate!" Dooley's eyes did not turn away from the guards as he spoke. "What started out as something decent turned into this, and all because of those dumb cowards, dumb yellow-bellied bastards!"

"What was all the yelling about to begin with?"

"The soldiers on the second floor caught a thieving mugger. They beat him to death and threw him out the window up there." Dooley pointed to a second-floor window that had been opened. "Do you see the one without the bars there?"

"Yeah, I do," I answered. Below the window, a crowd of fifty or more prisoners was milling about a boy sprawled upon the ground. "Was he a Federal?"

"Hard to say," he answered. "The top floor there is called the 'devil's den.' It holds some Southern turncoats, but mostly Union men who would cut your throat for your old boots or just to watch you bleed. On the other floors are mostly officers, taking turns to guard the doors to keep the muggers from them. That one," he nodded to the base of the building, "he broke through the door and was beaten pretty good and then thrown out that window."

"It's because of him we ran like fools?" Before Dooley could react to my sarcasm, the front gate opened and a unit of North Carolina regulars entered the compound. I followed Dooley's lead as he pressed into a space between prisoners standing against the side wall of the soup house, away from the direct wind.

"Get away!" A Rebel guard I hadn't seen pointed his musket at me and yelled, "Move out of here!" All four guards with him were leveling their weapons at the prisoners standing against the soup house. Pushed along by the others in an effort to obey the guards, we watched a jumbled column, nearly one hundred prisoners being led from the three-story building past the soup house. They walked tall, these Federal officers who had led us and would some day lead us again. Dooley stepped a few paces toward them and slowly, ostentatiously saluted. A grin crossed the face of the officer who returned Dooley's salute.

A cheer went up and then a spattering of a few more from the prisoners who stood and watched as the officers entered within the cramped quarters of the soup house. The guards then turned and marched to the main gate, leaving a unit of ten stationed outside of the soup house prison. It was over. Slowly the prisoners melted away as an eerie quiet fell over the yard. The gate had yet to close and as the last of the Rebel soldiers walked from the enclosure, I saw a wagon enter through the opening. Two large chestnuts were pulling the canvas-covered wagon. Slouched down upon the seat, a sutler, wearing a brown woolen coat and a black, broad-brimmed campaign hat, incongruent with his surroundings, urged his slowly lumbering vehicle down the center of the road leading from the gate. The clanging sound of metal pots striking against one another and the squeaking wagon wheels brought attention to the aberration; a trader of goods among men without food or clothes, many too sick to survive the week, undauntedly urging his steeds forward.

I followed the sutler away from Dooley and those who went to the aid of the wounded and dead, past newly-dug mounds of earth. Like the shell of a river turtle, each mound had a small hole at its end, with a ridge of dirt to shield those within from the wind and rain. Through the open holes, I saw faces looking out at the parade of men shuffling behind the clanging wagon. Oblivious to the rain and wind, I followed the squeak of the wheels and metal striking metal, sounds helping to dispel the helplessness of my existence. Walking gave me a feeling of purpose. I was in charge of my body. I had made a decision to act and was doing so.

"Reed!" Kalmbach's voice broke the spell-like concentration I had fixed upon the rear of the sutler's wagon. Watching it sway from side to side, bounce as it glided in and over the soft mud surface of the road, and then abruptly jerk forward as the whip cracked above the rumps of the team lulled me into a mindless daze. "Here! Over here!" he yelled. "This way, Reed! Where are you going?" I was too confused to answer him. Why was I here, on this road, with these people, behind the wagon? Would Ellen explain? Would my father look back at me or just drive the team away? Did I dig our hole deep enough? My eyelids were so heavy. If only the drums would quiet. If the shooting stopped, we will advance. It was so cold and my men needed me. If we were to survive this hell, I must remain strong.

"I will survive," I whispered as Kalmbach led me toward our hole.

"We found wood!" he said excitedly. "You need to get warm."

In their wanderings about the stockade, he and Hughes had confiscated an armful of branches and charred chunks of wood and while Kalmbach searched for me, Hughes had built a small fire a few feet from the opening of our hole. Holding my hands to the flames while struggling to withstand the falling rain, I looked down into the shelter to see small puddles of reddish water collecting in depressions on the floor bottom. Through the roof, water had saturated the packed mud and was now flowing freely to collect at the bottom.

"Shilton! Halleck!" I yelled. "Baker! Grab those extra sticks!" The three stood to their feet. Baker picked up the branches, each about one foot long. "Give one to Shilton and to Halleck," I said as I crawled to the edge of the hole. "We need to build a dam around the lip of this and a ridge to hold out the water. Now!" With my fingers, I began to pry into the clay in my determination to dig a four-inch trench. Halleck was already pushing his branch in the earth, plowing it back. "Can you get any more wood, Kalmbach?" My voice faltered as I gasped for air.

"I will try, Sarge."

"Do so," I pleaded. "We need to strengthen the roof as soon as we can." Without looking up, I continued to extricate small pieces of red clay with my fingers. At my side, I could feel the heat from the flames as they extended upward, cracking in their resistance to the steady rain.

Halleck was digging furiously, stabbing the stick into the mud and grunting as he pulled the clay free to form a trench along the edge of the hole. Again and again, he forced the stick into the ground lifting chunks that quickly channeled the incessant flow of water away from the opening. My fingers were numb. No longer were they responding to my commands. No longer could I wedge the clay free. Holding my hands to my chest, I slowly bent my fingers and then began to swing my arms, beating down upon the loosely packed clay of Halleck's ridge with the bludgeoning blows of my deadened fists. The surface water was flowing along the wall of the trench and down an incline created by Halleck's probing stick. With warm blood flowing into my fingers with each impact upon the clay, I was able to move my fingers and again lift the loose dirt. Grabbing handfuls of the clay that Halleck unearthed, the odor hidden by the surface water began to release and penetrate my nostrils. Mixed in the soil was human waste that flowed across the yard, settling in the soft clay. Halleck's sense of urgency was brought about by the sight and smell of the colored troops' shit washing down the gentle slope toward our hole.

"We have sticks!" Kalmbach had returned. I raised my head to look at the progress of our work. No longer was water running down the sides of our hole. The only water that entered it now came with the wind and seepage through the softening roof.

"The 24th Michigan gave us some of what they had!" Kalmbach's words came slowly. "There is no wood to be found. They gave us what they could..." He struggled for breath. I could see weariness in a tired face and maybe for the first time, sickness.

He dropped the armful of branches near my feet.

"You've done good!" I greeted him.

"It was Dooley," Hughes said as he bent over to lower three narrow logs to the ground. "It's him that got us this!"

"Those three there," Halleck pointed to the branches dropped by Hughes, "they can be used for supports for the roof. If we use them for support posts," he said quickly, "we can stack those smaller ones up on the roof." Reaching for Kalmbach who had crouched by the fire holding his hands near the flames, I patted him on the back and leaned down to him.

"You did well, soldier...you did well." I then stood and looked back to where Halleck was kneeling. "We'll take turns putting wood on the fire." I wanted all my men to hear. "We can put some of those smaller pieces on the floor of the hole to keep the water from us. Tomorrow, we'll spend more time fixing the floor and getting some of that water out of there." I looked at Kalmbach as I spoke. "Let's get into our huts and out of this rain. We're sick enough as it is."

I lay listening to the dull tapping sound of the rain striking against the branches of the roof overhead and knew that the water dripping upon me was oozing through the dissolving mud we had packed earlier. The warmth of the body pressing against me gave little comfort as I buried my head beneath my raised arm trying to hold back the world surrounding. With my left hand, I reached to the belt of my trousers. It was still dry beneath my shirt. My fingers gently massaged the firmness at the edge of Ellen's letter. Ellen, the aroma of her hair, the warmth of her eyes, her smile, the feel of her skin—images, blurred into the shadows of exhaustion.

The morning air eased through the hole as Hughes rose to his knees and crawled out into the light of dawn. His movement released the trapped warmth and brought a chill that swept my body and caused me to tremble.

"We must get a fire going," I stammered as I climbed from the hole and over the sunken fire pit, black with pooled water, and charred wood.

"I've got these left," Kalmbach, sitting a few feet from me, spoke as he guided a small bundle of sticks along the ground toward me. "But, I think it best to save 'em." I wrapped my arms around my chest knowing he was correct and that there will be no fire this morning. At that moment, his attention was not on the sticks or me, for he was absorbed in the sound coming from a single drum. Without words, we followed the tapping beat announcing the distribution of rations.

The cornbread, heavy and flat and composed of corn kernels and brittle husks, possessed a bitter taste similar to that of a dandelion stem. The chunk of pork I received was small enough to fit into the palm of my hand and within seconds would have been devoured had not Kalmbach convinced me to put it to flame. Hungry as a man is before starving, I agreed to wait until returning to our shelter holes and the pit fire at dusk.

The sun had yet to set before the feeble flame flickered and faded beneath the embers of the crumbled husks. Carefully, I placed the precious morsel of pork on top of the smoldering ash and vigilantly waited with determined attention. An aroma of cooked pork, unlike that of anything else on earth, began to rise within the white smoke. Anxiously, I probed the gray powder with a five-inch long stick, rescuing the prize and guiding it from its bed. My teeth crunching into embedded particles in the meat made faintly audible, popping sounds. I sat silently savoring the taste of the juice trickling into my throat, but too quickly, the bitterness of the charcoal permeated my mouth and enhanced my ever-present thirst. Rising, I sought the safe well.

Attempting to drive away images of creatures swimming at the bottom of the well or what had given the water its peculiar taste, I let the cup drop from my hand to watch it dangle at the end of the string. Having little reason to return to our shelter hole, Kalmbach and I began to walk in the opposite direction. Looking at the slowly shifting gray cloud mass overhead, I predicted that the next rains would hold off for a few more hours. Already the air was beginning to warm beneath the faint presence of the elusive sun and men were beginning to emerge from their shelters. With each passing minute, more appeared, a dozen, a hundred, an army of men, a brigade in size, not unlike the numbers I witnessed while standing in a clearing on a hillside above the North Anna. That night we had bivouacked and in the early morning light I stood in awe watching great columns of men that extended for miles, four across, stretching along winding roads and through tangled marsh brush. The number of soldiers imprisoned here would equal those of that day. We were once those men. We were soldiers.

"She must think me dead," Kalmbach interrupted my thoughts as we passed by the prisoners. "I mean, not hearing anything in these months, what else might my wife think?"

"You'll write to her as soon as we're freed."

"If she only knew now! God, it hurts when I think what she must be going through. It's got to be worse for her."

"Maybe it's best she not know you're here."

"No, it would be better if she knew I was alive. You're lucky, Reed, that you don't have anyone waiting for you."

"Yeah, I'm lucky about that."

"I don't mean that, Reed!" He reached to touch my arm. "What in hell is wrong with me? I just meant you ain't married."

"Look at that," pushing his arm away, I nodded toward the wall we were approaching. "That deadline couldn't stop us. Once we got to the wall we could pull ourselves up."

"You'd be dead before you reached the wall."

"They couldn't stop all of us! Some will die but in every charge that's to be part of it."

"If we could get to the sentries and turn their guns, maybe...," Kalmbach pondered.

"The regulars of the 68th North Carolina are soldiers. They can't like this duty. Hell, they even look distracted. They can't like this shit, not like those little bastard home guards. They'd be vulnerable. We could get on them and get their guns before they knew what was happening."

"Maybe..." Kalmbach nodded his head.

We walked away from the sentries to the west end near the sinks, nearer to the source of the insufferable stench that hung in the air. It was a pungent odor, bitterly sweet and heavy enough to cause a gagging reflex in my throat. Placing my hand over my mouth and nose, I inhaled the odor of the red clay dirt that still colored my palms. We turned toward the east, increasing our stride to escape the smell. In front of us stood yet another of the gates that offered a potential route of escape. Appearing to be a doorway cut out of the wall, I realized that this was not a gate at all, but rather an enclosure for a field piece. Four feet above the ground, resting on scaffolding, the hole of a cannon muzzle peered ominously from the shadows.

"It's a six-pounder," I whispered, more to myself than for the benefit of Kalmbach's hearing. Positioned there was the proof to the stories I had been hearing. Dooley had told me that there were three, another at the southwest and a third at the northern angle. Firing of such a piece could sweep an area from five to twenty yards with nails, stones, and iron trailings. If any escape attempt were to succeed they must first be captured.

"You know we won't get out of here, don't you, Reed?"

"If we can hang on, the army will get here." I slowed my pace. "We have to believe that."

"That shit about storming the walls won't work and you know it."

"It's a whole lot better idea than waiting to die and do nothing!"

"I don't know about that. The same thing that happened to those poor fools shot outside the cotton factory will be our fate too if we try something!"

"So what?" I snapped. "We'll die from that piss-water if we don't starve first! That poisoned water from Libby and now here, I'm probably dead already and too dumb to lie down." I turned to look back at the sinks. "Stop for a second and think about what we're drinking from those goddamn wells. All that shit is supposed to wash out of here in those trenches to the fields beyond the wall. There are so many of us here that there are no open trenches! They're filled to overflowing and all that crap is spread in piles everywhere! Where does it all go when it rains? Look! It's flowing along the ground right now over to those wells there! We're drinking it!"

"There can be no mistake," Crown said. "If any of us try to escape or overtake the guards, all will suffer for it." The sergeant stood before us, looking into the eyes of each man he had chosen for the water detail, the twenty to carry ten barrels filled with creek water. It was because of my size that he had selected me. The others were at least as tall, with the exception of the black man named Denton, a barrel-chested man with heavy arms and short legs.

We stood a few feet from the deadline, waiting for permission to approach the gate. A North Carolina regimental officer, a saber dangling at his side, strutted in front of our column. We proceeded across the deadline through the gate and beyond the walls of the prison. A breeze blew against my face, moving the hair on my head. My body shivered in reaction to the sudden change in temperature. It was a cool, damp breeze that lifted my spirits. Not since walking the streets of Richmond did I feel as free of the filth now lifting from my clothes and skin. Raising my eyes to look at the clouds hanging over the pine woods to the south, I drew in the moist air that cleansed my lungs and throat of the pungent, suffocating odors of death.

The creek flowed along the edge of a pine tree stand in a wide arc. In comparative size to streams I remembered in New York, it was little more than a drainage ditch I had often seen formed by the runoff of a thawing farm field in an early April. From one bank to the other side, it stretched seven feet at its widest, to four at its narrowest. The surface lay still, unbroken by a current too weak to bend tall grass at the water's edge. Many had trampled the mud and decaying leaves along the shoreline.

Lifting the partially-filled barrel, the wooden pole dug deeply into the bone of my shoulder. I placed my hand beneath it but only transferred the pain. I could hear the water splash and feel it sway, pulling the weight against me and then suddenly, violently in the opposite direction. Weakening under the strain of the load, I bent over, setting the barrel to the ground, gasping for air, staring at the ground so as to avoid making eye contact with Denton.

Standing upright, rubbing my shoulder bone, I looked toward the prison sitting as an island surrounded by a sea of red mud. Rising out of the cutover field of stumps and green pine trees, the brown-walled prison was like a beast emerging from hell itself. Within the enclosure, the bleak, brick cotton factory with peering windows, black and ominous, shielded by its surrounding walls, challenged the countryside upon which it glared. Incongruous to its setting, the prison, a monolith apart from the giant oaks to the northwest, the dark grove of pines to our rear and neatly rowed roof tops and church spires of the town of Salisbury to the north, was a great festering sore on the face of this bucolic land.

A faintly visible gray haze draped the field to the west of the prison. Appearing, as ghosts within the gently swaying shroud, were the dark figures of men, eight blacks, closely bunched together within a ditch that was as deep as a grave. With shovels in hand, slowly, methodically they stabbed at the earth, lifting and throwing soil to each side of the trench that extended nearly eighty yards. Talking among the barrel-carriers had ceased, as all stood silently watching the scene before them.

The trench was rectangular in shape and growing longer as the slaves continued to open the earth. Behind them, twenty yards to their rear, sat a dead-wagon loaded with corpses wedged together, three deep and six across. At the rear of the wagon stood another black, his vision fixed upon the driver who sat whip in hand, eyes forward, staring at this two-mule team. The section of the trench they had just passed had the appearance of a garden plot ready for spring planting. Dirt, darker in color than the untilled field, was packed down in an oval-shaped mound. Two slaves, ankle deep on top of the freshly-turned soil, were raising their feet, stomping the mound, leveling it with the surrounding land.

"Oh, my God!" someone near me gasped.

The black, reaching in the bed of the wagon, had taken hold of a body and pulling, dislodged it, allowing it to fall to the ground. While continuing to hold fast to its wrists, a second black, coming from the far side of the wagon, lifted the body by its ankles. Both men struggled to reach the ditch whereupon they swung the body, heaving it into the air where it folded momentarily, bending at the waist before falling out of view into the open trench.

"Move it!" the Rebel lieutenant yelled. "Sergeant! Move these men along at once, or the water will be left where it sits!" Sergeant Crown, who had been watching the burial of the dead, turned at hearing the lieutenant's voice.

"Step forward!" he yelled. "No one permitted you to stop!" He passed by me, walking to the lead. "There will be no more stopping for rest! Move along! Now!"

Being one of the last to pick up the pole, I grunted through clenched teeth as it settled upon my shoulder and the full weight of the barrel pressed down through my arms. The first step came slowly, my knees tightening as a stabbing pain passed through them. Pulled from side to side by the sloshing water, I strained the muscles in my arms, forcing the barrel to steady, to resist the pulling, to keep it moving forward. Directing my eyes to look upon the ground before me, trying to avoid stumbling in the ruts or in the tangled clumps of thickly matted, dead weeds, I slowed my pace. Desperately I wanted to look back toward the field where the bodies were being thrown into the trench but resisting this primordial urge to stare at the obscene, I raised my head and looked forward, above the weathered-plank boards and logs supporting the prison wall, toward the city on the hill, to the pristine, white steeple that rose above the roof tops silhouetted against the distant gray thunderclouds hovering on the horizon.

12

Rebel Retribution

November 1864
Salisbury Prison
Salisbury, North Carolina

Below sunken eyes, his skin was black and purple. Only now did I realize how thin Coroat's face had become.

"Stay here." I placed my hand upon his shoulder and felt the bones beneath his shirt. "Lie back down. I'll find some water for you." Before I could turn to crawl toward the opening of the hole, a low moaning came from deep within his throat as he slumped, his head flopping to the side, striking the ground with a dull thud. I knew he so desperately needed water and there was only that from the well. The barrel brought back yesterday contained enough creek water to last a day at best. We were to have no more today and tomorrow was too late for Coroat.

I had to turn to Welch for help. Although I knew he had no water to share, he would lend me the use of a cup. If I strained the water by picking out particles that I could feel, the well water would serve Coroat for the time being.

I lifted the torn blouse that covered the opening to our hole, exposing the darkness of its interior. Ashes from the fire of the night before, now cold and damp, smudged against the knees of my trousers as I crawled into the tunneled opening. A chilling dampness, permeating the air within the tomblike cavern, filled me with dread. The heat from Coroat's body and his breathing should have warmed the air, even with the flap at the entrance pulled back. As my eyes adjusted to the darkness, I saw him lying there. His mouth was open. I leaned closer to him and placed my hand beneath his head.

"Charles! Wake up!" His drawn eyelids failed to conceal an ominous streak of white that I had seen so often before. With trembling hand, I placed the cup to his lips. Water spilled over the brim of the cup, and rolled down his chin. His lower jaw failed to move and the water puddled in his mouth. I let the cup fall from my hand, spilling the water to his blouse and staining the red clay beneath him. Raising his head to my chest, I held him to me. My eyes closed, forcing the tears down my cheeks and onto the brittle hair of his head. Tears for a man I hardly knew! I didn't cry for all the others! What was different for this man? Were these tears for the death of yet another from the 24th, another from Buffalo, another one I had befriended? Or were they for a man who died, a man much like myself? Were these tears in the end, for me? No one would know of these tears. No one back home would know of Coroat's death. His mother knew nothing of where he was or even if he were alive at all. None in the Coroat family would know of what happened to Charles and that was good. I would not want them to see this hole in the ground or his emaciated body, the lice in his hair, or the sadness in eyes too dry to close. Maybe my tears were not for Charles or for myself after all, but rather for the shame of it all.

Kalmbach glanced toward Baker and then whispered to me, "Don't report him dead." I looked at him as he continued, "We need the extra rations."

"Baker wouldn't hear of us using Coroat like that," I too whispered.

Baker had been a neighbor to Coroat since their childhood. They acted like brothers, laughing at jokes only they thought humorous and arguing about every subject anyone discussed. Baker cried openly when learning of his friend's death. Much of his anguish had come from fear, for he too had become sickly, and now more alone to await his own fate.

I crouched near the fire I had built and stared at the ragged blouse that flapped over the entrance to the mound. Behind the curtain, from within the shadows of the enclosure, I heard Baker's voice and occasional laughter, the sounds of a friend's long good-bye.

Coroat's death had awakened me to our pending doom. I knew the sickness was inevitable, followed by the sleep of death and burial in the mass graves if we did nothing but succumb to this fate. The only alternative was escape. There was no choice but to overthrow the guards, take their weapons, eat the life-saving provisions they had denied us and fight our way out through the countryside. Coroat's death was the fire bell in the night, terrifying in its urgency.

Baker refused to leave Coroat's body unattended. He watched as we divided up his friend's portion of rations and knew that we waited to strip him naked when the opportunity presented itself. Kalmbach found that Baker had finally fallen asleep shortly before noon of the second day. Carefully, quietly, we removed the rigid, decaying body of Coroat from the hole and with some physical difficulties, his clothes as well. Kalmbach and I were standing near the wagon when the two Negroes swung Coroat's body onto it. I had turned away from what I knew would then happen. Faster I walked, unable, unwilling to look back.

In the eyes of the strangers I saw a fear and distrust that made them less human and more distant. With them, I had faced common enemies on the field of battle. We then had risked our lives for one another, but no more. I remained a warrior, but my enemies had changed. In this prison, my loyalties narrowed with each passing day and each fading life. All that drove me was my passion for life and its preservation.

There were fewer fires during daylight hours even though the air had grown colder. Gradually, the only smoke visible came from chimneys of the soup house and guards' hospital beyond the eastern wall. The press of bodies in the shelter holes became for many the sole source for warmth, a warmth that brought sleep with its hopeful dreams and denial of what lay ahead.

I knew the freezing temperatures to be brought by the fast-approaching winter would claim many more lives. Inadequate rations and drinking the piss-water would bring on insidious death, but exposure would kill quickly and broadly. My men would not survive winter. We must escape! I must find a way. I must!

"Reed!" Hearing my name called, I searched the bearded faces of those near me to see who had spoken. "Reed! Here!" Tom Barnett was walking toward me.

"What?" I asked hesitantly.

"You looking for Dooley?" he asked.

"Yeah..."

"Over there." Barnett pointed toward the soup house that now served as a prison for the officers. A dozen soldiers from the 24th Michigan were crouched some ten yards from the deadline, all facing the building. As I moved cautiously toward them, one of the Michigan men stood to block my path. Dooley suddenly appeared behind the soldier.

"Reed!" He spoke as he approached. "What is it?" he asked. "Something wrong?"

"No! No!" I tried to reduce the tension brought on by my approach. "I just wanted to see a friend."

"For what?" There was no lessening of the tension in his face. He guided me away from the building. "What is it?"

"What do you know about an escape?" My question caused Dooley to stop. Quickly, he turned his head towards the guards along the wall and then back to me.

"What are you asking?" His eyes narrowed.

"Do you know anything about it?"

"No!" He cut me off. "What about it?"

"Dooley! What the hell is wrong with you?"

"What do you know?" he pressed.

"Nothing! God damn it!" I leaned away from him. "If there is something, I want my men in on it." He grabbed my arm and began to pull me along with him.

"I'm sorry, Reed. There's a lot happening right now. You just caught me wrong, that's all." We walked a few paces. "There is a plan." Again, he spoke, but barely loud enough for me to hear, even though we were several yards from the nearest man. "The officers passed messages, plans for escape…" He paused as if to hear some reaction from me, before continuing, "We gotta make it this time!" His hands moved awkwardly at his sides. "If we do, we'll burn this sorry place to the ground!" He looked toward the guards on the scaffolding. "They're so damn dumb, they won't be able to stop us."

"Maybe they don't care anymore." I tried to hide the skepticism I felt.

"The hell they don't!" Dooley retorted. "Those devils up there would love nothing better than an excuse to shoot us!"

Dooley gave an accurate portrayal of the guards, but it remained commonplace to hear of attempts at escape; the secret, persistent digging to extend mounds into elongated shafts running beneath the walls or a maddened prisoner charging across the deadline and climb the wall screaming, only to be cut down and left to die before our eyes. I was convinced that Dooley's plan did not involve tunneling, but unaware of the details, I said nothing, hoping he would reach out to me and include the 24th New York.

"When it begins," he finally gave in, "I ask of you one thing." He looked into my eyes. "Make a lot of noise. If they're distracted long enough, it just might work."

It was a cold day. A steady wind blew out of the north, sweeping over the wall and across the hardening wastes of the sinks, smothering the flickering flame of our pit fire. The choking white smoke ushered into the hole's opening drove me to rise and crawl out over the smoldering ashes. Bending over to relieve the burning sensation in my throat, I slowly lifted my head upon sensing the movement of men to the north end of the prison where the main gate had swung open.

"It's happening!" Unable to form a loud noise, I emitted a cough.

"What is it?" Kalmbach reached my side. "What's happening?"

"I think it's an escape! Make some noise!" The crack of a single musket penetrated the air.

Through the open gate, hundreds of armed guards rushed, forcing the swelling surge of prisoners away from the front gate and toward us. Several shots rang out.

"Move back, Reed!" Kalmbach grabbed my arm. "Get back!" He pulled me away from the edge of the road, in the direction of our campsite.

"Tom Burness!" I saw one of Dooley's men. "This way!" The sound of my voice rose above the echo of musket fire. Burness, seeing me, fought through men to get away from the road.

"We were found out!" he gasped as he reached my side.

"What happened?" I yelled.

"They knew our plan! Someone had to have told them. They're going to know it was our regiment," he rambled. "They're going to come for us."

"What happened, Reed?" Before I could respond to Kalmbach's question, Burness spoke, "We had rocks and sticks. We would have made it." He turned to me, ignoring Kalmbach's question. "The officers smuggled out messages to Dooley. Some guard must have got one or someone ratted. Our men didn't talk..." He looked into my eyes, searching for some reassurance. "We were to begin by throwing rocks and baked balls of clay. Others were to rush the guards surrounding the officers' prison and take their guns and take out the guards on the wall." He paused, emotion filling his voice. "Dooley threw the first rock and then the big gate opened and there they were! Hundreds rushing at us!"

"What happened to the rest of the men? To Dooley?"

"They grabbed him right off..."

"Dead?" I asked.

"No, but they got him."

"There will be no rations tonight," was all that Kalmbach would say as he walked away from the two of us.

"You can stay with us tonight, Burness."

"No," he answered. "I need to find the others."

Throughout the night, torches burned along the scaffolding at the top of the south wall. The light from the buildings outside the eastern wall and main gate illuminated the figures of guards along the parapet. If I strained my eyes, I could see them positioned along the entire length of the palisades, facing into a yard void of prisoners. There will be no trips to the sinks or the wells, nor food, or water, only retribution, this night.

The screeching of brakes cut through the deep stillness of the sleepless night. Such sounds of incoming trains were heard infrequently as of late but still they came, more prisoners from the hellholes in Georgia and South Carolina. It was still dark when I heard the last train depart. The morning sky shone a pale gray with streaks of purple running along the edge of the horizon. The wind had disappeared, but cold, damp air greeted me as I emerged from the hole. To the north, I could see the main gate standing ajar.

"It's the officers." Halleck startled me. I didn't see him standing a few feet from me. "They took 'em. They're gone."

The sun had risen over the tree line on the distant hills to the east. Its direct light had crept down the side of the cotton factory, reflecting off the panes of glass of the second-story windows. Shadows along the ground were fading away in the light reflecting from the bayonets held high above the heads of the North Carolina regiment moving down the main road toward the center of the camp. Having reached a clearing in which a large post had been planted some fifty yards beyond the gate, the column came to a halt. In the center of the Rebel soldiers three bent figures walked incongruously out of step with the regulars that had progressed to the beat of a single drum.

The pole stood alone, conspicuous in its portentous silence. Rising to a height of twelve feet, it was encased in rusting iron slabs from its base to a foot from the top. Two U-shaped hooks welded to the sides gave this crude projection its purpose. The regulars had lined to each side of the pole, muskets to chests watching the gathering throng press closer to the open ring where Dooley and the other two leaders of the failed uprising were shackled together. The Rebel soldiers shifted from foot to foot nervously, knowing they could not reload before being swarmed over by a charging mob. Fear kept them from shooting and fear held us back.

"What we do here today," Commandant Gee yelled, "we do because of your dangerous and foolish actions!" I pushed through the prisoners, forcing them to give way for me to pass. No longer was I able to see Dooley. He had been released from his irons and was led away.

"No! No! Stop, you bastards! No!"

The guards lowered their weapons and leveled them as the cries of protest spread among the prisoners. Continuing to maneuver through the crowd, I again found Dooley. A rope that had been looped through the hooks tied Dooley's wrist to the pole above his head. "This man will be the first to feel the wrath of Confederate justice! All of you will learn obedience from the forty lashes he receives, but be grateful for my tolerance! For such behavior in the future will result in death in front of a firing squad!"

Jeers again rippled among the prisoners, but Gee had finished and stepped aside just as a distinct crack cut through the air and the crowd moaned.

Whirling, I saw Dooley's face pressed against the reddish iron. His mouth was open, but no sound came from him as the whip whistled through the cool, damp air and again found skin. Straining and wrenching to pull free from the taut, heavy rope, his eyes bulged from their sockets; saliva ran down his chin as the whip again tore into his flesh.

"No!" I leaped toward the Rebel guard as he drew the long black tail behind him. He was looking at the reddened streaks of his target and didn't see me coming. Having but one blow before being overcome by the other guards, I pushed against the ground, forcing my legs to take flight, to reach him before he lifted the whip. There was movement to my side and noise all about when I felt the pressure, the burning pain cutting into my back just below my shoulder blade. Above me I saw the legs of a guard, his musket raised, his bayonet driving deeper into me.

"No!" The declarations surrounded me, engulfing me before the simultaneous explosion of musketry deadened noise and movement. Violently, the steel blade cut deeper into my muscle as it moved sideways and then slithered from within me.

"Stop! Stop or we will shoot every damn one of you!" Gee screamed.

Raising my head, a sharp pain tore through my shoulder. Two bodies lay next to me, blood flowing beneath them, darkening the soil. At that moment, strong arms lifted me, opening the wound and sending pain exploding across my back. Abruptly, violently I jerked my head to the left in a feeble attempt to divert the suffering. For only a brief instant, Dooley's face had turned to me before tilting forward to rest against the iron-encased post as the bodies absorbed me.

In the fading light, I saw someone's face staring at me and then it was gone. Within the hole, I was alone. A humming came from deep within me, a humming that I had heard on stormy nights or when a fever had weakened and left me helpless. Mother had stroked my head and smiled, comforting me. I must feel her stroking my brow, gently dissolving the pain. Cool water flows from her hands and drips down my chin, upon my chest. Hearing her, I am lifted.

Sleep will preserve me, to hide beneath the cloak of sleep, within that place where pain fades away, where there is comfort and peace.

"Oh, Mother!" The words came in a whisper. "Let me sleep!" With every fiber of muscle in my body I willed to be still, to end the pain, to sleep.

"No!" I heard from within the veil of the shadows. "He's a mess! Be careful not to get that on you."

"We'll clean him." A familiar voice, and then darkness swallowed the light and I felt only the pressure of being lifted and pushed, and stripped of my clothes. With the touch of a singular hand, pangs ripped through my muscles and bones, bringing forth tears, tears of joy. I was alive and with my men! Darkness again descended as I was guided through an enclosure, into the warmth and familiar smell of the hole. My head was lifted and water entered my mouth and trickled down my throat. Mercifully, sleep came.

13

Survive Today

November 1864
Salisbury Prison
Salisbury, North Carolina

Seeing the angles of the sticks pressed into the hardened mud above, I suddenly became aware of the reality surrounding me. My legs and arms bolted with convulsive jerking sending spasms of pain tearing through my shoulder. Gritting my teeth, I fought to calm my muscles, to reduce the pain. I was alive!

"Reed!" Kalmbach was at my side. "I have soup." He placed his hand under my neck. "It's good to see ya awake. You've had a few tough days." A cup was held to my lips. "This'll help." He smiled. "Your wound will fester for a bit, that's all."

"How is Dooley?" I whispered after swallowing the tasteless broth.

"Better than you are right now," he responded. "Just go slow."

"I shouldn't have done that," straining to speak, I felt my throat tightening.

"Probably not." Kalmbach steadily lifted my head. "But it helped to remind us who we were..." The cup drained, Kalmbach crawled to the opening, leaving a chunk of bread where he had placed it on my chest. "We're still getting Baker's rations," he said as he held the entrance cover with his free hand. Pausing momentarily, he looked at something next to me and then dropped the flap and the shadows within darkened.

A coldness swept over my body, a feeling of trepidation. Slowly, ignoring the discomfort in my neck, I turned. In the shadows next to me, a body lay beneath a blanket. Reaching, I pulled away the cover to see the face of Lawrence Baker, his eyes closed in white death.

"Dear Jesus God!" I uttered as I fell backward.

Baker remained next to me throughout the night and all of the next day as part of Kalmbach's plan to add to our food allocation. But the deception could last no longer, for the smell of decay was now soaking into my hair, skin, and the very walls of the hole. I rolled away from Baker's body as Shilton and Hughes wrestled it through the small opening. Facing the wall and hearing the grunts of the men as they twisted the rigid limbs of their comrade, a sickness swept over me. Whether strong enough or not, I had no choice but to crawl from the putrid stench into the air of the new morning.

Of my men, I saw only Hughes, crouched at the side of the road, keeping vigil over Baker's body, waiting for the dead wagon to take it away. Without notice I passed by the two of them, but was unable to escape death that was everywhere. Along the roads, near tents, buildings, and in open spaces bodies lay. Prisoners had been dying since the first day of my arrival here but never had I seen so many waiting for the wagon as on this cold morning. Ignoring the pain deep in my shoulder, I walked. Alive!

The late November weather had left an early morning frost on the surface of the rooftops and shaded areas of the ground. I felt little wind against my face as I walked. Usually it was the wind blowing across the northwest wall, coming down from the great Blue Ridge Mountains that discouraged me from leaving the shelter of our hole. Today promised to be better. The few clouds above did not prevent the sun from warming the air coming from the west. Although too gentle to chill, it was strong enough to bring upon us the heavy stench from the sinks across the yard. Unwilling to tolerate the overpowering odor brought from them, I proceeded in the direction of Dooley's 14th Michigan where I would do as the others and pay homage to this man who stood in place of all of us at the whipping post. Humiliated and beaten, Dooley had been strengthened as a leader in the minds and spirits of his comrades.

He stood apart from the others. His back to his men, staring at the guards on the parapet, arms folded, he remained still as I approached.

"Dooley!" Hearing my voice, he turned. Through narrow slits, his eyes bore into me.

"I will make it." He finally spoke after a few seconds had passed. "There's no other way. If I fail, I die. If I don't try, I will still perish here."

"What can I do?" I asked.

"You will know, just follow the others." He didn't look at me. "Whatever ya do, Reed, do it smart. Carry through this time." With those words, he returned to his men.

"There will be an escape attempt soon," I told Shilton upon returning to my hole. "We must act when it happens."

"Yeah, I expect we can die that way a lot quicker, huh, Sarge?"

"We need to be ready, that's all I'm saying."

"With what?" Shilton snapped. "Look at us, for god's sake! Hell! Look at all of us! Those poor bastards coming in every day now are already walkin' dead, and we're damn close to them!"

"Be ready!" I stopped him. "I don't need you to tell me that! Just be ready!"

Shilton was speaking of the men most of us turned from when they arrived here. A sickly lot, gaunt, shoeless, filthy, the prisoners arriving with news of Sherman's advance huddled in the southwestern corner of the stockade, near the sinks, on ground, soft, saturated in waste. They had been evacuated from Andersonville as Sherman cut through Georgia. Those prisoners who still presented a threat to the Confederates were shipped north to more secure holding pens, while those remaining were left to die. Many arriving here had little more chance for survival than the poor bastards left behind.

"Ho! New York!" Glancing over my shoulder, I saw three men standing a few feet away. The shorter one, grinning, said, "What? Don't recall us?" They edged closer.

"He looks new, don't he, boys?"

"Indiana...," was the only word that came to me. I held back from saying the word "lunatics" to describe Jeremy Benson, his uncle, and the one named Wainright.

"N'er believed to be aseein' us kickin' agin, huh, New York?" Jeremy laughed. "They can't kill us, but they sure 'nuf try to do ya in, ya dumb-as-a-hog bastard."

"What is it you want here?"

"Well, damn it to hell!" The older Benson reacted. "Ya ain't got no manners!"

"Maybe Reed went 'n' had our good turn knocked outa his thick skull." Wainright stood next to me. "Or maybe he don't no more care 'bout his white friends long as the niggers be carrying him about."

"What do you want?"

"Just wanna sit fer a spell...," old Benson spoke. "Just like at Libby."

"Don't have time to sit. Too much work to do."

"Ya dumb bastard!" Jeremy stood to the side of Wainright, just beyond my reach. "Ya got niggers fetching fer ya. Take what they got or we will sure 'nuf."

"What?" I stepped backward.

"Now hold on there, Reed." Wainright blocked my path. "We got no bone to pick with you and you ain't about to mess up that shoulder of yers!"

"Then hold the reins on him!"

"I'm 'bout sick of ya talking, New York!" Jeremy threatened, but remained to the far side of Wainright.

"Hold it, goddamn ya, boy," old Benson lashed out. "We're here fer yer help, Reed." His voice calmed. "We can get ya food and wood if ya help with the niggers."

"What are you saying, you crazy son of a bitch?"

"No! No! No!" He raised his arms in the air. "I'm not here to bother ya, Reed. Only want yer help and we'll be on our way."

I took a step backward. A feeling of sickness swept over me, images blurred. I heard garbled voices and saw strange faces staring at me.

"What's with ya, New York? Afraid?"

"What?" I shook my head and struggled to gain my balance. "What do you want?"

"That's a whole lot better." Old Benson's words sounded clear to me. "Just git us close to the coloreds and we'll all have a bit more to eat 'n' drink."

"What in hell are you going on about?"

"Yer friends there," Wainright stood looking in the direction of the blacks' shelter holes, "they carried ya away from the whippin'."

"Ya kin git us close without 'em 'spectin' nothin'," Jeremy grinned. "We'll do the work. We just got to git at 'em close afore they see us a'comin'."

"Leave them alone. They have nothing."

"If they got any, it be a whole lot more than they should," old Benson answered. "No white need die if'n a colored have any food."

"Skin color don't mean much if we all die anyways." I shook my head to clear the sickness. "All our bones will be the same color in the trenches."

"They should die before us." Jeremy took a step toward me.

"Back off, you crazy little bastard." I raised my hand.

"Hell with ya, New York!" he yelled. "We don't need ya anyways!"

"Ya won't be gittin' any stuff, ya know, don't ya, Reed?" Wainright held Jeremy by the arm.

"Stay away from here." I stared at the older Benson. "If you go for the coloreds, you'll go for us here too."

"Come on." Old Benson turned away. "He said what he needed."

I squatted, watching the three lunatics blend into the prisoners surrounding me. To my right, on the parcel of dirt claimed by Welch's men, small, rounded piles of packed mud, cold as death and vacant as the devil's soul had become desirable treasure for the beasts some had become.

I rubbed the stick in the ashes to nurture the spark that had ignited it. The flirtatious flames had reduced its length to where it too soon would be added to the smoldering embers as the last of our fuel. A cold night lay ahead and I foolishly burned all the sticks the coloreds had brought back from their excursion. Had Kalmbach gone with them we would have more wood, but that was no longer possible for he too was sick. I could still carry wood and water but was forbidden to move beyond our sector. Welch's men could no longer help, for they had less than any. They were dying, many each day. Soon they would be no more.

Raising my head to avoid the trail of smoke that drifted from the fire, I looked to the soup house chimney for a sign that rations were being prepared. The same Rebel detail that had escorted the prisoners to the woods earlier in the day stood near the building. Along the top of the wall, the guards were walking toward the ladders leading to the ground. The main gate to the east of the compound had opened, and slowly the ten-man patrol stationed at the two sides of the hospital had formed into columns. The changing of the guard had begun.

The woeful whine of a steam whistle penetrated the silence and the repeating dull thud of iron coupling signaled the distancing of a departing train. As the lingering sounds faded into shallow echoes, someone began to yell, and then another. In a matter of seconds the voice had become many, carried along by the rush of prisoners toward the open gate.

"It's the breakout!" Hughes, struggling for breath had just returned from the sinks. Standing and turning in the direction of the guards who had formed at the far side of the hospital, I saw them lowering their muskets and quick stepping toward the front gate.

"Get them!" I commanded, pointing as I began running.

"Get the guns!" Hughes, ahead of me, in full stride, leaped over men struggling to extricate themselves from holes in the ground. A large contingent of men, a great blur of movement had joined alongside of Hughes. A sharp, immobilizing pain shot through my shoulder and back each time my left foot pounded into the ground. Vaulting over a domed dirt shelter, my foot sank into the mud roof, causing me to slip, stumble and twist my body in a frantic effort to retain my balance. Abruptly stopping, I reached to touch the wound in my shoulder. Taffner and Halleck were by me, moving towards the guards who had retreated to the hospital building. The sound of musketry penetrated the noise coming from the eastern quadrant of the compound. I glanced toward the wall to see puffs of smoke bursting from the guns lining the parapet and rising and rolling along its heights.

Hughes was in front, bearing down upon a musket leveled at his chest. Flame streaked from the muzzle and then I heard the crack of its explosion. Hughes rose in the air and suddenly and violently spun sideways. Reaching him, I fell to my knees and carefully lifted his head to see a great red gash where his right ear had been.

A scream came from my throat. No longer could I kneel and watch another life fade away. Leaving him, I rushed, leaping beyond where Hughes remained dying. Animal gruntings brought on by a frustration with the distance that separated me from he who had shot Hughes emanated from within me. Before I could reach him, before he could level his bayonet to receive the charging prisoners, he was overtaken. Three were upon him. The musket fell from his grasp as he disappeared beneath the tangle of men.

To the north, in the direction of the main gate, the roar of the unleashed was increasing in depth and scope.

"To the main gate!" They rushed onward, now with guns from the fallen guards. "Boom!" A great deafening thunder erupted to my right. Black smoke and flames lashed out from the dark recess in the wall near the front gate. The very air reverberated with a rush that pressed against my chest. Beneath my feet, I felt the ground tremble as an artillery shell exploded in the center of the first line of prisoners. For an instant, there was silence, apart from the echo of the blast sweeping the compound and then, another, and again.

All movement ceased. Only the motion of smoke trailing on a light, westerly breeze weaved above the prison walls while the six-pounders were being reloaded.

"Get back! Get back!" The tide turned. Pushing, shoving, tripping, the men pursued the safety of the brick buildings, back to where I stood. Grape and canister had cut into the prisoners, killing and wounding dozens. Bodies lay scattered along the main road; all trampled by feet of fear-stricken men, rushing pell-mell to escape the minié balls raining down upon them from above.

In through the partially opened front gate poured reserves, bayonets flashing in the late-afternoon light while from the parapets, the Rebels shot at will. Frantically, I pawed through the shirt covering the hole entrance and lunged headlong into the cavity, panting, pressing against the wall of dirt.

Already my legs were cold and my feet had lost their feeling. A faint, gray light filtering in through the opening of the hole indicated that the sun had set and the cold dampness of the night was beginning to penetrate the hut and steal away the warmth of our breathing. Kalmbach lay flat against the wall to my side, Shilton to my back, and Taffner, who had been prevented from reaching his hole, behind him.

There was to be no fire this night and no rations or water and few would leave their shelters. Fear forced men to behave like animals, to cower in their own waste. Struggling to deny my impulse, I turned on my stomach and hoped the soil soft enough to absorb the piss. With every movement against Kalmbach, I heard him moan woefully. His deep sleep was a blessing, I thought. Had he been awake and aware of the loss of Hughes and the threats posed by an enemy more frightened than we, he too would feel the agony gripping the three of us. We lay awake, listening to the musket fire and the voices of the guards directing it, yelling out when one of them spotted someone moving within the compound. Any noise—a cry, a moan, a plea—would bring death. It would be a long and deadly night.

A thin line of grayness appearing between the edge of the door flap and the wall of the hut signaled the coming of a new day. Desperate for water I knew we had to leave the hole and find provisions. Kalmbach's health had worsened during the night and he required water as soon as possible. Leaving him to sleep in his own waste, we each went a separate direction in our search. Escape was still on my mind. No day went by when it wasn't in my thoughts. But now, it must wait. To survive, I had to find food and water. Walking, I looked for any standing water or snow lying in the shadows but knew only the wells held enough to drink, only the wells had water, water we all knew shouldn't be drunk.

Whatever had fallen into the well and sunk beneath the green surface into the abyss below became lumps in the sour-tasting liquid, edible to a starving man. "June hardbacks" lining the shaft of the well were snatched by a patient hand as were the cockroaches hiding along the base of the soup house and beneath the lips of this well. Scurrying rats unearthed at the foundation of the hospital buildings were trapped and eaten. Food became my obsession and now believing that if I were of the earth, I then like the earth would survive.

It wasn't dark and too early for sleep, but the cold night air would soon descend upon the compound and we had nothing but our bodies to defend against it. Kalmbach's breathing was shallow and weak. Without good water and medicine, he would soon die. No one should be alone during their last hours, I thought as I rolled his body onto its side and pressed myself against it. The safety of the hole and the warmth provided by men hunkered down beneath the dirt roof was all I could offer Kalmbach. The sickness had taken away his strength. Deprivation of food and water for days would take his life. Placing my arm over his shoulder I could feel the coldness in him. No longer did he make a sound. We lay in silence, listening for Kalmbach's life to end.

The decision of the guards to end patrol of the grounds within the walls turned the prison into a jungle and muggers into predators. Few dared to venture beyond the hole and surrender the safety of anonymity. I lay with Kalmbach, listening to his breathing, and from beyond our hole, the cries and cursing of loosened animals. Shouting filled the early morning hours, close to where I knew Welch's men to be huddled. I arose and crawled to the opening.

Faint light cast from a burning torch braced at the top of the wall revealed darkened shadows bobbing up and down and scurrying across the ground. Desperate grunting and the deep thud of heavy blows caused me to rise up. Thick, gluelike mud pulled at my feet as I struggled to reach the men bending over a writhing body. Running past the first two mounds of the blanks, I stumbled and fell. Striking a rigid, embedded object, I reeled at the biting stings cutting into the palm of my left hand.

"Damn!" I cursed. "What in hell?"

Listening to the hollow blows of boot against ribs, I frantically pawed at the hardened chunk of wood, this weapon that lay before me. Wedging my fingers beneath the object, I lifted a jagged tree limb from its sunken entrapment. Raising up and holding the two-foot-long, arm-width branch above my head, I pounced upon the attacker who at that instant had turned to me. Wainright may have seen the waterlogged wood move through the darkness or heard it whistle in the cold air before it landed full against his cheekbone, violently snapping his head. While his body followed the momentum of the blow and slumped to the ground, I looked at Jeremy Benson rising from his crouched position over the lifeless Welch.

The gigantic black man lay on his back, his hands still on his chest in a defensive posture. His face, broken and opened, was distorted beyond recognition. Heavy muscled arms, too large to be contained by the ragged shirts of others, gave testimony to the identity of the fallen warrior. My eyes slowly lifted to see a rounded rock the size of a forage cap cradled in Jeremy's hands. The dim shadows failed to conceal Welch's blood smeared upon its surface.

"Here, New York," he uttered. "I got this to shove in yer big mouth! See if it tastes better to ya than to this big nigger here."

Holding the rock in his right hand, Jeremy extended his arm, exposing the right side of his chest. It was there I focused my thrust. Tightly gripping the sharply-splintered lance, I lunged my weight forward, sinking its end into the soft flesh below his rib cage.

"Aaahhh!" Straining to push the wood deeper and ignoring the biting pain of more shredded slivers entering my skin, I watched his eyes roll back into his skull. For five seconds he was lifted upward, his feet suspended above the ground before his head fell to my shoulders like a child in the arms of a father. Collapsing, he fell backward to rest upon Welch's body.

"Get off that man, you worthless bastard!" My arms trembled as I pulled Jeremy's body from Welch.

Before me like a swarm of bees, black soldiers beat upon the lifeless pulp that had been the older Benson. They had emerged from their holes, hoping with each blow delivered to return one more minute of life to their leader.

"He doesn't need you anymore." Halleck reached for my arm. "Let's go. Leave them be."

"He never needed me!" I snapped, taking steps toward our mound. "It was I who needed him and now he's gone."

I crouched to the ground, forcing my fingers into the cold clay, searching for grubs, for something that moved. Holding the soil between my fingers, rubbing it, breaking it into small granules and letting it fall to the ground I tried to ignore the approaching figures. Slowly, methodically they came nearer, growing larger as they plodded, heavy-hoofed upon the road. Behind, hidden from view by the broad-back mules, the wagon followed. Unwillingly, my eyes moved to gaze upon the naked body, upon the face of Kalmbach. I tried to remember the smile always upon those lips, his eyes, the swagger, and the sadness when he spoke of home and decisions ill chosen. No longer could I distinguish the features I had known. Tears blurred his image.

December 1864

They had made no promises of bread and I knew it was not for us, but rather the smell from a world beyond our reach. The sweet aroma of cornbread baking wafted from over the walls to be swallowed into my mind. We were to have none. Instead, some time during the early morning hours, partially-filled barrels of cornmeal had been set immediately inside the gates. Wrestling to reach the barrels and plunge into the remaining meal, I held fast to two fistfuls as I walked to where I had so often before shared a fire.

A stark, lifeless cold prevailed over the mounds of the blacks. Nothing moved with the exception of a scant trace of white smoke twirling from in front of a single mound where a solitary figure squatted over a pit fire. He didn't look up even with the noise of our approach. Stopping, Shilton and I stood in silence, awaiting his acceptance. His eyes remained fixed upon the smoldering flames struggling to escape from between small charred rocks in the pit. He nodded and I moved to the fire. The orange flame emerged from beneath the foot-and-a-half-long stick that rested upon the gray ash, igniting a blue streak that steadily lifted upward and cast warmth upon us.

"It's ready," Shilton spoke quietly, almost a whisper. Taking his tin of well water and letting single droplets absorb into the meal, he squeezed the dough into a ball. It was difficult altering the coarse, vermin-laden substance into something resembling cornbread, but easing the blackened ball of dough from the ashes I desperately bit into its tooth-breaking surface to reach the softness within.

"At least it's not moving when we eat it." Shilton spoke through teeth caked in charcoal flakes.

"And better than nothing, I guess," I reminded myself as I watched him lick his fingers.

"Yeah," he nodded. "This was a good day."

Shilton was right, for there were days when no rations were left at the gates or dumped over the walls, when no creek water was returned and only the silent stares of the guards on the wall and the ever-present death wagon told us they hadn't abandoned us.

Rumors of escape, nurtured and propagated, were of no further interest to me. No longer did I hear men speak of Sherman's advance or an end to the fighting. A resignation pervaded me, and acceptance that my fate and that of my men rested with me alone. For my body to endure, I must eat; for my mind to withstand the madness, I must believe I can save my men. If I survived this day, if I lived through this day, I promised myself that tomorrow would bring relief. Today is the challenge I must overcome, for tomorrow will mean freedom. I will survive, and so too will my men.

There was no definite color in the leather of Hughes' boots. Whatever it may have been now had faded with sweat and blood and urine to blend with the red clay dust of the earth. The toes were bent upward as if frozen in a grotesque plea for rest from their burden. I had removed them, paper thin and brittle, and then his clothes. To know that muggers waited to wrestle his corpse to remove any clothing and his fragile bones to be broken in such an attempt convinced me to strip his body. Sitting to his side, I guarded him until lifted to the wagon for his journey to the trench.

Halleck, Shilton, Taffner, and I from the 24th still lived. All sick, but Shilton, the worst, might last only a few more days. I alone was still strong enough to search for branches and scraps of wood. I would care for them and when they died, lay them by the far side of the road. I would do that for them.

January 1865

Shortly after daybreak, the slow trek began. Hundreds of men, bent with arms hugging their bodies in a futile effort to ward off the frigid air, walked toward the deadlines at the east and southwest corners of the wall. It now was anticipated. At that point in time when the sun edged over the top of the eastern wall, rations would be lowered from the parapet to the ground. During each of the past six days, the partially filled barrels of meal, corn, rice, or molasses were left for the prisoners. No longer following a pattern of distribution, those regiments larger in numbers, those men stronger or with makeshift weapons, claimed the bulk of the rations. That which remained was taken by the less brutal. Always, the blacks were last and often with no food.

Dooley's 24th Michigan had lost many to illness and failed escape attempts, but even with Dooley's death they remained one of the larger units and one of the most feared. The muggers watched and waited until the Michigan boys left before moving in ahead of the others. Dooley had adopted my men and saw to it we were provided whatever they gathered. Without him, we stood as the others.

Shilton slept his last two days on earth. Unable to chew the charred ball of meal cooked for him, I no longer attempted to force it down his throat. It was sometime during the night that he stopped breathing. In the morning, Halleck and I removed Shilton's clothes and placed his body near the road; Taffner, growing weaker, was unable to help. As the others had done, he now slept much of the time. In the cold murkiness of the hole, with enough light filtering in through the openings of the door cover, I saw the outline of his body, trembling, his arms moving, his head twitching. Placing my hands to his shoulders, I felt the bones beneath the layers of ragged cloth. I removed one of my shirts and laid it over his shoulder, tucking its edges between his ribs and the damp ground. It would not help I knew, as I crawled from the hole, leaving him to tremble alone.

Halleck, expected soon with a tin of water, could care for Taffner and free me to search for wood. Wood, so desperately needed, to warm Taffner. Anything to prolong his life, to delay his coming to this place. Here, with those I now passed, discarded alongside the road, swaddled in a dusting of snow, awaiting the wagon.

At the wall where the ration barrels were lowered, I saw a dark object, a piece of wood protruding from beneath gray, powdery snow. Walking faster, looking to my left and right, I anticipated a great rush of competitors for the split-barrel stave. Reaching for it, pulling it from the grip of the frozen ground, I saw it to be much smaller than I had hoped. But there had to be more hidden beneath the snow. Kicking at the ground, forcing frozen dirt and ice into the opening in the sole of my boot, I pounded away in bold determination to rescue the life-saving wood. Breathing with greater difficulty, steam bursting from my mouth with each gasp, I found there to be no more.

Above my desperate breathing, I heard a noise coming from the top of the wall, from the boy guards, those I hadn't seen in a week, the killers. I was too close to flee. They would shoot me if I ran. It would be safer to remain still, ignore them, not provoke them. They didn't see me as they struggled to drag a barrel to the edge of the wall. Struggling, grunting, cursing in protest, they tilted it over the lip, to send yellow, dark red fluid oozing down the wall, chunks plopping to the ground in a rounded pile at its base.

Repulsed at the sight, I stood while men hurriedly passed me, rushing to pounce upon the bloodstained snow. Inhaling the pungent stench of the offal, I saw in the pile a white, twisted tube of a cow's intestines intertwined with something colored black and purple. The sac of the stomach, the heart, lungs, eyes, and ears mixed with chunks of hair and skin were wrapped in heavy red fluid. Prisoners were reaching, probing into the mass to retrieve fistfuls of organs that were then placed in the makeshift pouch of their shirts. Taking lead from one prisoner who ravishingly devoured that which he had held in his hand, I raised my head toward the sky as I reached for a rounded red and purple chunk. Standing there above us, the three guards looked at the scene unfolding below them, watching as the pile diminished before their eyes.

14 Unbeaten

February 1865

Soot-laden smoke from the chimneys of Salisbury drifted over the land, soiling the snow to shades of gray, but within the shelter of the woods lay a blanket of pristine white that banked the trees and tapered to a depth of six inches. Small, barren saplings broke through the wind-leveled snow to stand in proud defiance against the cold mantle covering the floor of the forest. Miniature bouquets of yellow and brown prairie grasses lifted their seeded heads to move gently in the breezes. The same breezes had blown the soft snow to coat the north side of the great oak and elm guarding the edge of the woods, within which a shaded sanctuary grew more inviting with each step taken away from the prison.

The Rebels were willing to risk the loss of a guard detail by escorting prisoners into the woods rather than suffer an upheaval of greater numbers from those desperate for water and warmth of fire. The guards trusted our need for water to be more pressing than a desire for freedom. But was it so? To choose between subsistence or escape, was it not reasonable to believe I would have water and wood? What of my desire for freedom? What might I do if faced with a safe haven within the woods, a place where escape was not only possible, but the very attempt itself to restore human dignity?

"Stay in line!" An abrupt command startled me. "Keep together!"

Frost covering the slope of the field was threatened by the rays of the midday sun struggling to penetrate the heavy gray clouds hanging above the treetops and the steeples of the Salisbury churches in the distance. No longer serving the purpose intended, my boots, but paper-thin remnants of leather unable to resist the freezing moisture against my skin with its biting pain of a hundred probing pins, glided through the crusty snow embedded in the tall grass. I held no hope for our halting, to permit the rubbing away of the numbness in my feet, as the guards had grown increasingly uneasy. Holding their muskets level, they prodded us onward, hoping to shorten the time before their return to the warmth and security of the guardhouse.

Taffner had died in his sleep. His clothes, removed by Halleck and me, will better serve us as a buffer to the cold ground. The tattered rags we so jealously guarded would be the only tangible reminder of Taffner.

"We can't let it be," I spoke quietly. Halleck did not look up. He remained silent, holding Taffner's shirt in his hands. Satisfied that he hadn't heard me, I didn't wish to say that the rag he held was the measure of Taffner and soon there would be no one to remember any of us.

I heard the snow crunch beneath my feet but the numbness prevented any feeling as each step took me closer to the woods and the shadows that might shield my escape. Could I do it? If I died in the attempt, how much longer would Halleck survive without me? He too had weakened and with the loss of Taffner was growing more despondent with each passing day. A night without heat in the hole might also take his life. He needed me. Together we had survived. I clenched my jaw and fought to erase the doubts from my mind. Behind me, I sensed the presence of the Rebel guard, only ten feet away. I could feel his stare, hear his breathing as he pushed through the thick, frozen grass. This was not the time for escape. Maybe later for both of us. Together, Halleck and I will carry on the memories of Taffner and the others.

We reached the crest of the incline. Before us, less than fifty yards away, was the cutover section of the woods. To our rear, resting dark and sinister against the white landscape was the prison, to the left, the trenches. Without receiving a command, the small detail of wood gatherers and water carriers had stopped walking. No one spoke as all had turned to the field which had once produced the staff of life, corn or oats, land on which cows grazed or pigs rutted, now the grave of thousands. Snow hadn't fallen in two days but overhead the gray mass of clouds that had settled over the land from horizon to horizon, pressed closer to the ground in suffocating proximity, adding to the gloom cast by the presence of the trenches.

Three more long and narrow swaths recently cut into the soil of the field awaited the corpses decaying in the dead house. Snow-dusted mounds of earth crested above another fourteen trenches, a fifteenth having been filled with freshly dug dirt for three-quarters of its length. Along the edge of the last remaining twenty yards of the still-open trench, a dozen black men methodically toiled. Two, with shovels in hand, stabbed at the cold-hardened earth in their deliberate effort to further expand the depth of the trench.

Mid-point between the prison's water gate entrance on its west side and the first trench, an open buckboard slowly and rhythmically bounced along the blackened path cut into the thin layer of snow covering the field. The echo of a snapping whip turned my attention back to the trenches where a hitched wagon slowly moved under demand of the skinner's switch. In the bed of the wagon, white and pink-hued shapes, distorted and massed, distinguished the load as human cargo.

The blacks, following along two together, walked in slow routine to where the wagon stopped at that portion of the trench yet to be sealed. One black struggled to dislodge a body from its place on the buckboard, while the other then dragged the fallen burden along the ground to the edge of the trench where another team of two lifted the jumbled body, swung it backward and then forward, releasing it into the air above the open pit. Falling into the trench with arms and legs jerking spasmodically before resting in its own unique and grotesque distortion, it lay until altered by impact of another following. Body after body was piled in the row of the once living, heaping, rising to ground level. A solitary black man, ten yards behind the wagon leaned over the unsealed trench and with shovel in hand poked at the top layer of pale-pink forms. Pushing a protruding leg or arm into a level plane some foot or less below the surface of the ground, he struggled, slowly and unmercifully against the deads' unbending and offending limbs. He moved quickly, swinging his spaded weapon against brittle bone, poking, shoving, and pounding the extremities into a congruent mass.

"Move!" I braced myself at hearing the sound of wood and iron slapping against the palms of soldiers who pointed their gun barrels, chest-high. "Move along!" the lieutenant repeated. "We return to the stockade in thirty minutes, water or no water!"

Momentarily, I glanced in the direction of the trenches. The image, blurred by the low light and haze rising from snow-covered fields, burned into my mind. In the field between the bordering tree stands, eighteen elongated mass graves clashed with the bucolic serenity of the winter landscape. Below the stirred topsoil of these frost-gripped tombs rested as many as ten thousand soldiers, nameless and forgotten.

I turned away and followed in the steps of those before me. Passing by the lieutenant to my right, I looked into his face. His eyes met mine and for a moment, held.

The flames were no longer visible above the orange and yellow glow pulsating from crevices in the burning log. Smoke continuing to drift along the roof of our hole was thinning now and disappearing into the blade-wide slits of the closely packed branches overhead. Having covered Halleck with the three shirts we had been using for bedclothes, I pressed the extra pairs of pants onto the dirt floor beneath him.

The heat cast from the smoldering embers was succumbing to the coldness of the air seeping into the interior of our hut. If I delayed in taking him from here, there existed little hope for his survival through this night.

Sitting, holding my knees to my chest, the thought of carrying Halleck though the tunnel dug beneath the western wall deeply troubled me. I slumped in resignation of what lay ahead. Death surely awaited in the woods if we made it that far, but to die there, frozen in the snow to await the decomposing thaw, was more desirable than to be beaten down by a shovel and flattened into the obscurity of entangled corpses.

His was a familiar sound, the shallow, raspy breathing of Halleck, this harbinger of death that I heard all too often. The light shining through the cracks in the roof penetrated the shadows and shone a peaceful aura upon this face. He had finally accepted death, surrendering to the hunger, cold, and sickness. I closed my eyes.

"Free! Free!" The yelling, muffled and distant, was not that of pain or distress. It was that realization which drove me to crawl through the flap covering the opening, out into the cold, moist air blowing from the east. The sun, directly overhead, illuminated the thinly veiled cover of clouds with a glare that forced me to shield my eyes. "Free!" It was repeated again and again by those running toward me, inspiring a growing swell advancing to the southern end of the compound.

"We're being exchanged!" they yelled. "Tomorrow, we'll be free!" There was no mistake in the words I was hearing. "The gate will be opened!" Someone facing me said, "We are to be freed!" More words followed among the screams of men maddened in disbelief.

A smile curled Halleck's lips when I told him of the pending release.

"We did it," he whispered. "We did win."

"Yeah, we did." I held him close to me through the night and into the early morning daylight, listening to his gentle breathing, that fragile sign of life, tenuous and fading, never to survive our trek to freedom.

The glow in the ashes had faded along with the trailing tails of white smoke rising above the pit. Cold air had overcome the interior and caused Halleck's body to again shake. I had to leave him. There was no choice but to join the others lining the road to the main gate. He was too weak to walk on deadly roads and across snow-packed fields in search of Federals and rescue. Major Gee had promised that Halleck among the very sick would be delivered by rail to Danville. There was no alternative, it was my only hope.

His eyes remained closed. He was at peace in these remaining minutes within my embrace. Beneath my fingers I could feel a slight tremble in his body. I looked into his face for the last time. Wrinkles had creased his brow. No longer did his shallow sleep conceal the pain. Already his body was shaking in the air that would soon turn colder.

From deep within his chest came a moan that rumbled as I dragged him through the hole into the brightness reflected from the overcast sky. His fragile arms dangled doll-like as I pressed his body to my chest and stepped cautiously over mounds of clay. Clenching my jaws and pressing my eyelids together tightly, I implored God to protect this man, to find him medicine, to sustain his life.

Lifting the flap covering the entrance to the hospital tent, I turned back to see where Halleck lay upon the floor, between two men from Welch's regiment, there to die among those who had known him.

The gate began to move, edging only inches, slowly, inextricably, methodically, as if to tantalize and frustrate those who held their breath, fearing it may stop. Air, cold and fresh, brushed in through the opening when the heavy wooden barrier swung aside. There were no guards before us, only those above staring down the barrels of muskets. The column nudged forward, the lead already beyond the wall. I saw the guardhouse and the lighted windows, and guards along the road before us, channeling the march away from the church spires rising above Salisbury. Step by step, we proceeded onward.

Fearing that the images fading behind me would forever burn into my memory, I diverted my eyes to the black fingers of the treetops beyond the railroad tracks before me. Refusing to look into the faces of the guards, I shuffled along with this ebbing throng, beyond the guardhouse, the tracks, tree line and city of Salisbury, away from its citizens frightened of their still dangerous enemy. Freed, I wanted to look back to the opened gate gaping like the mouth of a great devouring monolith. I needed to look back to humanize the nightmares, to eradicate the specter, by the light of this day, to lift the rotting sinews that bound me and dissolve them in the gales of the frigid air and the cleansing sunlight. But I couldn't. Wishing to be free of the hellish place, I found no more battles here. To look back now might by some corruption entangle me within this dismal miasma from which my mind would find no escape.

Below the bridge we crossed, the brown rust of the tracks cut their long lines through the soot-stained snow in the roadbed. To the east, the iron rails darkened to black and disappeared in the shadowy distance. Beyond the curve where the tracks could no longer be seen was the route that had brought me to this place. It was that which would lead us to Greensboro, some fifty miles away. With each step came physical, bone-penetrating pain but also the satisfaction that I was nearer the Federal lines and moving farther from

Salisbury. One step and then another, not to achieve distance but rather goals. To walk where I must was more than I could endure, but to walk to the next tree line or out-building or rail fence was within my reach.

Nearing the crossroads of a main turnpike leading back to the town of Salisbury, a group of men huddled to the sides of their buckboards, facing into the cold wind, their flintlocks resting across folded arms, silently watching as we labored past them; stares reflecting acceptance of the unacceptable.

The head of our column was a half-mile before me. Unlike those who paused exhausted, I refused to stop until the few Rebel guards who continued on with us ordered it to be done. I had slowed considerably, dragging my feet through the light dusting of snow that had become the color of red dirt. Each step became more agonizing than the last, but I found support from the others, those sickly, weakened, and determined. Onward, away from these lowlands where frigid water lurked beneath the cover of tall weeds, onward, toward the hills rising in the northeast, to shelter, to food and rest.

The setting sun cast long shadows across the wooded landscape. A pale gray and pink light muted the distant objects. On the porches of farmhouses close to the road darkened figures watched our passing, their eyes studying the spectacle parading by them. The dirt road we followed intersected with a turnpike that ran north to south. On the far side of the wide and level plank road that connected Salisbury to the adjoining farm country surrounding Lexington to the east and Virginia beyond to the north, two carriages sat.

A gray-bearded man, his white hair protruding from beneath a black, floppy hat, stood stiffly, several yards in front of the team harnessed to the lead buggy. Having the appearance of a merchant, his Sunday-best suit of clothes could not betray his profession nor deny the weathered, wrinkled face of the old farmer. Standing alongside him, slightly to the rear, straining to shield herself from our sight, a tiny girl of four or five held tightly to the old man's left hand. With right arm extended upright, his hand pressed to his forehead in a gesture of military salute. He stood erect, back straight, a look of resolute determination upon his face.

On the bench of the buggy sat a solitary figure wrapped in a heavy blanket, wearing a sky-blue colored bonnet that struggled to contain the old lady's thick gray hair that flowed down to her shoulders. Deep furrows wrinkled her cheeks and forehead in an expression of anguish, her clutched hands were pressed to her breast, as if in prayer. Raising one hand, she abruptly wiped her palm across her eyes and then determinedly stared into me. There was sadness in her reddened eyes, a forlornness reserved only for the soul of a mother.

Looking into the faces of our men for what must have created such anguish in this Southern lady, I found no fear or sadness. More than the rags they wore or the filth embedded in their skin, I saw only brave men, soldiers who came and conquered. A dozen at my side, a hundred before me and a thousand behind, we are soldiers of the Union army, the Army of the United States of America. Bent, slumping forward, clutching onto one another so we might take one more step, shuffling in the red-earthen-hued snow on this nameless path, rendering pity from old women and children, we remain unbeaten. My eyes blurring from tears swelling within them, I could no longer see the face of the woman. Blinking to clearly focus upon the old farmer, I stopped and raised myself to stand tall. With shoulders back, heels together, I returned his salute.

"It mattered, Welch...it mattered, Morgan and Kalmbach and Dooley and Halleck...it mattered...it must," I whispered.

The End

Epilogue

Black clouds appearing to rise out of the dark waters of Lake Michigan assumed an ominous threat as the cold breeze having blown steadily from the north all morning changed to an easterly direction. Gusts of wind pressed the skirt of Ellen's blue woolen dress to her legs. The knitted purple-dyed scarf given to her by James at Christmas of 1871, flapped against her shoulder. Her hand grasped the loose end and urgently tucked it beneath the collar of her coat. She thought it appropriate to wear the scarf on this day. He would have been pleased to see it wrapped around her neck now, knowing how she smiled when opening the gift.

Leafless, sentrylike trees stood over mausoleums and the square, white headstones dotting a sweeping panorama broken only by sporadic, rusting iron fenced enclosures in which elongated marble slabs rested. Ellen and her eldest son, Alvin, stood facing the wind, looking out across the wide vista and down the incline of the gently rolling hill land, unaware of the location of the grave they sought. Alvin reached for his mother's hand and gently guided her down the first row of what were thousands of green markers dotting the brown, dormant grass covering the grounds of the Federal cemetery. Together, with heads bowed, intently reading the etchings on each marker, they walked slowly, careful to avoid stepping on that soil under which a body lay resting.

Feeling her hand tremble within his grip, the young man looked into his mother's face, into her reddened eyes. The corner of his mouth curled into a smile, an expression all too unfamiliar to the humorless nature of the nineteen-year-old. At that moment a sudden gust of cold air blew across his face, blurring his eyes. He blinked to clear them as he squeezed his mother's hand, attempting to calm its steady trembling. She stood still, unaware of Alvin's hand upon hers and weary from the memories racing through her mind. Alvin, sensing her growing discomfort, could little resist his urge to place his arms around her shoulders, to extend warmth and a barrier to the wind and to the pain the memories still held.

"Do you wish to go on, Mother? It's getting colder out here."

"I would like to wait here for just another second," Ellen replied.

"There's a bench." Alvin looked toward a stand of ornamentally trimmed pine trees arranged in a semi-circular pattern enclosing an eight-foot long concrete bench resting on a marble slab bearing the inscription "For God and Country." A light dusting of freshly fallen snow that had resisted the blowing wind coated the seat of the gray-cement bench. "We don't have to find his grave," Alvin spoke as he slowly brushed away the snow for his mother to rest.

"Yes we do!" Ellen's voice was soft but stern. She had grown impatient with the oldest son of her union with James. "If you don't wish to accompany me, then you can wait for me here!"

"Please, Mother." Alvin, making one final sweep of the snow that had collected in the corners of the bench, gestured for his mother to sit down. He chose to ignore her words, aware that his behavior had disappointed her, and for that he was saddened. He was becoming what he had hated in his father, indifferent, withdrawn, and hurtful.

Fluffy, dry snow that had fallen in the pre-dawn hours and accumulated on the arms and backrest of the bench swirled in the gusty breezes, coating the bench that Alvin had just cleared.

"Damn!" Alvin cursed, swinging his hand angrily at the recalcitrant snow.

"Don't, Alvin." Ellen frowned as she leaned on the arm of the bench. "I know this is difficult for you too." Gently Alvin held his mother's arm, guiding her to the bench where she rested against the cold cement, eyes closed, drifting into a blur of memories.

"I don't understand, Mother." Alvin stared out across the frozen landscape of the cemetery.

"What?" she blurted out, causing Alvin to stop talking.

He turned to look into his mother's eyes. "I'm sorry."

She sat straight, pressing her back to the bench. "What is it?" she asked awkwardly.

"This is too much for you, isn't it?" he said, attempting to read the thoughts hidden within her eyes.

"No, Alvin, please don't do this!" She spoke softly, struggling to control the emotion building within her. "What is it you were saying?"

"Nothing, Mother. It wasn't anything important."

Ellen smiled at her son's childlike resistance to do that which he dreaded so. He had avoided accompanying his mother on this trip in search of his father's grave and still held hopes he could discourage her from going any further.

"I know how you feel about this, Alvin, but you must respect my need to be here."

"I do understand." Before Alvin could finish stating his apology, Ellen interrupted him.

"No you don't, son!" She paused, attempting to gain control of her breathing, to quell the emotion rising to pour forth in tears. Squeezing her son's hand, she smiled. "It's not your fault or anyone else's." No longer able to speak and stop from crying, tears began to form in the corners of her eyes. The smile had disappeared and with it the maternal shield she had built around her first son, day by day and crisis by crisis. She had again become the wife of James.

Her thoughts of him as he now lay within reach of her, somewhere in this field, overwhelmed her. "He didn't let people get close to him." She turned her head and gazed out across the field of marble markers and snow. "There were many days that I felt so distant from him." Her mind wandered to those many hours of silence when James had blocked Ellen from the world she now tried to enter.

Alvin had often seen this deep sadness in his mother, the desolation that drained life from her. Growing into manhood, he could see that behind her laughter and reassuring words, there existed a deep melancholy. Hidden within the smile was the heavy burden of loneliness and tears. Her tight embraces lasting too long created fear within a small boy struggling to breathe, feeling the trembling in his mother's body as she searched for composure before releasing her grip on him. He felt pity for the helplessness in his mother and a hatred for his father of an intensity reserved for the hearts of the defenseless and powerless.

"I thought I had lost him in the war." Her eyes were cast down to where her hands nervously fidgeted with the buttons on the front of her wool coat. "I had convinced myself that he would not return. The day the letter came...," she paused, opened her mouth to breathe deeply, to calm herself. Slowly releasing a sigh, she continued, "...it was the happiest day of my life. I felt reborn, alive again!" She lifted her hand to draw her fingers across the corner of her right eye. "God had given me a miracle without my prayers in return." She looked at her son through tears that swelled in her eyes. "I didn't pray for his return! I couldn't, not to a God who would take him from me like that!" Lowering her eyes to stare into her hands, she said softly, "My only hope was that he hadn't suffered before his death." Tears flowed down her cheeks. No longer could she speak.

Alvin reached for his mother's arm, his mind searching for words of comfort, words to distract her from the suffering she was enduring.

"You told us that he came home and then returned to his regiment." Alvin spoke as he placed his arm around the shoulders of his mother and held her close to him.

"Not at first," she sighed. "He was too sick. He was in a hospital for nearly a month and then went to Clouds Mill outside of Alexandria where his regiment was mustered out in mid-July of 1865." Ellen lifted her head to look into the eyes of her son, searching for understanding, for a bridge that would connect him and his father in a manner that had eluded them. "Your father was a hero, Alvin," she smiled. "You should have seen the parade for them in Buffalo!" Alvin squeezed his mother's arm. He too smiled.

"I wish I could have been there," he responded. "Father didn't share much about the war with me."

Ellen had not taken her eyes from her son. She was pleased with the thoughtfulness of his words. On too many days she had watched his withdrawal from his father, often observing the longing in her son's eyes that soon became indifference. When very young, Alvin would press his face to the kitchen window, watching and waiting for his father to return from chores. She remembered the look of joyful anticipation in her little boy's face when he saw his father open the door and step into the kitchen. She also remembered seeing the vacant look in Alvin's eyes when his father left without a word, disappearing through the doorway into the cellar or hallway leading to the upstairs bedroom. The day came when Alvin no longer looked for his father's return.

"He loved you so much." Ellen's words were familiar to her son. Seldom did a day pass without her expression of support for the love between father and son. The words had become only hollow sounds that Alvin would accept as expressions of love, not from a distant father but from a mother who became both a mother and father to him. The rationale for the sins of a father became testimony to the love of a mother. It was that love that brought Alvin to the cold, foreboding cemetery, and only that love.

"Do you ever wish to return to Angola?" Alvin was unwilling to respond to his mother's confirmation of his father's love for him. As always, he would change the subject and go on. "To be close to your family, I mean." It was a safe question, one that had been asked many times since hearing of the death of James.

"I don't think so. That's not my life anymore."

"Why did you and Father leave the farm there?" Alvin had heard the stories of life in the big house where the Eddy children lived with their parents, of tales of long trail rides on broad-backed plow horses, of chasing sea gulls feeding in spring-planted fields, hayrides and skating on frozen ponds, all bringing a faraway look in his mother's eyes.

"We wanted to start a life of our own...together," Ellen answered. Alvin looked at his mother and saw that she was distracted in her thoughts and knew it wasn't worth pursuing the worn questions she so often answered. "We didn't get married for few a years following his return," she continued, looking out across the fields dressed in winter-white, indistinguishable and stark. Behind the blank stare, in eyes that didn't move, she saw only James, embracing her, kissing her, smiling as he looked into her eyes. "His father was very sick," she spoke. "He died that first autumn. The farm wasn't theirs anymore. Your father had no place to go." Ellen paused, rubbing her hands to fend off the pain deep within the joints of her fingers. "Your grandpa gave him a job and a place to stay." It became increasingly difficult for her to speak. "That was hard for your father." She looked out to the rows of grave markers lining the field. "When we were married, we were given a house on the land Grandpa had always promised." Tears had already formed in her eyes. The wind blew harder, drying the moisture on her cheeks. Dark clouds, heavy with snow, rolled across the lake and hovered off the near shore. Alvin moved closer to his mother, placing his arm around her. He knew it was not the time to suggest they seek shelter in the buggy parked alongside the road. "James was proud." She placed her hand to her face. "He never felt it was his land." Each sentence, each word came hesitantly, reluctantly, as if great care was required in peeling back the shroud covering her past. "He was a hero. There were so many who said so, but he saw only his failures."

Alvin held tightly to his mother, straining to remain still, fearing that any sound or movement would silence her words and shield from him this portrait of a father he had never seen.

"Following your birth and then your brother Edwin's, it seemed the nightmares increased." Ellen stared at her cold, reddened hands held in her lap. "The yelling in his sleep, calling out names of men I had not heard." It was difficult for Alvin to understand what he was hearing. This man she was describing had shown no emotion, never anger, sadness, or pleasure that Alvin could ever remember. "When he spoke of moving us to Wisconsin, of giving the farm back to my parents, I believed he could escape the nightmares and find peace and I, the man I loved."

"How could you ever forgive him for leaving us, you with young children?" There was no empathy in Alvin's words. A lifetime of growing anger could not be denied him.

"He didn't leave!" Ellen pleaded. "You can't say that! You don't know what he did or why!"

"I know he abandoned us!" Alvin had always been patient with his mother when she spoke of his father. In her kindness, she described a man created from love, not reality. Alvin knew only a man who worked the fields and sat silently at the supper table, but his love for his mother was too great to ever challenge the myth she had long attempted to establish in her children's minds. With his words today, Alvin had said more to challenge her than any time before.

"He didn't leave us, Alvin," she said softly, turning to look into her son's face. There would be no more tears on this day. Her body moved to an erect position, slowly withdrawing from her son's hold.

"He never left, because in many ways, he hadn't returned." The corners of her mouth curved to form a smile, a gentle, maternal smile reserved for mothers imparting life-lessons to children. "The war took his heart. The James Reed that I knew did not return from Virginia. Something important inside of him died in the war. He loved me and he loved you, Alvin, very much, but he was unable to tell us or show us his because something inside was lost. There may have been too many deaths to endure, too much suffering, too few answers for the questions he had. The deaths of his mother and then his father, when he came home...he lost so many. It was as if he expressed love for anyone, they too would be taken from him. To keep us at a distance may have been his way of saving us from harm. He blamed himself for so much of the misery he witnessed. When it became too much, when he couldn't escape his love for us, when he could no longer resist taking us into his heart...he protected us as best he could." Ellen's voice broke. She sighed deeply to regain her composure. "He removed that which would bring us harm...himself. He didn't leave, son, he protected us."

Snow began to fall. At first it was only glittering specks of light particles in the air but soon turned to large flakes, falling heavily, collecting on the shoulders of Ellen's wool coat.

"I wish I could have been with him during those last days in the hospital here." Ellen lifted her head to look in the direction of the Milwaukee Veterans Hospital that stood out beyond the ridge to the west of the cemetery. Lights glowed in the second-story windows visible above the ridge line. "I wish I had been there to tell him that we loved him...to thank him for what he did for us...and the others...those names he cried out night after night."

Alvin stood to his feet and reached to gently brush away the snow that had fallen on the shoulder of his mother's coat.

"Come," he held out his hands. "Let us find Father's grave."

Together, Ellen's hand resting on the forearm of her son, they walked. Having gone less than twenty yards, passing by two long rows of headstones that seemed to fade away into the distant snow cover to the north, Alvin again spoke. "This way, Mother. I think it's over there." Walking a few more feet, they came to a stop. Ellen's face, familiar with harsh winter weather of northern Wisconsin, began to suffer the brunt of the wind that had picked up moisture as it skimmed the smooth surface of the lake, but she didn't feel it strike her or hear it moaning as it blew through the branches of the great oak and sycamore trees thirty yards to the right. Her senses were narrowed upon the stone that lay at her feet. Both she and her son stared down at the letters carved into the flat face of the white marble.

James E. Reed
Sgt Co. M 1NY
June 23 1896

The wind cut into Ellen's eyes causing tears to swell within them. She blinked, allowing her to focus on the single word, "James."

"He's here, Mother." The sound of Alvin's voice was low, hoarse. Ellen turned toward him.

"Yes," she tried to control the emotion in her voice, knowing that crying would only make it more difficult. They stood there for several minutes, alone in their thoughts, images, memories blending and fading, a kaleidoscope of dreams, events, words spoken and unspoken.

"I thought more would be written than that," Alvin spoke, searching for more appropriate words.

"We know he was more than that." Ellen swallowed. She wanted her son to hear her clearly. He needed to know what she was about to say. Squeezing Alvin's arm, her head bowed, blinking her eyelids to clear the tears brought by the now steady wind, struggling to focus upon the name chiseled into the stone at her feet, she continued, "In your heart, you will know your father. Your heart will reveal more than any words written upon a stone."

She bent her knees and slowly lowering herself to the ground, extended her hand, reaching for her husband. Fingers separating blades of the brittle, dead grass, touching the wetness of the cold soil, probing its stiffness, Ellen pressed to feel the softness of James' face. No longer able to see the inscribed words through her tears, she whispered, "My darling, you were lost...confused...just a boy in a great war. In that terrible place where too many were lost, I have to believe that you found some peace. To me you will always be the husband that I love so much. I know you loved me and I know you loved our children. Please God," tears blinded her as she raised her eyes toward the gunmetal clouds pressing down from above, "bring him peace. Let him know that what he did mattered and let him find peace."

Afterword

The Prison

A gray, unfinished, plank-board fence ran the perimeter of a sixteen-acre enclosure. Within, a dominating four-story structure, once the prosperous and promising Maxwell Chambers textile factory, built in 1839, closed in 1853, rotting and deteriorating in 1865, stood along with six smaller, one-room utility buildings, among them, a soup house, hospital, prison, and dead house. Designed to hold 2,500 prisoners of war, more than 10,000 captives had been delivered in October 1864. In spite of the increasing daily death toll, the steady influx of prisoners over the next four months kept the population consistently above 10,000.

On February 19, 1865, the main gate was opened and nearly three thousand Union soldiers walked free. Several hundred more men, sickly and diseased, struggled to follow over the next month, and another thousand, near death and unable to walk, were transported by rail to Richmond. On April 12, 1865, General George Stoneman's Union Cavalry raided the area surrounding the city of Salisbury, North Carolina, and burned its nearby prison to the ground. Today, on the knoll of a gentle rise, a granite monument looms over a National Cemetery in silent testimony to the more than 11,000 men who remain behind, buried in unmarked mass graves beneath sweeping fields of neatly-mowed grass.

The Commandant

On August 24, 1864, Confederate General Braxton Bragg assigned John H. Gee the command post at Salisbury Prison. Following Confederate surrender to Union forces led by General George T. Sherman in April of 1865, Major Gee was free under terms of the peace agreement. However, in November 1865, he was arrested and imprisoned at Old Capital Prison in Washington, D.C., the same prison where Andersonville Commandant Henry Wirz was hanged on November 10, 1865. Gee's court-martial trial began on February 21, 1866. On June 13, 1866, he was acquitted of war crimes by unanimous verdict. On August 13, 1876, Gee died of burns suffered in a self-ignited dynamite explosion in Quincy, Florida. His remains were laid to rest on land that was once a family plantation in Gadsen County, Florida.

The Soldier

James Reed, treated in a series of hospitals from Greensboro, North Carolina, to Washington, D.C., eventually received two months of intensive care in Michigan and recovered sufficiently to return to his regiment outside of Appomattox Court House, Virginia. He, along with the survivors of the 24th New York Mounted Cavalry, was mustered out of service on July 18, 1865, at Clouds Mills, Virginia.

Returning to Angola, New York, to marry Ellen and ultimately father eight children, Reed remained haunted by images frozen deeply within him. In searching for a peace he was unable to find, he moved his family to Wisconsin, only to be mysteriously struck down on the streets of Milwaukee while serving as a National Guardsman. He died alone in the city's Veterans Hospital, bequeathing to his father-in-law in Angola, his solitary possession, a pocket watch left him by his father.

Military History of James E. Reed

FIRST TOUR OF DUTY

21st New York Volunteers ("1st Buffalo")

October 1861 * Enlists in Buffalo, N.Y., under command of Commander William S. Rogers

March 1862 * Joins regiment at Upton's Hill, Va. (Brigade Commander James S. Wadsworth)

May 10, 1862 * Fredericksburg, Va., I Corps prepares for invasion of Richmond * General Marsena Patrick is appointed military governor of Fredericksburg

Shenandoah Valley Campaign April–June 1862

June 1862 * The 21st moves west in pursuit of Thomas J. "Stonewall" Jackson to curtail potential invasion of Washington, D.C.

* Under command of:

I Corps—Irvin McDowell

1st Division—Rufus King

Brigade—Marsena Patrick

Regiment 21st N.Y.—William S. Rogers

* 21st engages in Battle of Front Royal

Battle of 2nd Bull Run August 29–30, 1862

* George B. McClellan commanding Army of the Potomac is 20 miles from Richmond on the Peninsula but Lee drives him back in "Seven Days' Battles."

* Frustrated President Lincoln appoints John Pope to strike Richmond from the west with newly created Army of Virginia:
  General in Chief—John Pope
  III Corps (18,500 men)—Irvin McDowell
  1st Division—Rufus King
  Brigade—Marsena Patrick
  Regiment—21st N.Y.—Colonel William Rogers
* Patrick drives men to prepare for coming campaign
* Pope's "Order No. 5" encourages widespread looting throughout Virginia
* Colonel Rogers suffers ball to groin but stays with regiment
* John P. Hatch replaces King as division commander

Sept. 2, 1862 * Rout of Federals lead Lincoln to fire Pope and puts all eastern forces in Army of the Potomac under McClellan's command

Battle of South Mountain September 14, 1862

* Federal army marches north in pursuit of Lee's incursion into Maryland
* Army of the Potomac—George McClellan, General in Chief
  I Corps—Joseph Hooker
  Division—Abner Doubleday
  Brigade—Marsena Patrick
  Regiment (21st N.Y.)—William S. Rogers

Sept. 13, 1862 * Maryland Campaign
Federals passing Frederick, Md., discover "Lost Order No. 191"

Sept. 14, 1862 * 21st take the right in advance up South Mountain to secure Turner's Gap

Battle of Antietam September 16–17, 1862

* Armies clash at Sharpsburg, Md. (Antietam Creek). In this battle, more men are lost than in all American wars combined in history to that date

Sept. 18, 1862 * Armies rest and Lee withdraws south

Sept. 19, 1862 * Federals bury the dead and for next 30 days remain on the battlefield

Oct. 8, 1862 * Patrick is assigned to provost marshal general in Washington

Oct. 14, 1862 * Gabriel R. Paul takes command of brigade and Rogers is given furlough for health reasons

Nov. 1, 1862 * Army of Potomac march back to Virginia

Nov. 16, 1862 * McClellan is replaced by Ambrose Burnside & Army of Potomac continues toward Fredericksburg

Dec. 6, 1862 * Rogers returns to command 21st N.Y.

Battle of Fredericksburg December 12–13, 1862

* While Federals delay crossing Rappahannock, Lee fortifies defenses

* Army of the Potomac—Commanded by Ambrose Burnside

Left Grand Division—William B. Franklin

I Corps—John Reynolds

1st Division—Abner Doubleday

3rd Brigade—William Rogers (Replaces G. R. Paul)

21st N.Y. Regiment—George N. Layton

Dec. 12, 1862 * City is bombarded throughout day and Federal army crosses Rappahannock at sunset

Dec. 13, 1862 * 1st Division takes lead and moves directly to left flank where they meet intense Rebel cannon fire. * Sullivan A. Meredith retreats to leave flank exposed. Center of Union lines is devastated in assault upon Marye's Heights

Dec. 14, 1862 * Flag of truce permits burying of dead

Dec. 15, 1862 * During night, Federal forces retreat back across river and pull in pontoons

Dec. 20, 1862 * March toward Potomac 10 miles away

Jan. 6, 1862 * 21st N.Y. is detached from front and assigned to detail at Acquia Creek under former Commander General Patrick

May 18, 1863 * 21st N.Y. mustered out in Buffalo

SECOND TOUR OF DUTY

24th New York Volunteers Cavalry

January 1864 * Enlists in Buffalo under command of Colonel William C. Raulston

April 1864 * Assigned to Department of Washington

Battle of Wilderness May 5–9, 1864

* Generals Ulysses S. Grant and George G. Meade march Army of Potomac on to Richmond and meet in the Wilderness

* Federal army leadership consists of:

General of the Armies—Ulysses S. Grant

Army of the Potomac—Commanded by George G. Meade

IX Corps—Ambrose Burnside

1st Division—Thomas G. Stevenson

Brigade—Daniel Leasure

24th N.Y.—William C. Raulston

* Battle is confusing and costly to both sides. Federals retreat south

Battle of Spotsylvania Court House May 10–12, 1864

* Armies again meet in deadly clash at Spotsylvania

May 10, 1864 * Federals attack Lee's entrenchments and IX Corps move to within 300 yards of Court House before pulling back

May 11, 1864 * Nearby Battle of Yellow Tavern—J.E.B. Stuart is killed

May 12, 1864 * On this date battle begins at 4:30 a.m. against Rebel salient—Grant threw the IX Corps into the breach in support role at "Bloody Angle," sustained heavy losses but prevented Rebel forces from attacking Winfield S. Hancock and John Gibbon's forces opposite them * Stevenson is shot and killed

May 20, 1864 * Sporadic fighting stalls and Federals pull out and march south

May 21, 1864 * Battle of Genova Station begins series of running engagements

May 23–24, 1864 * Armies collide on banks of North Anna at Hanover Junction * Federals continue to march south toward Cold Harbor

June 2, 1864 * Battle of Bethesda Church—24th N.Y. is heavily involved and then continue onward to Cold Harbor

Battle of Cold Harbor June 3–10, 1864

* Again Federals encounter Lee's army entrenched behind fortifications

June 6, 1864 * 24th N.Y. take right flank but hold position during Federal assault upon Rebel defenses that see 7,000 Federals fall in less than 30 minutes (stand only ten miles from Richmond). That marks the end of the Union strategy to make frontal assaults upon entrenched defenses * Federals march east and south to Petersburg

Siege of Petersburg June 17–August 19, 1864

* Siege of city begins as Lee builds defensive positions encircling it

June 17, 1864 * Series of probing actions begin to find weaknesses in Rebel defenses

July 30, 1864 * Battle of Cemetery Hill ("The Crater")

Massive explosion to disarm fort leads to crushing Union defeat. Ambrose Burnside is relieved of command along with Edward Ferrero and Leasure. John Parke assumes command of IX Corps. Wilcox assumes command of Leasure's Division

Aug. 18–19, 1864 * Battle of Weldon Railroad (or Globe Tavern)

1,303 Union men are killed, 2,152 are missing and 60 men from the 24th N.Y are captured, including James E. Reed

Libby Prison, Richmond, Virginia

Aug.–Oct. 1864 * Held as P.O.W. in warehouse building in heart of Rebel capital city

Salisbury Prison, North Carolina

Oct. 19, 1864 * Moved deeper into South and farther away from potential rescue

Oct.–Feb. 1865 * P.O.W. in Rebel death camp where 11,700 captives perish

Feb. 1865 * Returned to hospital in Michigan

May 1865 * Having returned to the 24th N.Y., Reed is mustered out at Cloud's Mill, Virginia